Wine
Red
Wrath

Wine Red Wrath

EMILY OBERTON

Nolan Publishing
Company

Cover art by DLR Cover Designs

Internal images © Julien Eichinger/Adobe Stock; Tartila/Adobe Stock

Wine Red Wrath/ Emily Oberton. — 1st ed.

ISBN 978-1-7347003-6-7

For Noelle and Landon

CHAPTER ONE

"Hi, Aunt Deb," I croaked. "I have to bail on our shopping plans today—" I paused, eyeing the small bucket next to my bed as another wave of nausea ripped through me. "I've come down with a nasty stomach bug."

The mere mention of 'stomach' and 'bug' in the same sentence sent me flying to the bucket again. I collapsed next to it, curling up into a pitiful ball of agony as I clutched the plastic pail against my chest. It was six in the morning, and I'd been violently ill since midnight.

"Hadley," she croaked back. "It's not a stomach bug. It's food poisoning."

"But it can't be!" I protested. "I followed all the instructions on the turkey's tag."

"It's food poisoning alright—salmonella, most likely. Roy and I have it too. Been up all night."

I wanted to cry. Just yesterday, I hosted my first Thanksgiving dinner at my new house. I'd spent weeks preparing for the special day. The meal had gone off without a hitch, and my aunt's boyfriend, Detective Roy Sanders, surprised us all when he placed an engagement ring atop her slice of chocolate cake and

1

asked for her hand in marriage. It was unbearable to think they'd spent the night suffering from food poisoning.

"Oh, Aunt Deb! I'm so sorry. I thought I did everything perfectly. I thawed the turkey and used a meat thermometer to check the internal temperature. And I kept my counters clean."

"The turkey was fine. It was the stuffing, hon." Her voice was strained, each of her words requiring an obvious effort.

"The stuffing?" I asked, incredulous.

"It's the only thing Michael didn't eat—he never has liked it—and he's fine and dandy this morning."

Though I was relieved Michael wasn't ill, my heart raced at the thought of Dennis and Carmella, my close friends who had also joined us for Thanksgiving dinner. Were they sick too?

"I don't understand," I said. "How could stuffing make us sick?"

"Did you stuff the turkey before you cooked it?"

"Yes."

"Did you check the temperature of the stuffing before removing the turkey from the oven?"

I closed my mouth.

After waiting a moment for me to respond, she sighed. "This is why you shouldn't stuff a turkey before you cook it. The stuffing absorbs all those nasty raw meat juices, which can contain bacteria. You have to make sure the stuffing is cooked to the same temperature as the turkey. It usually takes an hour longer to cook a stuffed turkey."

"Oh," I said softly.

Roy moaned in the background, saying something about wishing he would just die.

"I need to help Roy," she said. Her voice was no longer the kind, motherly one I was used to. Aunt Deb was miserable and angry. "You'd better call Carmella and Dennis. Find out if you food poisoned them too."

"It sounds so intentional when you say it like that."

"There's a fine line between negligence and intent. Ignorance of food safety rules is no excuse. You need help, Hadley, and I know just the person who can straighten you out. I'll make all the arrangements, and if you ever want to cook for our family again, you'll follow through with the planned intervention."

"Intervention? Isn't that a little extreme?"

"Extreme would be letting you continue to wreak havoc in the kitchen without any sort of guidance. For now, stay hydrated and drink plenty of fluids. Chew on ice chips if you must. They're easier on the stomach than swigs of water."

Aunt Deb hung up, and I immediately called Carmella. Though the sky outside my bedroom window was still dark, she would likely be awake—either getting ready to go Black Friday shopping with Aunt Deb and me or writhing in agony if she'd eaten my stuffing.

I prayed it was the first scenario.

"Hey, Hadley." She sounded tired, but not miserable.

"Are you feeling okay?" I held my breath as I waited for her answer.

"I've never felt worse."

"I'm sorry," I managed to say. A new swell of nausea tugged at my stomach, but I clenched my jaw and forced out my words. "Aunt Deb says it's food poisoning."

"So it seems."

"Can I bring you anything? Juice, maybe?"

She gave a short laugh. "If you're feeling half as bad as I am, you'd better stay put and take care of yourself. I took some medicine, which helped a little. I'll be okay."

"Everything was supposed to be perfect," I said, choking back tears. "I should just give up on cooking. Let's face it, I have the worst kitchen karma ever."

"You know what I love about you, hon? You never stop trying. Most people don't have half the grit you do. They would've thrown in the towel ages ago. I know I did. I hate cooking. But if

3

you keep practicing, then you'll get there. I've never turned down your dinner invitations, and I won't start now—well, except for turkey. I might skip that meal."

I laughed between sobs. "It wasn't the turkey. Aunt Deb says the stuffing was the culprit."

Carmella grunted. "I can't think about food right now. How's everyone else feeling?"

"Michael didn't eat the stuffing, so he's fine, but Aunt Deb and Roy are having a tough time. I haven't talked to Dennis yet, but he's probably sick, too. He ate everything I made." My stomach fluttered at the thought of calling him. He'd been through so much in the past couple of weeks—a gunshot wound in the line of duty and a bad breakup with his girlfriend. I desperately hoped I hadn't topped off his week with a case of food poisoning.

After saying goodbye to Carmella, I spent a minute collecting myself before calling Dennis. I'd known him since moving to Darlington Hills, Virginia, early this year, but we became closer friends in the past several weeks when I went along with his crazy scheme to keep his relationship with another law enforcement officer a secret.

The relationship had imploded, as did the one I had with my ex-boyfriend, Reid. But last night's dinner was the sweet ending to a series of crimes, drama, and break-ups.

And now the salmonella.

The soft motor-like purring of Razzy, my Siamese-tabby cat, sounded above me. She jumped off the bed and nuzzled her head against my leg. I scooped her up into a hug, setting aside the bucket. Taking a deep breath, I called Dennis.

He answered on the third ring with a strained grunt. My heart sank. I'd ruined his Thanksgiving weekend as well.

"You're sick, too?" I confirmed.

"Mm-hmm." His labored mumbles spoke volumes of his agony. He was in bad shape.

"I'm sorry, Dennis. This is my fault. We all got an awful case of salmonella."

"Mm-hmm," he agreed.

"Aunt Deb said it's from the stuffing. Apparently, I shouldn't have cooked it inside the turkey."

"Hmm," he responded.

I wanted to jump in my car, drive to his house, and do whatever I could to help him feel better, but the thought of even making it down my own stairs seemed impossible. My stomach cramps were so bad, it felt as though someone were wringing my insides like they would a damp towel.

"I'm so sorry I ruined your weekend."

"Mmm," he reassured me.

"I'll make it up to you soon, and I promise it won't involve a steaming pot of stuffing."

"Mmmphf—gotta run! Gonna be sick—"

CHAPTER TWO

"During the next ten classes, we will delve into the sacred realm where food mirrors the essence of our inner being. Just as the simmering pot unveils its rich flavors over time, so too does our soul reveal its unique essence through the art of cooking." Madame Camille Balleroy, head of the Madame Balleroy Cooking School, gestured with swan-like grace as she paced in front of the classroom. "Each ingredient we select, every delicate stir of the spoon, echoes the rhythms of our heart."

I scanned the faces of the other students in the classroom. Did anyone believe this nonsense?

One young woman in a faded jean jacket sure seemed to. In the row behind me, she nodded eagerly along with our teacher's words, her eyes filled with admiration. Madame Balleroy was a renowned chef who co-owned the five-star French cuisine restaurant next door to the cooking school. We were in the presence of a culinary A-lister.

Our teacher continued, her words oozing with sophistication. "Cooking, my friends, is no mere chore—it is a meditative dance with the universe, a symphony orchestrated by the soul's yearning for expression. The kitchen is a sanctuary of transformation, a divine place of opportunity, solace, and—"

"Torment," I piped up, then cowered back in my seat when Madame Balleroy shot me the stink-eye. "Sorry, but my kitchen didn't come with even an ounce of divinity. It has conspired against me. Its wrath knows no bounds."

It was the first Thursday in December, exactly one week since I served my guests salmonella-laced stuffing. Even though everyone had made a complete recovery, I still felt the bitter sting of humiliation and frustration each time I stepped into my kitchen.

"That's why you're here, hon!" Hal Stenner, who sat to my right, clapped a firm hand against my back. He was Darlington Hills' most sought-after bachelor among the over-sixty crowd, and the sole male member of Aunt Deb's ever-growing hiking club. I was certain my aunt had told Hal, along with half the town, about my Thanksgiving dinner failure.

"Indeed." Madame Balleroy said, her gaze locked onto me. Her eyes were as dark as her hair, which had shimmering silver strands woven throughout. She was likely in her late forties; early fifties at most.

Madame Balleroy glided to the back of the classroom and lifted a book from her desk. Its cover was green, the same shade as the silk scarf around her neck, which added a feminine touch to her white button-up chef coat. "Before I forget, Hadley, this is for you. Read it cover to cover and etch these words into your memory."

With a loud thud, she dropped the book on the table in front of me: *The ABCs of Kitchen Safety: 500 Easy Steps for Beginners*.

Hal chuckled. "Your aunt's a tough cookie. She isn't letting you off easy this time."

It was true. Aunt Deb had pestered me into enrolling in Madame Balleroy's Cooking School, which was nestled in a wooded area on the southern edge of Darlington Hills. Classes were three hours a night, four days a week, during the busiest time of the year. I would have refused, but I desperately needed to improve my kitchen karma. I was prepared to serve time for my culinary misdeeds.

Only hitch was, there were some strings attached to my enrollment in Madame's school—actually, a lot of strings. The tuition was absurdly expensive, so Aunt Deb had negotiated a lower rate in exchange for my interior design services for the upcoming Christmas Eve brunch, a well-attended event held every year inside the large red barn on Madame Balleroy's property.

Truth be told, I was more excited about decorating for the event than the cooking classes. But they were an early Christmas gift from Aunt Deb, and I couldn't turn down her generosity.

Opening her arms wide, Madame Balleroy gestured toward the doorway leading to the school's kitchen. "Over the next two weeks, you will learn a variety of cooking techniques and recipes —exquisite hors d'oeuvres, delightful desserts, and everything in between. I encourage each of you to embrace the kitchen as a temple of self-discovery, where food becomes a mirror reflecting the beauty of our inner world."

A tall man with a square jawline and steely gaze came through the doorway to the classroom, joining Madame Balleroy at the front. He wore a white chef coat dotted with two rows of black buttons, along with a pair of loose-fitting black slacks.

"Tonight, we're lucky to have my sous chef, Seth O'Boyle, helping us in the kitchen. Though he's usually busy barking orders to my restaurant's crew, you'll see him around the school a few times each week.

Seth acknowledged us with a cool, indifferent wave before Madame Balleroy escorted us to the adjacent kitchen and divided us into three groups of four, handing us recipe cards for our first cooking assignment: crispy fried zucchini sticks. After walking us through the list of ingredients and instructions, she let us loose in the kitchen.

I tied back my hair, covered it with a baseball cap, and donned my apron before slipping on a pair of disposable gloves. It was time to begin my kitchen redemption.

The recipe turned out to be straightforward. I didn't hit any snags until it came time to fry the zucchini.

"Any idea why my sticks are turning brown so quickly?" I whispered to Hal, whose frying pan sat on the other gas burner at our table. Our group's station was equipped with two ovens, a dual gas stove, and a spacious stainless-steel prep table.

Hal shrugged. "Mine are cooking fast too. The recipe says to fry them for two-to-three minutes per side, but these lil' fellows are browning after only a minute."

I glanced at the other two ladies in our group, who were waiting for their turn to use the stove. Although both would probably know the answer to Hal's and my question, I didn't want to ask either of them.

Darcy, a sixty-or-so-year-old woman wearing a floral apron, hadn't spoken a word since Madame Balleroy divided us into groups. If I had to guess, I'd say she was overcome with shyness around Hal and his gemstone-green eyes.

Then there was Mitzi, the young woman in the faded jean jacket who had earned the title of Teacher's Pet within the first half hour with her flawless vegetable-slicing technique. She didn't hold back on giving me tips as I cooked, each one dripping with irritation. I didn't want to flatter her by seeking her help.

I turned around, spotting the sous-chef at the cooking station next to ours. He was talking to a middle-aged woman in bright pink lipstick with wavy, chin-length brown hair, and showing her how to slice the zucchini.

At least I knew more about chopping veggies than she did. It was a much-needed confidence booster.

I waited for Seth to finish helping the woman, then raised my hand when he passed by.

"Our zucchini sticks are frying too fast," I told him. "I'm using medium-high heat, just like the recipe says."

Seth closed his eyes before responding. "Madame Balleroy went over this already, and I don't have time to reteach everything just because you didn't listen to the instructions."

"But you were helping her," I argued, pointing to the woman hunched over the cutting board.

Seth stepped closer to me, lowering his voice. "I have to help her; she's my future mother-in-law." He sighed, then motioned to the stove's knob. "This unit cooks faster than the others. Just turn down the heat." He turned it down for me, giving me an ego-smashing smirk. "Don't assume a recipe was written exclusively for you. Adjust as you need to."

Seth grabbed the tongs from my hands and plucked a zucchini stick from the sizzling oil and held it up for my group to observe. "See how lumpy this one is? This is what happens if you don't shake off any excess flour mixture or allow the egg to drip off first. This step is articulated in the recipe."

Hal gave me a reassuring smile. "They look good to me." No wonder Aunt Deb's hiking group was so large. 'Hal the Heart-throb,' as they called him, wasn't only easy on the eyes, but was also a genuinely nice person.

There was a squeal of delight near the doorway, where Madame Balleroy greeted an attractive blonde woman wearing a long red coat and matching heels. The women hugged before Madame Balleroy ushered her guest to the center of the kitchen.

"Attention, everyone! I'd like you to meet Chloe Johnson, the food and restaurant reporter at the *Darlington Hills Dispatch*. She is working on a feature-length article about my restaurant, cooking school, and preparations for the upcoming Christmas Eve brunch." Madame Balleroy gestured around the kitchen. "Chloe, meet my latest group of students. Tonight is their first class, and as you can see, they're making a delicious alternative to French fries."

"It smells amazing in here," Chloe said. With delicate precision, she freed a tendril of her blonde hair from behind her ear, reshaping its spiraled curl before sweeping it to the side of her cheekbone.

"Just wait until my class learns to make sherried lobster bisque on Monday! That aroma is heavenly. Even though none of my students are professional chefs, many are culinary enthusiasts seeking to broaden their expertise." Madame Balleroy aimed her beady blue eyes at me. "Some, however, are beginners."

Chloe joined Madame Balleroy at a stainless-steel workbench with a two-tier shelf. She removed her fleece gloves, then scribbled into her small spiral notebook as Madame Balleroy spoke.

Seth returned my zucchini stick to the sizzling oil, clumsily placing the tongs back on the spoon rest. He left our station, heading for the exit, but another student stopped him to ask a question.

Hal and I finished frying our zucchini sticks, then exchanged places with Darci and Mitzi so they could use the stove. Ten minutes later, a woman who looked to be in her nineties entered the kitchen. Her wrinkled face was framed by silver hair, pinned back neatly with clips. She had a slight hunch in her posture but moved with surprising agility.

"The cakes need frosting," the woman announced to Madame Balleroy in a thick French accent. She shared the same whisper-thin nose as our instructor and held herself with the same air of authority.

"Who's that?" I whispered to my group.

"That's Zelia Balleroy, Madame Balleroy's grandmother," Mitzi said. "But everyone calls her Grand-mère, which is French for grandmother. She co-owns the restaurant with Madame Balleroy."

"Perhaps *you* can frost the cakes," Madame Balleroy countered, her accent only barely noticeable. "I'm planning to take Chloe, our guest from the *Darlington Hills Dispatch*, on a tour of the grounds now." She turned towards Seth. "I'd like you to come with us. I want you to tell Chloe about the holiday menu you prepared for the upcoming brunch."

Seth nodded in agreement, hastily placing a spoon back onto its ceramic resting plate before hurrying toward his boss.

"Hadley, dear," Madame Balleroy cooed, "I want you to join us so you can see the area you'll be decorating for the event. Everyone else, you are free to leave once you finish. Remember to practice what you learned tonight. Practice, practice, practice. You'll hear me say it a hundred times, but it is the only way to improve. Oh, and don't worry about the mess; my crew will take care of it. Chefs never do their own cleaning."

"Lord knows we're paying enough to skip dish duty," a man said from the table next to me.

I frowned. How much had Aunt Deb paid for my tuition? I hoped it wasn't too much, since she was saving for her wedding early next year.

After placing my zucchini sticks into the storage container I brought, I followed Madame Balleroy and the reporter into the adjoining classroom. I removed my hat and apron, placing them next to my bag, before slipping on my black puffy coat. Though the early-December temperatures weren't quite bone-chilling, it was too chilly for me to wear my lightweight jean jacket.

I hoped the tour wouldn't last long. It was two minutes before eight o'clock, and I had a full day of work tomorrow at Walnut Ridge Furniture and Decor—my full-time job where I staged rooms for catalog and website photoshoots.

Chloe placed her bag on the opposite end of the lengthy table in the first row, but held onto her spiral notebook, pen, and phone.

"Have we met before?" she asked, making her way over to me.

I smiled. "No, I've been told I have a familiar face." Apparently, according to one of my ex-boyfriends, if you've seen one woman with wavy light brown hair and dark brown eyes, you've seen them all. "Hadley Sutton," I said, shaking her hand.

Madame Balleroy opened the door and gestured gracefully for us to leave. Before turning to follow Chloe, I snuck a few zucchini sticks from my container to silence my growling stomach. I would enjoy the rest later—lumps and all.

We toured the restaurant's dining area first, spending twenty minutes amid soft chatter and tinkering glasses as Madame Balleroy boasted about the restaurant's history and the famous patrons who'd dined at their tables. We browsed her extensive wine collection, each bottle nestled in custom-built racks lining the walls.

As we walked through the swinging double doors into the kitchen, the atmosphere changed drastically. The air was heavy with competing scents of simmering sauces and fresh herbs. Chefs in white uniforms and towering toques bustled between stainless steel stations, their movements a well-rehearsed sequence of culinary expertise.

Madame Balleroy introduced her team, each chef nodding curtly before returning their focus to the dishes in front of them. I immediately recognized the station chef, Natasha Antonov, with her coppery-red hair and wide, expressive eyes. She was a frequent customer at Whisks and Whiskers Cat Café, which had recently reopened after being closed for several weeks.

Madame Balleroy then directed Chloe's attention to Seth, who described the special Christmas Eve menu.

My stomach growled fiercely as he spoke of charcuterie boards, French quiches, crepes, goat cheese and walnut salads, and buttery brioche sandwiches filled with ham and gruyere cheese. Fortunately, I would get to indulge in these delicacies, since part of Aunt Deb's negotiation with Madame Balleroy included a table at the brunch. We would dine in style on Christmas Eve.

"That sounds amazing!" Chloe told Seth. "If I didn't have plans to go out of town, I would most certainly buy a ticket."

Madame Balleroy dismissed Seth, instructing him to return to work, before turning her attention to a man with sharp cheekbones and deep-set eyes who had just strolled into the kitchen. His cobalt blue dress shirt, crisp and tailored, stood out among the sea of white chef coats in the bustling kitchen. He stopped in front of Chloe and shook her hand. "Thanks again for coming out tonight. If you have questions after your tour, be sure to let me know."

Madame Balleroy turned to me. "This is Jared Bernardi, our program director. He handles all our special events, from weddings to corporate functions. He also assists with marketing efforts, like this media opportunity with the *Darlington Hills Dispatch.*"

Jared extended his hand with a quick smile. "Nice meeting you, Hadley. Madame told me earlier you're in charge of decorating the barn for this year's brunch."

"Oh, I've heard so much about the barn," Chloe chimed in eagerly. "My husband's company hosted a sales event there last year, though unfortunately, spouses weren't invited. I was quite disappointed to miss out."

"What a shame!" Madame Balleroy said, shaking her head. "I will take you there in a few moments, just after I show you the herb forest."

Chloe raised an eyebrow. "Herb forest? I'm intrigued."

We left the kitchen through the back, which led to a room with lockers, a small sofa, and a TV—the staff break room, I guessed—then stepped outside onto a narrow crushed-granite walkway that wound between mature oak trees with sprawling branches.

The so-called herb forest was a dense, sprawling garden with rows of trellises forming tunneled pathways. For the next thirty minutes, Madame Balleroy talked about all the herbs thriving under her care—which plants required more sunlight; which shared similar growing conditions; how nutrients from one plant could affect the growth of surrounding ones; and which herbs she used in the dishes that made up her award-winning menu. It seemed she either had no clue what time it was, or she simply didn't care that it was nine o'clock and well past dinnertime.

Finally, she motioned us to follow her back onto the sidewalk, prompting a loud sigh of relief from Chloe. We strolled up the gently sloping hill, with Madame Balleroy still droning on about her precious herbs the entire time.

At night, the barn's enormity was amplified by warm, golden lights flooding the exterior, casting a soft glow across the cabernet-colored walls, making the rich red hue appear even deeper and more dramatic. Instantly, my mind swirled with images of Christmas-themed decorations—rustic yet enchanting; simplistic yet captivating. It would be a fun design challenge after all.

Madame Balleroy pulled on the long rustic handle, ushering us inside. "My grandfather built this barn in—"

Chloe's phone interrupted the conversation with a loud ring. Glancing at the screen, she slipped it back into her coat pocket.

"Please, take the call, dear," Madame Balleroy said.

Chloe waved a hand. "It's just my husband; I'll see him soon."

Or maybe not, I thought, if Madame Balleroy gave us a history lesson about the barn.

Madame Balleroy persisted, her tone gracious. "No, I insist. I wouldn't want to intrude on your personal call."

After a moment of hesitation, Chloe relented and answered the call with a gentle smile. "Thanks, sweetheart," she cooed. "Yes, salmon sounds perfect. I can hardly wait. Okay, see you soon." Ending the call, she checked her watch.

That was a hint if I'd ever seen one.

"Would you like to invite your husband to the restaurant for dinner tonight?" Madame Balleroy offered. "My treat, of course."

"Thank you, but he already bought the fish."

Madame Balleroy's smile faltered. "I understand. The invitation stands should you change your mind. Now, where were we? Ah, yes, as I was saying, my grandfather—"

This time, it was Madame Balleroy's phone that rang. Color rose to her cheeks as she raised the phone to her ear. "Very well, thank you," she huffed. Returning the phone to her pocket, she faced Chloe. "It just occurred to me that I should have snipped some fresh dill for you in the herb forest earlier. It's a cold-hardy herb, and you simply must try it. Please excuse me for a moment."

Chloe raised her hand to protest. "Thanks, but really, I—"

"I won't take no for an answer. It will be a beautiful—and tasty—addition to your salmon tonight." She motioned to me. "Hadley, please take some photos inside the barn so you can start working on your design plans. I'd like to see a draft next week."

Chloe let out an audible sigh, then yanked her phone from her coat pocket, fixing her gaze on its glowing screen.

I wandered through the enormous barn, snapping photos as I explored. The rustic atmosphere struck me with its charm—weathered wooden walls and rafters strewn with fairy lights that had likely twinkled during countless weddings. The long walls to the left and right overflowed with hay bales, relics of the barn's more utilitarian past.

A small stage stood at the back of the barn, equipped with various microphones and sound gear. A floor-to-ceiling curtain behind it completely concealed the back wall. I pulled back the heavy black curtain, peering into a dark space holding dozens of folded tables and chairs leaning against the wall in orderly rows.

Returning to the center of the barn, I tried to visualize various design themes, but my thoughts kept drifting to my rumbling stomach, reminding me it was time to head home and eat—not start a large-scale design project.

Five minutes later, Madame Balleroy burst back into the barn, holding a fistful of dill.

"Here you go," she panted. "Fresh dill for your trout tonight—or was it flounder?" She handed the herbs to Chloe, then loosened the scarf around her neck, fanning herself as she spoke.

"Salmon," Chloe corrected dryly, brushing some dirt from her coat that had fallen from the dill's scraggly roots.

"Right. Salmon. Of course," Madame Balleroy acknowledged with a nod. "Well, I've given you enough dill to whip up a creamy lemon garlic dill sauce to accompany your fish. I'll provide you with the recipe before you leave."

Madame Balleroy's gaze swept quickly around the barn before swiveling back to Chloe. "Unless you have questions, we will head back to the classroom now so you can collect your bag and head home."

"No questions," Chloe responded hastily.

"Great, and Hadley, did you—"

"Yep! I got what I needed." I interjected, eager to avoid any lingering lectures on barn history.

Chloe was the first to exit the building, and I stayed close behind her. We zipped down the walkway leading back to the cooking school, winding around the perimeter of the small asphalt parking lot designated for students, which was now empty except for my blue car and Chloe's white SUV. In the distance, thin slits of brake lights illuminated as a vehicle slowed before turning onto Picket Lane, exiting Madame Balleroy's property.

The walkway forked near a wooden bench situated under a vine-wrapped trellis. The left path led to the front of the school, while the right would take us by the herb forest before leading to the kitchen.

I veered left. We had heard enough about herbs for one night.

Inside the classroom, notebooks, pens, and other forgotten items were strewn across three long tables. I made a beeline for my bag, keeping my eyes fixed on my container of zucchini sticks. My stomach grumbled with the rich aroma of our culinary creations lingering in the room.

Just ten more steps and I would pry the lid from my container and finally savor another veggie stick.

Madame Balleroy remained by the front door, her hand poised on the handle as if eager to usher us out.

Which was fine with me.

"Oh, wait, my gloves—" Chloe began, turning towards the kitchen. "I think I left them on the workbench."

Madame Balleroy's gaze snapped towards the open doorway, and she hustled to catch up to Chloe. "Are you certain you didn't leave them in the barn? I seem to recall—"

Both women halted as if they had collided with an invisible barrier.

"*Seth?*" Madame Balleroy demanded. "Are you okay?"

I caught up with them as they hurried into the kitchen. Seth lay on his side near the doorway leading to the herb forest, his legs propping open the door.

Madame Balleroy lunged toward him with her arms outstretched. "Seth!" she cried, crouching next to him.

She jumped back with a shriek, accidentally nudging his shoulder and causing him to roll onto his back. His once-white chef coat was now stained with blood, and the large handle of a kitchen knife protruded from his chest.

CHAPTER THREE

"Don't worry about getting it perfect. Just tell me what you remember happening from the time your class started tonight." Detective Sanders, sitting in a chair next to me, placed a reassuring hand on my shoulder. "You don't even need to talk in complete sentences."

I wasn't sure if I could utter a coherent word, let alone a full sentence.

Before Detective Sanders arrived, the first officers on the scene asked Chloe and me to wait for questioning inside the classroom, and they told Madame Balleroy, Grand-mère, and all their employees to wait inside the restaurant next door.

I would have rather waited in the restaurant instead of smack-dab in the middle of the police action. The blue and red lights flashing outside cast eerie shadows on the walls of the classroom, and the constant sound of boots thudding back and forth between the kitchen and classroom made my heart race.

Even with my coat wrapped tightly around me, my whole body trembled. I felt lightheaded, likely from the shock of finding Seth in the kitchen and from needing to eat—even though I no longer had much of an appetite.

"I didn't notice anything out of the ordinary tonight." I spoke slowly as I struggled to recall everything that had happened. "There were no arguments involving Seth—well, none that I saw."

As I narrated my first cooking class and the subsequent tour, Detective Sanders listened intently. Officers moved behind me with purpose and efficiency, and at the other end of the long table, Chloe sat slumped in a chair, her face buried in her hands.

Detective Sanders's eyebrows rose when I mentioned the vehicle I saw leaving Madame Balleroy's property. "Can you give me any details on the make or model?" he asked.

I shook my head. "Sorry, it was too dark. I only saw the brake lights."

"Do you know if it was a car or a truck?"

"They looked like any other brake lights—red and bright."

He made a note in his spiral pad. "There are more differences to these lights than you might think. We'll find out which cars entered the premises tonight and get photos of their lights. Then, maybe, you'll be able to identify them. A brake light line-up, so to speak."

"I'll do whatever I can to help."

Detective Sanders sighed. "I know you will, and we appreciate it. Are you doing okay, all things considered? Your aunt was awfully upset when I told her you were one of the three who found the victim. I told her not to forget these classes were her idea, and let me tell you, she didn't appreciate the reminder."

I gave a small smile to my soon-to-be uncle. Detective Sanders was a good man, and I was thrilled Aunt Deb had found love for the second time in her life. Her first husband, Uncle Bill, was my dad's older brother, who died on a fishing trip five years ago.

"Where's your partner tonight?" I asked, glancing around once more for Dennis, known to everyone else in the room as Detective Appley. "He's still confined to desk duty?"

Detective Sanders peered at me through his bushy gray eyebrows. "Officially, yes. But you and I both know that even a bullet wound couldn't keep him away from work."

Until several months ago, Sanders had been the sole detective in Darlington Hills, but because of a drastic uptick in homicides, the police chief promoted Dennis to detective. Sanders was slowly warming up to the idea of sharing his duties with a partner.

"I tried telling Appley that I could handle this tonight, but he insisted on coming," Detective Sanders said. "He'll be here soon; he just had to drop off Kinsley at your aunt's house first."

"Oh, that's right! I completely forgot she arrived this morning." I cringed at the thought of Dennis's five-year-old niece having to stay with a stranger her first night in Darlington Hills. Kinsley was staying with Dennis for a couple of weeks while his older sister, Kate, her husband, and parents went on an African safari. They had enrolled her in a day camp during the work week, but I doubted Dennis had expected needing to work after hours while she was in town.

"I'll stop by Aunt Deb's on my way home and see if she needs any help."

He shook his head. "She'll be fine; in fact, she was more than happy to watch little Kinsley. And Michael's there to help entertain her."

My cousin Michael had recently returned to Darlington Hills from Chicago and was staying with Aunt Deb as he figured out his next career move. He had finally landed a job doing what he loved—acting and directing—and he was planning to move into his own apartment soon.

"Okay, but I can help—" I began.

"You need to take it easy tonight; go grab some dinner. Your stomach hasn't stopped rumbling since I sat down to talk with you. Besides, Appley will pick up Kinsley when he's finished here and head back to their hotel."

I pulled back my chin. "Hotel? Why aren't they staying at Dennis's place?"

Detective Sanders looked around the room, then lowered his voice. "Someone broke into his house through a window yesterday while he was at the station, and then he received a threatening letter in the mail."

"That's terrible!" I exclaimed.

He nodded. "It's most likely related to a suspected money laundering investigation he's been working on while recovering. Though Chief probably would have stuck him on the case even without the injury, since he's the numbers guy at the station." Dennis had majored in math at a university in Texas before he enlisted in the Army. "Until he nails the perp who threatened him, they're staying at Hotel Darlington out of an abundance of caution."

I shook my head. "They can stay with me. I have plenty of extra rooms." It had been nearly four months since I moved into the Ladyvale Manor after I inherited it from a former client, for reasons still unknown. The iconic ivy-wrapped mansion and its sprawling estate, complete with a full-size labyrinth of hedges, had turned our sleepy town into a tourist hotspot. And since my new home was now open for public tours, it was constantly filled with people from all corners of the country.

"Your aunt already made that suggestion, but Appley said he ran out of favors to ask you." Detective Sanders stood and gathered his pen and notepad. "I have a long list of other folks to talk to tonight, but please call me if you remember any other details worth sharing. Now go home and get some rest."

He gave me a reassuring nod, then headed toward Chloe and introduced himself. I got up from my chair but sat back down immediately as a wave of dizziness hit me. Detective Sanders was right—I really needed to eat something.

Peeling back the lid of my storage container, I gathered several zucchini sticks to munch on. Dennis strode into the classroom with a notebook in one hand, pointing towards someone in the kitchen behind him. "I'm gonna need prints on the disposable gloves. *All* of them."

"You got it, Detective," a woman responded.

Dennis stopped when his eyes landed on me, and he hurried over. I stood and greeted him with a hug, keeping a hand on the table to steady myself.

"Are you okay?" he demanded. "You're pale." Dennis didn't look like himself either. Despite his experience in law enforcement and as a military police officer, the weight of the homicide still weighed heavily on him. His eyes held traces of sadness and guilt, as though he believed there was something he could have done to prevent the tragic event.

"I'm okay, thanks." I eased back into my chair. Somehow, I felt better, now that Dennis was here. "I just gave my statement to Detective Sanders, but I can share the highlights with you if you'd like."

Dennis glanced at his partner, who was taking notes as Chloe spoke. Her cheeks were streaked with tears, and she fidgeted with a piece of twine around her bag strap. I wondered if her news article would now turn into a report on the homicide instead of a review of Madame Balleroy's restaurant and cooking school.

I shared more than just the highlights with Dennis. He sat on the table as I repeated everything I'd told Detective Sanders, plus a few more details I remembered, like Madame Balleroy's brief outing to the herb forest while Chloe and I were in the barn.

"Do you know who had access to the classroom and kitchen after classes ended tonight?" he asked.

"As far as I know, the doors were unlocked the entire time. We didn't use a key to enter when we returned from the tour." I grabbed the container of zucchini sticks and held it out to him. "Want to try one?"

He peered into the container but held up a hand. "No, thanks."

"You're just scared I'm going to make you sick again," I teased.

The corner of his mouth twitched upwards. "They look good, but I already had dinner with my niece. We went to the Nuggets 'n Such joint tonight." He made a face that told me it wasn't the best meal he'd ever had.

"Oh! That reminds me," I said. "Detective Sanders told me you and Kinsley had to—"

"Excuse me, Detective. Regarding the weapon, has anyone checked the kitchen inventory?" Officer Ben Stevens, nicknamed 'The Bulkster' by his precinct buddies for his massive biceps, approached Dennis, gripping a hand-held radio that looked tiny in his hands.

"Officer Patel is working on that now," Dennis replied. The weariness in his eyes betrayed the calmness in his voice. "Our preliminary sweep suggests it's one of the cooking school's own —part of a set used by the students."

"From what I could tell, the butcher knife looked just like the ones we used tonight to make these appetizers," I said, pointing to the veggie sticks.

"It's not a butcher knife; it's a boning knife, used to—" Dennis started.

"Ugh, please spare me the details," I said, holding up a hand. "I don't want to hear about what type of knives slice what right now. I'm woozy enough as it is."

"You made these?" Officer Stevens asked, eyeing my zucchini sticks.

I held out the container. "Would you like one?"

He didn't hesitate. "Thanks, I'm starving." Popping two sticks into his mouth, he turned to Dennis. "Medical Examiner said she'll—" Officer Stevens swiveled back to me, his eyes gleaming with surprise. "Dang, Hadley! These are amazing. What are they?"

It was one of the few times I'd seen Officer Stevens veer from his all-business demeanor. Apparently, zucchini sticks brought out his lively side.

"Panko-crusted zucchini sticks," I said. Despite the trauma of finding Seth's body, despite my still-shaking body, I couldn't help but feel the tiniest sense of accomplishment.

Officer Stevens perched on the edge of the table next to mine, then told Dennis the medical examiner's whereabouts. He mindlessly grabbed more zucchini sticks as he talked, finishing them in just under a minute.

I sighed. My poor stomach would have to wait for dinner a little longer.

Officer Stevens brushed his hands against his slacks, leaving behind dozens of tiny crumbs. "Chief says I need to clear my schedule this week to help Detective Sanders since, theoretically, you're on desk duty," he said, grabbing a lime-green plastic container next to him and digging in.

"You let me worry about my availability," Dennis told him. "Desk duty is a metaphor for surrender. No offense to all the pencil-pushers, but I need to be out here, where the clues aren't filed away in police reports."

"Not sure Chief sees it that way, but whatever you say," Officer Stevens said, crunching loudly. "Just know I'm available if you need me." He stood and gestured for Dennis to follow him. "I want you to look at the murder weapon. There's a weird doo-dad attached to it that I've never seen before. And if anyone knows what it is, it's probably you."

Dennis was indeed known for his cooking skills and even had a popular social media channel where he shared videos of himself cooking meals with ingredients from his own garden.

He stood and tucked his notepad into his pocket. "Alright, let's go see this 'doo-dad'."

"Wait," I said, holding out my hand. "Detective Sanders mentioned that you're staying at a hotel with your niece."

Dennis looked at Officer Stevens. "I'll join you in a minute."

Then, facing me, he explained, "Someone sent me a threatening letter and then broke into my house yesterday. I believe it's connected to a money laundering case I've been investigating. The suspects are the stereotypical white-collar types who probably wouldn't follow through on their threats, but I'm not taking any chances since my niece is staying with me."

"Why don't y'all stay at my house? I have plenty of extra rooms."

A slight dimple appeared on his cheek. "Thanks, but I've already asked enough favors of you lately. The last one was a big one."

"Don't worry, you haven't reached your limit yet."

He wrapped a hand around the back of his neck and grimaced, as though he wasn't so sure about accepting my offer. "There are a lot of breakable things inside the Ladyvale Manor, and my niece, God love her, is a live wire. She's like a ping-pong ball that never stops bouncing."

"All the more reason for you guys to stay with me! I must admit, it is a little awkward having tourists roaming the first floor, but they are only there for part of the day, and there's more than enough space upstairs for us to relax away from them. And I promise not to serve you salmonella again—or your niece. She will adore Razzy, and—oh!—I almost forgot about the labyrinth! Imagine how much fun she'd have running through it." Standing, I gave his arm a reassuring squeeze. "I insist."

A grin broke across Dennis's face, but he quickly caught himself amid the somber atmosphere and tightened his lips into a more reserved smile. "Thank you. I'm gonna take you up on your offer, Miss Hadley, but we need to keep it quiet that we're staying with you. Even though I doubt anyone you talk to runs in the same circles as the suspects in the money laundering case, I don't want to put you or Kinsley in harm's way. I'll be busy at the station tomorrow, but if you're sure you don't mind, we'll come on Saturday. I'd be the worst uncle in the world if I deprived Kinsley of staying at a house with a labyrinth."

CHAPTER FOUR

My doorbell rang at precisely seven-thirty this morning. Then it rang five more times in rapid succession.

I scurried towards the front door, my smile growing with each sock-footed slide through the marble-tiled entry hall. Since leaving the horrific crime scene Thursday night, every spare moment had been a mad dash to prep for Dennis and his niece. Fresh sheets, squeaky-clean bathrooms, and a few (okay, a lot) of girly decorative touches in Kinsley's room so she would feel comfortable and welcome.

Counting the two times I nodded off while applying pink floral wallpaper to her bathroom, I got a whopping four hours of sleep last night.

I smoothed down my hair one last time and opened the door.

Despite the early hour, Dennis looked like he'd spent more than a hot minute in front of a mirror. His usually unkempt sandy-blonde hair was styled (with gel!), and he wore a casual-cool jacket over a simple white shirt. He had a black duffle bag slung over his shoulder, and a small purple suitcase in hand.

Kinsley clung to his leg, clutching a stuffed rabbit and peering up at me with big, curious blue eyes that looked remarkably similar to those of her uncle. Her stick-straight hair was gathered into pigtails that were more than a little lopsided, and adorable light-brown wisps of hair framed her sweet face.

There was an awkward moment of silence as Dennis's eyes met mine, his sea-blue gaze flickering with...nervousness, perhaps?

"Good morning!" I said, resisting the urge to smooth down my own hastily thrown-together jeans and baggy sweater combo. "Please, come in."

"Sorry about the doorbell," Dennis chuckled as he stepped inside. "Seems someone here"—he pointed discreetly to the little one still attached to his leg—"got a bit trigger-happy with it."

I laughed. "Doorbells are meant to be rung, right? And why push it once when you can push it five times?" Leaning down, I met the curious gaze of Dennis's niece. "Hey there, Kinsley! I'm Hadley. I've heard so much about you."

Family was everything to Dennis. Framed photos occupied prime real estate on his desk at the station and on tabletops, bookshelves, and kitchen counters at his home. Behind each photo were stories that he eagerly shared. Even though the rest of his family lived in Texas, Dennis traveled home a couple of times every year.

Kinsley peeked out from behind Dennis's leg, her eyes darting around the entry hall. "Uncle Dennis told me you have a cat," she said, her tone hinting at skepticism, as if she were conducting her own little investigation into the matter.

"I sure do! Razzy usually hangs out upstairs, but she likes to play hide and seek, so it might take us a minute to find her. She's really good at the game."

With a gleeful squeal, Kinsley peeled away from Dennis's cover and bolted up the stairs, her voice echoing through the hall as she called for Razzy at the top of her lungs.

"If Razzy wasn't already hiding, she sure is now," he laughed, shaking his head in amusement.

After helping Dennis bring in a few more bags from his unmarked patrol car, we made our way upstairs. The Darlington Hills Historical Society would begin hosting tours at nine o'clock, so we had the house to ourselves for a solid hour and a half. Just enough time to get them settled and show Kinsley around before tourists started rolling in.

"Kinsley's room is at the end of the hall on the right, and Dennis, you're across from her in Irma's old room. It has a great view of the labyrinth," I pointed out.

Irma Murdoch, the Ladyvale Manor's former homeowner, occupied the largest room upstairs before she died. After inheriting the home and moving in, I selected the smaller room next to hers. It felt like the respectful thing to do, especially considering the tragic circumstances of her death.

Aside from a deep cleaning and fresh layer of paint, I'd left Irma's room untouched—traditional oak furniture, a desk with a vintage bronze lamp, and three rows of shelves holding Irma's extensive porcelain doll collection. A bit creepy, maybe, but it added to the house's charm.

Dennis wasted no time in settling into his room, dropping his duffel bag with a grateful sigh. "You're a lifesaver, Hadley. Can't thank you enough."

The soft rumbling of tiny feet echoed down the hallway, and moments later, Razzy burst in, darting under the bed before anyone could blink, closely followed by a giggling Kinsley. Dennis swooped in and scooped up his niece before she could join Razzy in her hiding spot.

"Let's give Razzy a break," he suggested. "I bet she's tuckered out."

Kinsley shook her head. "She's not tired. She just ran down the hall. I want to play with her—" She stopped, her eyes transfixed on the display shelves. "Dolls!"

Dennis followed her gaze. "Yes, but those are the fragile kind," he said with a note of caution in his voice. "They're more for admiring than playing with."

Kinsley looked puzzled, probably wondering why anyone would make dolls you couldn't play with.

"How about some breakfast before I show Kinsley around?" I asked.

He shook his head, gently setting down his niece. "Thanks, but we ate at the hotel before we left. And don't worry about feeding us. I'll do the grocery shopping and cooking while we're here. You don't need to go to any more trouble for us."

"Madam Balleroy told us at least a hundred times we need to practice what we're learning. And boy, do I need the practice," I chuckled.

His cheek dimpled. "Alright then, we'll cook together. It'll be fun."

I showed Kinsley her room, which I had livened up with a new purple blanket, a matching fluffy rug, and a cuddly teddy bear perched in front of the pillows. She squealed when she saw the bear, then oohed and ahhed at the bathroom, declaring it fit for a princess.

My crazy, last-minute re-wallpapering project, despite the sleep deprivation it caused, was totally worth it just to see her face light up.

"Just a head's up, these rooms can get chilly at night if you don't leave the doors cracked open," I said as we left her room. "The heater is old, and it functions best when there's more airflow up here. But don't be surprised if Razzy pays you a visit in the wee hours."

We took a whirlwind tour of the upstairs, stopping by the family room, my office, the exercise room, and the makeshift kitchen—soon to be fully equipped to avoid disrupting the tourists below. Next, we headed downstairs, walking through the formal rooms that were part of the historical home tour.

Kinsley's blue eyes sparkled as we moved through the halls adorned with twinkling Christmas lights and festive decorations. Each room was decked out with themed displays, adding a touch of holiday magic to every corner. With tours booked solid for the month, my mission was clear: dazzle every guest who crossed the threshold. After all, there was no better marketing than word-of-mouth, and with the profits rolling in from tours and events, I had a hefty decorations budget.

"You have a lot of Christmas trees," Kinsley observed. "We only have one in my home."

"Just wait until you see my nutcracker collection!" I told her, leading her into the formal parlor. "What do you think? Each one's dressed as a character from a popular children's story." Smiling at Dennis, I said, "They're completely out of place amid the rest of the eighteenth-century decor, but that's what makes them so fun. Tourists can't get enough of them."

The towering figures, each about as tall as Kinsley herself, stood proudly next to an artificial balsam fir Christmas tree frosted with a layer of white flocking. "Look, there's my favorite —the Pinocchio nutcracker, with his signature long nose and yellow hat."

Kinsley's eyes lit up with recognition. "And a Peter Pan nutcracker!"

Dennis chimed in with a chuckle. "I don't see Captain Hook in your collection. Do you have something against pirates?"

"Hook and the Neverland pirate nutcrackers are busy pillaging the gingerbread village in the next room," I said with a wink. "They're causing quite the ruckus among the sugary inhabitants."

"Do you have any princess nutcrackers?" Kinsley asked.

"I should, shouldn't I? Just to keep my Prince Charming nutcracker on his toes..." My voice trailed off as I scanned the room. "That's weird. I'm down a nutcracker. The prince is missing."

"He must have marched off to save the gingerbread folks," Dennis said.

I nudged him playfully. "Detective Appley, always on the case. Let me know when you find him. He's supposed to be on guard in here, you know."

He smiled. "I'll make this search and rescue mission my top priority."

As we made our way out, I quickly checked the storage room and the Historical Society's office for any sign of the missing nutcracker. No luck. It seemed unlikely a tourist had made off with it, given its hefty size.

Outside, we zipped up our jackets against the chill of the early morning. Two sleepy-eyed young women in Whisks and Whiskers T-shirts were busy opening the shutters of the café's food truck, which had been parked outside my house for the past several weeks after the original location was forced to close temporarily. Despite the café's reopening in the town square, we continued running the food truck on my property. It was a lucrative venture, and it satisfied the cravings of tourists visiting the Ladyvale Manor.

Long shadows stretched across the backyard, but gleaming patches of sunshine hinted at warmer temperatures to come. By noon, we probably wouldn't even need our jackets. Dennis planned to spend most of the day at parks around town, and I had gladly accepted his invitation to join them.

"Speaking of sleuthing," I began as Kinsley dashed ahead, "any leads on the homicide case?"

He brightened. "Actually, yes. Let me fill you in."

I did a double-take, astonished by his willingness to talk about his case.

"We have conclusive evidence indicating the victim died from a stab wound." He gave me a definitive nod, then jogged to catch up with Kinsley, who was heading for the entrance to the labyrinth.

I hurried after him. "Wait! That's all you've got so far?"

Dennis shot me a sideways glance, his teasing smile in full force. "No, it's the only info I'm sharing with *you*."

I lowered my voice, mindful of Kinsley's innocent ears. "Any early suspects in mind?"

"Yes." His eyes crinkled at the corners. Clearly, he enjoyed torturing me by withholding information. "I can tell you the culprit was present on Madame Balleroy's property for a period of time on the evening of the victim's death."

I groaned and shot him a mock glare. "That doesn't tell me anything! Can you at least say—"

"Not a chance."

"But I—"

"Nope." His playful laughter came in deep rolling waves, momentarily holding me captive. That smile of his! It sparked a flutter in my chest I couldn't quite explain.

Today wasn't the first time Dennis had left me breathless, but it was the first time I let myself get lost in his gaze without an ounce of guilt. With Reid out of the picture, I no longer had to suppress the feelings that stirred within me whenever Dennis was near. I was free to let my heart lead the way.

Or was I?

My heart had been wrong before—twice in this year alone, when two out of two relationships ended with me getting dumped. First by Ricky, which had prompted me to move from New Orleans to Darlington Hills, and then, only a couple of weeks ago, by Reid. Maybe it was just a string of bad luck, or perhaps my heart was simply incapable of distinguishing genuine love from a convincing counterfeit.

It was probably best to proceed with caution. I didn't want to risk jeopardizing my friendship with Dennis by jumping into another misguided romance.

I sighed. My breath formed tiny clouds in front of me, dissipating as quickly as they appeared, much like the remnants of my relationship with Reid. My phone rang, and I welcomed the interruption, eager for a momentary escape from the swirl of emotions. I needed to clear my head and talk some sense into my stubborn heart.

"Good morning, this is Hadley," I answered, slipping into my most professional tone since I didn't recognize the number on my screen. You never knew when a call could be a potential new client.

"Hadley, it's Camille Balleroy. How are you, dear?" Her voice dripped with its usual saccharine sweetness, tinged with an air of superiority.

"I'm hanging in there, all things considered."

"Good to hear. I trust you'll be continuing with my classes?"

I hesitated. "Actually, I haven't given it much thought." Okay, that was a bit of a fib. I had secretly hoped Madame Balleroy would cancel the remaining classes in light of the homicide. With Dennis and his niece under my roof, spending evenings with them sounded far more appealing than cooking classes. "Are any of the other students returning?"

"Yes, most are."

I blinked in disbelief. "Seriously?"

"I've been calling everyone to reassure them of their safety. It was likely a random homicide, and although the police don't expect additional attacks, I've hired a security guard to be present for the rest of the classes—or at least until the police put the killer behind bars."

I mulled over her words. "I'll have to think about it. I'm not sure I'd feel safe returning."

Madame Balleroy let out an impatient grunt. "You can't quit now. Must I remind you how much you need these classes?"

It was a hard truth to swallow, but she had a point. These classes seemed like my best shot at redemption after the Thanksgiving disaster.

"I'll consider it," I replied cautiously. "Safety is my top priority."

"You'll be perfectly safe. We're beefing up security with cameras, an alarm system, and a badge entry system for staff."

I sighed, feeling torn. It seemed like there was no easy way out of this culinary imprisonment.

I glanced over at Dennis and Kinsley. Three hours of cooking classes each night meant three hours less with them. Who knew how long they would stay? They'd leave as soon as Dennis caught whoever had broken into his house and threatened him.

"I don't know…"

"Quitting now is not an option. There's a lot riding on the deal I worked out with your aunt."

"What do you mean by 'a lot riding on—'" I started, but she had already hung up.

I scrunched my nose, staring at my phone's screen in confusion. Madame Balleroy's words echoed in my mind as I tapped on Aunt Deb's number, wandering further into the labyrinth, out of earshot from Dennis and Kinsley.

The hedges glistened with early morning dew as sunlight filtered through the tall shrubs. Without tourists in the area, the air was quiet, interrupted only by Kinsley's soft giggles—growing more distant as I moved away from them.

"Good morning!" Aunt Deb's cheerful voice greeted me. "You're up early on a Saturday morning."

"What were the terms of the agreement you worked out with Madame Balleroy?" I asked, cutting straight to the chase. "She made it sound like I'm bound by blood to complete the cooking classes. Like I'm some kind of indentured servant."

"Oh, well…um… I'm sure she just wants to make sure you're committed to decorating her barn for the Christmas Eve brunch. It's only a couple of weeks away, and finding another designer on such short notice would be difficult. She's been rather stressed as of late, what with the homicide and all. I'm sure you can understand."

"I guess so," I admitted.

"Now, let's talk about the important news this morning," she exclaimed, changing the subject. "Roy told me you invited Dennis and his niece to stay at your house! What a kind, generous offer. It's moments like these that make me proud to be your aunt."

I turned left into an opening in the hedges, following the winding path deeper into the labyrinth. "Well, the Ladyvale Manor isn't the most ideal place for them to stay, but I figured it was better than a hotel room."

"Of course it is! Oh, and while Dennis is staying with you, make sure he doesn't get any wild ideas about Hal being involved in the homicide. My hiking group would implode if he ended up behind bars."

"Hal?" I whispered, feeling a jolt of surprise. "Is that who they have their eyes on? Madame Balleroy said it was likely a random crime. Has Roy said anything?"

"He's being particularly tight-lipped about this investigation, but I know that Hal was on Madame Balleroy's property at the time of the homicide, even though the other cooking school students had left."

"Why didn't he leave with the others?"

"He headed over to Madame Balleroy's restaurant after classes. He was supposed to meet up with his new girlfriend for dinner, but Sheila had car trouble and never showed up. Hal left the restaurant shortly before you found the sous chef in the kitchen."

"But why would Roy and Dennis suspect Hal? What motive would he have?"

"Exactly! That's what I keep trying to tell Roy, but he says it's for him to decide who does and does not have a motive."

I laughed softly. That sounded exactly like something Dennis would say.

"If you ask me, Roy has something against Hal. I'll bet he's jealous because Hal's in my hiking club and has all the ladies chasing after him."

"Roy doesn't come on your hikes?"

"I've invited him, of course, but he says he's not the eye-candy type like Hal."

"Okay, I'll let you know if Dennis mentions anything about him," I promised, though I doubted he would share much about his investigation.

"Thanks, hon. I've reached a record number of members in my group this year, and I don't want to lose anyone else. Just last week, Mary Jean and Collette quit when Hal started dating Sheila Moody. If the ladies find out the police are eyeing him as a suspect, I can only imagine how many more will leave."

After hanging up with Aunt Deb and tucking my phone back into my jacket pocket, I turned around to rejoin Dennis and Kinsley. But as I tried to retrace my steps, I realized the Ladyvale Manor's roof looked farther away now than when I'd gotten off the phone.

Yikes. Where was I?

"Dennis?" I called out. Oh, how embarrassing—to get lost inside my own labyrinth!

I waited a moment for him to respond, then tried again. "Dennis? Where'd you go?"

Kinsley let out a tiny giggle seconds before Dennis snuck up behind me and started tickling my sides, making me laugh uncontrollably.

"I...couldn't...find...my...way...out," I gasped between laughs as his fingers moved relentlessly across my stomach.

"Is that so?" he said, his voice a playful hum close to my ear. "Or could it be that you wanted to be caught?"

"You are impossible, Dennis!" I struggled and squirmed, desperately trying to break free from his tickling assault. My heart pounded—half from the breathlessness of laughter, half from the thrill of being so close to him.

Finally, he relented and turned me around to face him. I drew in a quick breath at the proximity, feeling suddenly shy under his mischievous gaze.

"Sorry I lost you guys," I said, still panting slightly. "I was chatting with Madame Balleroy, and then my aunt."

Dennis's face-splitting smile vanished. "I'd like to hear what Madame Balleroy said."

CHAPTER FIVE

As the clock ticked closer to the start of our second cooking class, only seven out of twelve students had arrived. Madame Balleroy paced around the kitchen, glancing at her watch every few seconds and stealing hopeful looks towards the doorway. Tonight was the first night the restaurant and school were open to the public after being closed while the police conducted their investigation.

The kitchen felt empty, and yet somehow heavy with a mix of tension, grief, and death. I was alone at my prep table, and the other two tables were only half-full. When Madame Balleroy had said "most" of the class would return, either she was being overly optimistic, or trying to coax me back.

As promised, a security guard stood in the corner, arms crossed, watching everything.

Only problem was, I doubted he would intimidate anyone. He couldn't have been over twenty, was stick-thin, and his duty belt held only a flashlight and a small canister of pepper spray. Clearly, Madame Balleroy had found a good bargain.

Her shoulders slumped with relief when the sound of clicking shoes signaled a new arrival. My eyes widened at the sight of the woman in the doorway—it was the lady Seth had claimed to be his future mother-in-law. Her short brown hair was messy, and she wasn't wearing any makeup, which made sense given the recent tragedy. But why had she returned?

Madame Balleroy hurried over to greet her. "Eileen!" she exclaimed, wrapping her in a dramatic hug. They exchanged some hushed words and dabbed at their eyes before Madame Balleroy led Eileen to the table next to mine and pulled out a stool for her.

"Hadley, this is Eileen Riggs. I'd like for you to join her table group tonight." Madame Balleroy nodded towards an open stool. "There's no reason for you to sit by yourself."

I moved over and introduced myself to everyone, then turned to Eileen. "I'm so sorry about Seth's passing. I understand he was your daughter's fiancé, and I know how devastating this must be for her and your family."

Eileen dipped her head in silent thanks. "My daughter, Cindy, is...beyond heartbroken—especially considering how Seth died. Their wedding was supposed to be at the end of the month. She hasn't slept or eaten since the police gave her the news." Her voice was heavy with emotion, each word a pained effort to utter.

"I understand it may not be much of a consolation," I said softly, "but the detectives assigned to this case are highly skilled. They will quickly bring Seth's murderer to justice."

"Thank you, hon. I've tried reassuring Cindy of the same, but there's really nothing I can say to ease her pain." Eileen's watery brown eyes flicked toward Madame Balleroy, and she lowered her voice. "Honestly, I'd rather be with Cindy right now than at these cooking classes. But Seth paid for my tuition, so I feel obligated to come. It was his way of trying to bond with his future mother-in-law, even though I'd rather wrestle with a grizzly bear than cook a meal. It's important to Cindy that I finish the classes; otherwise, I'd be throwing away Seth's gift."

I gave her a sympathetic smile. "Believe me, I understand.

There are a dozen places I'd rather be tonight, too. My aunt gifted me these classes—supposedly as a Christmas gift—but in reality, they're a punishment for a long list of culinary misdeeds."

"Well, I'm glad I'm not the only one here who doesn't know a spoon from a spatula," Eileen said with a smile that didn't quite reach her eyes.

At the top of that list was hanging out with Dennis and Kinsley. Yesterday and Saturday had been a blur of laughs, giggles, and squeals of a five-year-old's delight during trips to nearby parks, walks around town, and a cartoon movie marathon while Dennis worked on his laptop, occasionally stepping out to call Detective Sanders.

Of every second that had ticked by this weekend, two moments continued to replay in my mind. First, the tickle session in the labyrinth. What *was* that? A friend-to-friend tickle, or something more? Like me, Dennis was fresh out of a relationship. Was it possible he had already shifted gears to someone else—i.e., *me*?

Second, Dennis's barrage of questions about my conversation with Madame Balleroy. After I'd recounted every word spoken during the five-minute phone call, Dennis excused himself to make a series of phone calls before we left for the park.

The squeaks of sneakers on the tiled floor signaled the arrival of Mitzy and Hal, with Grand-mère guiding them in from behind. Madame Balleroy narrowed her eyes at the two of them. "Next time, be more prompt to my class." Her stern gaze followed them to our table.

Mitzy looked mortified by Madame's censure, but Hal waved off the reprimand with a lazy two-fingered salute, rolling his eyes as he took his seat.

"Hadley, please return to your table group," Madame Balleroy commanded. "That way, we'll have three groups of three."

"Good luck," Eileen whispered as I stood to switch tables again.

Darcy, the fourth member of my table group, must have bailed on the cooking classes—either because of the homicide or because Hal made her too nervous. Maybe both.

Madame Balleroy introduced her hired security guard as Officer Butch, though his unofficial uniform told me he wasn't actually on the police force. Grand-mère remained near the doorway, her arms crossed, and feet spread wide as though blocking the exit. With a pinch-faced glare that darted continuously from one student to the next, she looked far more intimidating than our pip-squeak security guard.

Madame Balleroy spent the first five minutes of class giving a eulogy for her fallen sous-chef. Her words were eloquent, but her tone was cool and detached—like she was reading a weather report rather than mourning a close colleague.

The kitchen was silent, except for the occasional creak of a stool. Madame Balleroy finished her speech, then clapped her hands sharply. "Now it's time to begin tonight's lesson," she declared. "We will honor Seth's life by striving for excellence in our craft. Can someone please tell me what all chefs have in common?" She peered out at her students expectantly.

"They all love to eat," guessed a man sitting at the table to my left.

"Wrong," she snapped. "And we're not all chubby sloths who over-indulge in our own creations."

"That's not what I was—" he started.

"Any other guesses?" Madame Balleroy said.

Mitzy raised her hand. "They're all creative and have an attention to detail?"

Madame Balleroy looked impressed. "While these are indeed hallmark traits of a successful chef, it's not the answer I'm looking for. The most prestigious chefs I know have one thing in common."

She held up a finger as she paused, as though her silence would put us on the edge of our seats. "They all have a signature ingredient, something beyond your traditional seasonings and spices, which they use in nearly every dish they create—both savory and sweet. Mine, of course, is the—"

"There are more than two types of dishes," Grand-mère interjected. "What Madame Balleroy meant to say is there is a wide range of flavors and culinary styles into which a chef incorporates his or her signature ingredient: savory, sweet, spicy, sour, bitter, and umami, to name a few."

Madame Balleroy's eyes narrowed. "As I was saying, my signature ingredient is citrus zest. It adds a refreshing kick to my dishes and enhances everything from seafood to desserts with its subtle bitterness and tangy aroma. Seth, God rest his soul, incorporated pomegranate seeds into nearly all his dishes, showcasing his truly unique culinary style. Grand-mère's signature ingredient—"

"Is truffle oil," Grand-mère said, lifting her chin. "It adds a luxurious depth of flavor to all my dishes."

As Grand-mère spoke, the kitchen's back door opened, and Natasha Antonov, the station chef I met Thursday night in Madame Balleroy's kitchen, strode inside. Her coppery-red hair was pulled into a sleek ponytail beneath her chef's hat, and long, chunky gold hoop earrings swayed with each confident step. Natasha's cool, inscrutable smile suggested she either didn't know she was walking over the spot where Seth's body had lain, or she didn't care.

"Mine's vanilla bean," Natasha proclaimed, somehow knowing exactly why Grand-mère was talking about truffle oil.

Madame Balleroy gestured to Natasha and introduced her to our class. "I have named Natasha as the new sous chef for my restaurant. Likewise, she will be available periodically during these classes to assist you."

Natasha gave us a friendly wave. "And I can help you brainstorm ideas for your Christmas Eve brunch—"

Madame Balleroy shushed her with an impatient wave. "I

was just getting to that part. Class, I have a special surprise to announce. As students of my December cooking classes, you will prepare a unique dish for this year's Christmas Eve brunch!"

Mitzy clapped her hands excitedly, nearly squirming out of her seat. "Can I bake a cheesecake?"

"Absolutely! Anything you'd like—dessert, appetizer, a main dish—the choice is yours. Your creations will be presented alongside my restaurant's dishes, showcasing everything you've learned in my classes. The only requirement is that you create a dish that is truly unique, and you must include your own signature ingredient. I will invite guests at the brunch to vote on their favorite one and the winner will receive a prize."

I rolled my eyes over to Eileen and gave her a supremely sarcastic thumbs-up—as if this was the most exciting opportunity I'd ever been granted. She raised a hand to her mouth, stifling a smile.

Madame Balleroy went around the kitchen, asking each student to name their signature ingredient. There was a Szechuan peppercorn fanatic, a molasses devotee, a lavender enthusiast, and several hot pepper zealots. Even Officer Butch had one—coconut shavings. Either everyone truly knew what their signature ingredient was, or they had made it up.

When it was my turn to share, I confidently announced, "Pepper."

"*Pepper?*" she demanded. "That isn't a signature ingredient, unless you have the imagination of a doormat."

"But another classmate said peppercorns, and it's essentially the same thing."

Madame Balleroy just stared at me. No words, no expression, nothing. Most likely, she was cursing herself for entering into the agreement with Aunt Deb in the first place. "You will need to figure out what your signature ingredient is before the Christmas Eve brunch," she said at last. "Consider it a homework assignment. Speaking of which…did you finish reading the book I gave you?"

"Sorry, I had a busy weekend."

"We're all busy, Hadley, but that's no excuse. You need to finish it before you prepare a dish for hundreds of guests on Christmas Eve. I'd hate for you to ruin the holiday for half of Darlington Hills."

Ouch. That one stung a little.

Madame Balleroy described the recipe we were learning tonight—sherried lobster bisque—and explained the instructions on the recipe cards she'd given each of us.

"If you were first to use the oven and stove in the last class, please let someone else in your group go ahead of you tonight. Let's all be considerate of one another, and most importantly, practice what you learn at home. Otherwise, you're wasting your money on these classes."

Mitzy finished chopping her vegetables in record time, so she claimed the oven and stove first, and then Hal finished slightly before me. I cursed my slow chopping skills as I watched the minute-hand traipse slowly around the clock on the wall.

Kinsley would probably be asleep now. Maybe Dennis too. I'd visited with them for a whopping ten minutes between the time I got home from Walnut Ridge and when I left for cooking classes. It had only been two days since they arrived, but I greedily wanted to spend more time with them. Their presence filled my home with warmth and laughter, banishing the stony silence that seemed to swallow me whole.

I scanned the other two prep tables, hoping others who got first dibs on their appliances might finish before Hal or Mitzy so I could get my lobster in the oven and veggies on the stove.

No such luck. My classmates to my left had forgotten to preheat their ovens before they started chopping, and Eileen and another woman at her table were even slower veggie slicers than I was.

Fifteen minutes later—though it felt like at least thirty—I donned a pair of oven mitts, removed my two lobster tails from the oven, placed them on the prep table, then twisted and pulled the head from the tail.

"Yeow!" I exclaimed as a splash of hot butter landed on my chin.

"You need to let them cool before you remove the meat from the shells." Natasha stood behind me, reaching her gloved hand out and pointing to the recipe card, where this step was written.

"I skipped that step because I want to leave soon." I gave her a weak smile and braced myself for a reprimand or condescending remark, but she laughed quietly through her nose.

"You and me both, girly. Here's a tip to speed things up: just pull the fins off and poke the fork into the tail to loosen the meat, then push it out through the other side. Here, I'll write it down for you." She removed a purple pen from her pocket and made a note in the column of my recipe card.

"Thanks!" I said, then hurried to do as she instructed. "Oh, and congrats on your promotion, although I know the circumstances are tragic."

She sat on the empty stool next to me and sighed. "Maybe I'll feel grateful once the shock of what happened wears off, but now all I feel is guilt for taking Seth's position. Does that sound crazy?"

"No, it doesn't," I assured her. "There's no perfect way to think or feel during a time like this. Sometimes crazy is the only sane response we have."

Her voice dropped to a whisper as she quickly scanned the room. "There's a lot of 'crazy' going around this place tonight—the kitchen crew, the wait staff, Madame Balleroy, and Grand-mère. Those two have been at each other's throats more than usual."

"How so?" I asked. Hal and Mitzy were busy debating whether

bisque could ever be served as a main course, but I kept my voice low anyway. "They don't get along?"

"Grand-mère opened the restaurant years ago, and ran it by herself until fifteen years ago, when she made Madame Balleroy co-owner and Head Chef. Even though Grand-mère officially retired, she still has strong opinions about how they should run the restaurant."

"And the cooking school?"

Natasha's eyes flicked once more towards Madame Balleroy. "No. The school is Madame Balleroy's pet project. It's what she's most passionate about these days, probably because she enjoys being revered as the expert—but you didn't hear that from me."

"Of course not," I promised. "Does Grand-mère like to teach too?"

Natasha shook her head. "She never has liked the school. She thinks Madame Balleroy should spend more time in the restaurant because the food—and ratings—were better before she started teaching."

"I've always heard such good things about the restaurant. It's the nicest one in town. When did ratings dip?"

Natasha hesitated, chewing on her lip. "It was about a year ago," she said at last. "That's when Madame Balleroy started spending more time at the school and less at her restaurant. She hired Seth to oversee the kitchen crew, but ratings continued to slide from that point on. Critics noticed, regulars murmured, and then a couple of scathing internet reviews made Grand-mère panic. She accused Seth of tarnishing the restaurant's reputation she'd spent decades building."

"Why didn't they replace him?"

Natasha leaned in, her voice barely above a whisper. "He may not have been the best chef they could employ, but he was the reason the restaurant was booked solid every weekend."

"Oh? Why's that?"

"Seth was incredibly charming. He had a way with the

customers, especially the regulars. He made everyone feel special, like they were part of an exclusive club. People came back just to see him. I'm sure Madame Balleroy felt overshadowed by her sous-chef's growing popularity, but she knew it was good for business."

"Well, I hope the restaurant continues to thrive, despite Seth's passing."

Natasha stood, her eyes already on a student with his hand raised at another table. "I hope so, too. We've already had ten cancellations for the upcoming weekend. *Ten*. And that might not seem like a lot, but in the restaurant business, where profit margins are as narrow as a sharp knife, it could spell disaster—or at least the beginning of one."

"Last Thursday—"

"Hang on a sec." Natasha lifted her chin, sniffing gently. "Smoke!" she hissed. She ran toward a nearby oven and yanked a kitchen towel from her chef coat pocket. She folded it once, twice, and then used it to grip the sides of the baking dish from the smoking oven.

"Who forgot to set a timer?" she called out, then set it down on a hot plate in front of a red-faced man at the table next to me.

Finally, a kitchen mishap that I hadn't caused.

Natasha strolled over to my table again, making a face at the unpleasant burnt lobster odor in the room. "Sorry for the interruption. You were saying?"

"Just one more question for you: last Thursday, Grand-mère came into this kitchen and told Madame Balleroy that the cakes needed frosting. Was that code for something, or did she really need her granddaughter to frost some cakes?"

"It was a code for, get your butt to the restaurant because there's an unhappy customer who just found a beetle in his short rib bourguignon."

CHAPTER SIX

After acing the pastry-wrapped cranberry baked brie appetizer in our cooking class the next night, I felt a resurgence of confidence —so much so that I called Dennis on my way home and offered to make dinner. Neither of them had eaten yet, so my timing was perfect. Class had only lasted an hour and a half, which left me plenty of time to swing by Darlin' Mart to pick up the ingredients for a recipe Mitzy had suggested: baked salmon with basil, lemon, and thyme. I couldn't wait to try it out.

As I entered my kitchen, I found Dennis and Kinsley sitting at the breakfast table—Dennis glued to his laptop amid a sea of scattered papers, and Kinsley hunched over a coloring book, going to town with a purple crayon.

He jumped up to greet me, taking the bags from my hands and setting them on the counter. "You sure you don't want me to cook tonight? You must be beat after a full day at work and cooking classes."

I shrugged off my coat and folded it neatly before placing it on the counter. "I'm sure, but thanks. Madame Balleroy says practice is the only path to culinary greatness."

"Alright, but holler if you'd like help." Dennis turned back to the table and grabbed his laptop bag. In his comfy joggers and a snug rusty-red athletic top, he looked like he'd snuck in a workout—especially with those wild sweeps of hair on his forehead.

"Mind if I borrow some thyme and dill?" I nodded towards the potted herbs perched on the windowsill. Dennis had swung by his house earlier with Detective Sanders to check on Sadie, his pet goat, and to pick up a few essentials, including more clothes and several small pots of herbs.

"Help yourself; that's what they're here for. Oh, and before you get started, can you look at these for me?" He dropped a big yellow envelope onto the table. "They're photos of brake lights from all vehicles present on Madame Balleroy's property the night of the hom—"

Dennis stopped himself, catching Kinsley's eye. "—last Thursday evening."

"Sure thing." I dropped my keys on the counter, then sidled up to the table where he was spreading out the pics. "Wow, who knew there were so many brake light shapes? Circles, rectangles, crescents…" I leaned in, studying the photos. "…ovals, X-shaped ones, thin slits—"

I straightened my back as recognition dawned on me. In an instant, it felt like I was back on that narrow walkway near the cabernet-colored barn, squinting at the parking lot and the long road stretching away from Madame Balleroy's.

"This one." I tapped the photo that showed slits of red light shaped like a backward letter C, which narrowed in the center.

Dennis hovered beside me, eyeing the collage. "You're sure?"

"Absolutely. I remember them because they're so unusual. Whose vehicle is it?"

He chuckled, nudging me playfully with his elbow. "You know I can't say."

I threw my hands up in mock surrender as I retreated toward the stove. "Fine. Then I won't share the super-secret technique I learned tonight for unfolding a puff pastry sheet without ripping it. It would have blown your mind, Dennis. It's a life-changing cooking hack, and unfortunately you'll never know it."

Dennis swaggered over, his thick eyebrows knitting together over mischievous eyes. "Oh, really? I guess that means you'll have to unfold all my puff pastry sheets for me. Forever and ever—"

Before he could finish, Kinsley's cheery voice cut in. "H...al... st...en...ner," she said, carefully sounding out each syllable while studying the back of the photo I'd pointed out.

In a flash, Dennis was at her side, plucking the photo from her little hands. "Whoa there, little genius! I didn't know you could read. You haven't even started kindergarten yet!"

She beamed up at him proudly. "I'm in *pre*-kindergarten, Uncle Dennis. It's serious business. I already know my level one sight words, and I can write all my letters."

"I'm impressed, kiddo, but we better put these pictures away." He scooped them into a messy pile and shoved them into his laptop bag. "Believe it or not, Miss Hadley can read too. And now that she knows I've labeled the backs, I wouldn't put it past her to sneak a peek herself." He shot me a toothy grin, which nearly made me snort with laughter.

"I don't need another look," I said. "Kinsley just told me everything I wanted to know. Thanks, sweetie!"

She gave me a thumbs-up before turning her attention to the grocery bags on the counter. "What's for dinner?" she asked.

"Salmon with lemon, basil, and..." I trailed off as her nose scrunched up like she'd just sniffed a skunk, disgust plain in her eyes. "Or, I have some chicken nuggets if you'd rather—"

"Nuggies!" Kinsley screamed, leaving no doubt about her preference.

Dennis's eyes twinkled as he watched me shuffle over to the freezer. "You like chicken nuggets?"

"I always keep some on-hand for when I have a dinner fail. They're my safety net."

Opening my freezer, I grabbed the bag of nuggets and heaved it onto the counter. Kinsley's eyes widened with pure joy, like she'd just won the dinner lottery. Christmas had come early, and it was shaped like dinosaurs and breaded to perfection.

Dennis's lips parted. "That's…a lot of nuggets."

"Value-size," I said, tapping the bold, red words on the bag. "Might as well get the big one. You can freeze them for a million years, and they're still edible. Please, help yourself."

Dennis strolled toward me, a smile forming on his lips. "So this is your culinary secret, huh? Prehistoric poultry?"

"Absolutely," I replied with mock seriousness. "They're my sacred fallback that surpasses all cooking disasters."

Kinsley, oblivious to our banter, stood in her chair to get a better view of her dinner. "Can I have ten?"

"Sure, I'll heat them up when the fish is almost ready," Dennis replied, gesturing for her to sit down.

I removed a small mixing bowl from the cabinet and added lemon zest, lemon juice, and minced garlic. Dennis dropped a handful of thyme sprigs beside my cutting board, as though he knew exactly how much the recipe called for.

With a paring knife in-hand, I bent over the counter and got to work, meticulously separating the tiny thyme leaves from their stems. Two minutes later, I'd amassed a grand total of approximately twelve leaves.

"Want me to show you a trick?"

I jumped back, bumping into Dennis. He steadied me with a gentle hand on my shoulder, his quiet chuckles filling the small space between us.

"Of course," I said. "Let's see it."

Dennis stepped closer behind me, took the knife from my hand, and placed it on the counter. "You don't need a knife. Just your hands."

He held onto the top of the stem with one hand while pinching and sliding his fingers down the stem with the other, cleanly stripping off the leaves. The tiny green flecks gathered in a neat pile on the cutting board.

It was an excellent trick, but all I could focus on was his arms encircling me and the heat radiating from his body.

"Show me one more time?" I asked, hoping to prolong the moment.

He demonstrated again, this time drawing me closer into his embrace. I lifted a stem and mirrored his movements, trying to concentrate on his instructions rather than the closeness of our bodies.

After removing all the leaves, he stepped back and wiped his sleeve against his brow. The kitchen was now a furnace, ignited by his leaf-pulling session.

"Need anything else?" he asked.

"Thanks, but I'll take it from here. I just need a few sprigs of dill, and then I can get this fish in the oven."

Kinsley sprang from her chair. "I want to help! Can I pull the leaves?"

Dennis took a pair of scissors from my knife block, then knelt beside the dill plant and motioned her over. "It's best to take leaves from the top of the plant so it will grow fuller."

Kinsley grabbed a fist-full of stems and leaves and tugged, but Dennis quickly stopped her. "Here, use the scissors." He showed her how with a few easy snips. "You never want to pull up the plant's roots."

I stared at him as a wave of chill bumps rippled across my arms and neck. "Never?"

He shook his head. "Not unless you want it to wilt and die. Why?"

"Remember how I told you that Madame Balleroy took Chloe and me to the barn Thursday night during the tour and then stepped out for five minutes after receiving a text?"

Dennis's gaze sharpened with interest. "Yes."

"Well, before she left, she claimed she was heading to the herb forest to gather some dill for the fish Chloe's husband was making for dinner."

"I remember you saying as much. Anything to add?" He glanced at Kinsley, who was now carefully snipping dill sprigs with the focus of a miniature gardener oblivious to the gravity of our conversation.

"When Madame Balleroy returned, she gave Chloe a handful of the dill—roots and all. Seems like she would have known the right way to harvest her own herbs."

He nodded curtly. "I'm sure she knows. Question is, why didn't she take the time to do it properly?" Dennis gathered the sprigs of dill Kinsley snipped, along with the scissors, and placed them on the counter in front of me. "I need to make a couple of calls. If dinner's ready before I'm done, please go ahead and eat."

For the rest of the night, until I drifted off to sleep, I replayed his hands-on thyme demonstration, savoring the lingering shower-fresh scent of him on my sweater, and wishing I had leaned back into his arms just a little more.

CHAPTER SEVEN

I could count on one hand the number of times I skipped class during college, and I never missed work unless I had a darn good reason. But today, while I worked at Walnut Ridge, the temptation to skip tonight's cooking class grew stronger with every passing minute.

Dennis had spent most of last night on the phone, only breaking to join us for dinner and do the dishes. He didn't put Kinsley to bed until ten o'clock, and she had taken full advantage of the late night to give all her dolls a complete wardrobe change. This morning, Dennis and Kinsley had the same groggy blue eyes, and Kinsley even fussed about going to her day camp.

So, there was a good chance they would both be asleep by the time I got home from Madame Balleroy's tonight, which meant zero opportunities for more herb-cutting lessons, playful tickle sessions, or sitting down to chat about our day.

As he left this morning, Dennis mentioned he had a lead on his money laundering case and was getting closer to identifying whoever had broken into his house. I'd wished him good luck, but secretly, I wouldn't have minded if it took him a while longer to crack that case. In seven days, my two-week vacation would begin, and I could spend even more time with them if they were still staying at my house.

But first, I had to tackle my mile-long to-do list at work. Vincent was launching a new line of wallpapers and framed art next spring, and I needed to plan which patterns, furniture, and decor would pair nicely for upcoming photoshoots. This was on top of a slew of last-minute photo retakes needed for the next catalog.

"Hadley, come tell me what you think about the chandelier in the dining room." Vincent stood in the doorway to the upstairs bedroom, where I was spreading out wallpaper samples. He motioned for me to follow him with a casual wave and easy smile. His mostly gray hair looked slightly disheveled. The deep crease between his eyes softened briefly, though it never fully disappeared.

This was not the same man who had hired me to work as his interior designer earlier this year. Vincent had been so unpleasant to me and the rest of his crew during my first few months at Walnut Ridge that I'd even considered looking for another job.

I guessed his dramatic personality reboot had something to do with the tiny beagle sitting smugly in the front-carrier backpack that Vincent now wore every day. With his crew hauling furniture in and out of the house, doors were often left open, and he worried Lexi would escape. Though judging from the content, princess-like expression in the pup's big brown eyes, I was certain she wouldn't stray too far if she got out.

Or maybe Vincent's shift in attitude towards me was from guilt—or worse, pity—after his younger brother, Reid, broke up with me last month. Vincent reacted by giving me a small raise and reassuring me that he thought his brother was a jerk. Combined, these two things were a nice consolation to getting dumped.

"Of course!" I replied, jumping to my feet and smoothing down the fabric of my sweater. "Did the guys finish hanging it?"

"Yes, but then I told them to swap the Sonoma Chandelier with the twelve-light brass one. I thought it would make the room look more sophisticated, but now I'm not so sure."

I could have told him without even looking at it that the brass chandelier most definitely would *not* work with the dining table and chairs we were shooting, but I held my tongue as I followed him downstairs.

"Any plans for the Christmas break?" he asked.

"Nothing big. I'll be spending a lot of time in the kitchen—"

"*Cooking*? Really?" His half-grin made it clear that Reid had shared stories of my culinary mishaps.

"I'm taking cooking classes," I continued. "And I'm decorating a barn for an upcoming event." I left out the part about housing a hot detective and his sweet niece.

Vincent chuckled. "That doesn't sound like much of a vacation. Most people like to catch up on sleep or binge-watch Netflix."

"I plan to do those things on my next vacation."

"And your parents—they live in Japan, right?—are they traveling home for the holidays?"

"They usually come home for Christmas, but this year they are staying in Tokyo since they're flying home for my aunt's wedding early next year."

Vincent slowed his pace, his expression knitted with concern. "You said you're taking cooking classes? Where? Because I heard a chef was recently murdered at Madame Balleroy's school. Please tell me you aren't—"

"Yep. That's where I'm going. I was there the night of the homicide."

His eyes widened with bewilderment. "And you're still taking the classes?"

"Mmm-hmm," I squeaked. He didn't need to know my attendance wasn't completely optional. "Madame Balleroy hired a security guard. Officer Butch will keep us safe."

Vincent's brow furrowed with skepticism. "Just promise me you'll be careful. We need you back here in one piece."

"Promise."

"And the barn you're decorating...is it for Madame Balleroy's annual Christmas Eve brunch?"

"That's the one! As of right now, she's still planning to host it. Are you going?"

His gaze shifted uneasily, momentarily cracking his confident facade. "Not this year. Reid will be with—well, you know who— and I don't have any other family around."

We stepped into the dining room, where the muted afternoon sun filtered like wisps onto the Cotterhill dining table and white upholstered Parsons chairs. I'd spent two hours this morning decorating the space with popular Walnut Ridge accessories—the Hamlin wool rug, white-tailored curtains, sculptural vases, and a rectangular mirror with a thin black frame—all which would have looked better with the chandelier I had recommended.

"I know the brass chandelier is a popular item," I started, keeping my tone light, "but it doesn't meld well with the more modern decorations I selected for this space. A room needs to be cohesive. Otherwise, it feels like walking into a conversation where everyone's talking about a different subject."

He pressed his lips together, giving a tight nod. Vincent didn't like to be wrong, but he knew I was right; I could see the begrudging acceptance in the slight droop of his shoulders. "Well, Hadley, you have a better eye for these things," he said, with an attempt at grace that didn't quite mask his irritation. "I'll have the guys swap it out with the one you selected initially."

I returned to my project upstairs before he could question my advice or change his mind. For the next hour, I jotted down notes on recommended groupings of wallpaper, furniture, rugs, and decor. Rather than actually apply and reapply wallpaper to all the rooms, Vincent's graphics team would superimpose it onto the walls after the photoshoot.

It was a relief to focus on my work and forget about the craziness of the past few days. As I scribbled down notes and ideas, I found myself smiling, looking forward to another evening with Dennis and Kinsley. The cooking, the laid-back conversations, the futile attempts to get Kinsley to bed on time, and even the flirty exchanges with Dennis were feeling like a new kind of normal.

At five o'clock, I stretched my arms high above my head, releasing the tension tugging at my neck and back. It was time to go home. After stacking all the wallpaper samples into the corner of the room, I switched off the light and practically flew out the door, unable to suppress the smile on my lips. I'd made up my mind: tonight, I would skip cooking class.

I bounded down the hallway but skidded to a halt when a familiar voice drifted up from the entryway below. It was Reid—laughing, loud-talking, boasting about his day chugging along the James River on his paddlewheeler. He sounded so *happy*.

I pressed my back against the wall, staying out of sight from the bantering brothers. Through the forged iron balcony rails, I saw the top half of Reid's face. His eyebrows shot up and down as he talked, as though he were sharing exciting news with his brother.

Clearly, he wasn't the least bit sad I was no longer in his life. He'd moved on to another woman, and now I was nothing more to him than his brother's worker bee.

A hollow pain tugged at my chest. It was a reminder of what I thought we had, and what he so easily discarded. Even if Reid ever changed his mind, I wouldn't go back to him—not after what he had done.

Still, it stung. I felt foolish for once believing Reid's sweet words and promises, for believing someone like him could truly value me.

And yet, here I was, flirting my little heart out with Dennis. Flirting with another opportunity for failure.

I hadn't needed that second thyme leaf demo, and Dennis didn't need me or my hospitality. He and Kinsley would have been just fine staying in the hotel—in fact, she might have enjoyed it even more since it had an indoor pool.

As for the tickle session and thyme-cutting demo, they probably meant nothing to Dennis. He was an absolute flirt—had been since the day I met him, when his sea-blue eyes stole a tiny piece of my heart. Even though I liked to think of myself as a smart woman, I could not unravel his playful behavior—was it because he was interested in me, or was it simply his personality?

Perhaps my sudden desire to spend time with Dennis was nothing more than a frantic rebound from Reid. I needed to slow down, to rebuild the walls around my mess of a heart and give it time to heal.

Vincent muttered something below about Lexi, and Reid's laughter rumbled throughout the house, shaking me to my senses. With a deep breath, I peeled myself away from the wall, determined to leave the house without looking at either of them.

I wouldn't skip class tonight. Dennis and Kinsley would be fine without me, and I needed cooking lessons more than I needed a man.

Digging a hand inside my tote bag, I removed a spool of plaid ribbon and other small decorative items, then placed them on the classroom table. Everyone else was in the kitchen, but I'd snuck into the classroom to retrieve some Christmas decorations I just so happened to have in my bag. I'd grabbed them from home this morning, planning to tie them around napkin rings for a Walnut Ridge Christmas-themed social media post.

Now, I planned to use the leftover decorations to jazz up the red velvet dessert loaves we were baking tonight. Madame Balleroy said they'd make exceptional gifts for friends and neighbors—and what was a gift without a bow?

Problem was, I didn't know who I'd give them to. Not Dennis —it might send the wrong message. Aunt Deb probably wouldn't eat them. She wouldn't trust my cooking until I completed the classes. Michael, maybe? Carmella?

Cindy Riggs, Seth's grieving fiancée, ambled from the kitchen into the classroom, her mom's arm looped around her shoulders. One look at Cindy's tear-streaked face made my own troubles seem trivial.

"Call me if you need anything," Eileen said. "I'm here if you need me." She gave her daughter a parting hug before returning to the kitchen.

Head sagging, Cindy made her way to the red leather purse on the table next to me. She'd arrived twenty minutes ago, just after we started mixing ingredients for the red velvet mini loaves. Madame Balleroy had asked Grand-mère to assist us while she took Cindy to the restaurant to collect Seth's belongings.

Cindy eyed the spool of Christmas ribbon I held, her eyebrows raising slightly.

"It's for the mini loaves," I explained. "Decorating my food distracts from any potential shortcomings in flavor."

Cindy offered me a faint smile, then set the box she was carrying on the table as she zipped up her coat. I sneaked a peek at the items inside—a water bottle, a picture frame facing down, a sweatshirt, sunglasses, and a sleek black container that looked like a sunglasses case, only smaller.

"Would you like help carrying this to your car?" I offered.

"I got it," she replied a little too sharply. Then, softening, she looked up at me through long, damp eyelashes. "I'm sorry."

"It's okay. I know how hard this must be for you. To come back here, where—"

"I had to. I want to know—I *need* to know who killed my

fiancé. As crazy as it sounds, I hoped I'd see something…
anything…that would give me a clue about who took him from
me." She whisked a hand across her cheeks, brushing away tears.
"Finding Seth's killer won't bring him back, but I have to know
who to hate because right now, I hate everyone."

"Did you find anything?" I asked. "Or do you know anyone
who would have a reason to hurt him?"

She hesitated just long enough to make me think she had
someone in mind. "Seth had a big personality that won him just
as many friends as…well, those who couldn't bear to be around
him. Half of his kitchen crew adored him while the others—"

"Hey, Cindy."

We jumped at the deep voice behind us. It was Jared Bernardi,
the program director I'd met on the tour Thursday night.

He placed his hand on Cindy's shoulder. "Sorry I couldn't say
hi earlier when I saw you in the restaurant. I was dealing with a
customer…sighting, so to speak."

I wrinkled my nose. Hopefully, "sighting" didn't mean another
beetle had shown up in someone's dinner.

Cindy stepped out from under Jared's hand. "I'm fine. I have
to leave now. I'll text you later to let you know when my mom
can pick up my things from the apartment. It's too difficult for
me to go back there." Turning to me, she explained, "Seth and
Jared were roommates."

Jared nodded. "Let me know if you ever need anything," he
said, before heading back to the kitchen.

"Everything okay?" I asked, noticing the sneer she gave Jared
as he left.

"That man is awful. A sorry excuse for a human being," she
seethed. "Don't let his polished front fool you. He's the reason
Seth suffered severe insomnia and heartburn the past several
weeks."

"They had a falling out?"

Cindy nodded. "Have you heard of the KnuckleKnight?"

"No."

"Seth and Jared invented it to protect fingers while cutting, since those who aren't pro chefs often slice their fingers when they go too fast." She removed the black case from the box and opened it, revealing a small stainless-steel tool that looked like a shield with wings. "Unlike other finger guards on the market, this one stabilizes whatever you're slicing and can be hooked over your fingers or attached to the top of the knife."

I recognized it immediately. It was the same tool I'd seen around Madame Balleroy's kitchen. The same 'doo-dad,' as Officer Stevens had called it, that was attached to the murder weapon.

"I've seen it before," I told her.

"Well, after Seth and Jared designed it and had a prototype made, they talked about patenting it, but then Winterbridge Supply Company approached them about buying their invention, and it seemed like a better deal. Then, one day while Jared was out of town for a family wedding, Seth met with Winterbridge to discuss the potential sale. Jared had urged Seth to get a signed nondisclosure agreement before sharing the design plans, but Seth was too trusting. Winterbridge ran away with their idea and started manufacturing it without paying a dime, even after we invested so much money into the invention."

"Oh, how awful!" I gasped.

"Hadley, it's your turn to use the oven." Grand-mère stuck her head through the doorway, her pinch-faced expression clearly showing she wasn't thrilled with my absence.

"Be right there," I promised. "Or, better yet, could you please put them in the oven for me? All four of my pans are filled with batter and ready to go." She turned and grunted, making no promises whatsoever to help me.

I turned back to Cindy. "So that's what caused their falling out?"

"It was more than a falling out. Jared went nuclear. Three

weeks ago, he became so angry that he threw Seth's heirloom China dishes out the window, shattering them all."

"I can see why Seth had insomnia. I'm sorry he went through that." Though, honestly, I could understand Jared's anger. Sharing the design plans without a non-disclosure agreement? No one should be that trusting.

Cindy returned the KnuckleKnight to the case, then dropped it into the box. The sleeve of her jacket rode up, revealing a dainty braided bracelet with three shiny beads shaped like pomegranate seeds. Frayed from time and use, it was clearly a well-loved piece of jewelry.

I pointed to her bracelet. "That was Seth's signature ingredient, wasn't it?"

She sighed, her eyes softening at the memory as she ran a finger over the largest of the seeds. "Yes, he gave this to me. He made it himself after watching a YouTube video explaining how to use epoxy resin and red dye to make the beads. It's something I'll treasure forever."

This time, Madame Balleroy stepped through the doorway, her pale skin a stark contrast to the bright-pink silk scarf billowing over the collar of her chef coat. "Hadley..." she warned.

I said goodbye to Cindy, gathered the ribbon, and then followed Madame Balleroy into the kitchen.

"Bread doesn't bake itself." Her tone carried a stern bite that made me flinch. "Never ask someone else in my kitchen to do your work for you. Understand?" She stared at me a moment longer with razor-sharp eyes that seemed to narrow with each passing second. I held her gaze as long as I could, my stomach twisting with anxiety as I wondered if she'd found out I told Dennis about her hasty uprooting of the dill.

Forty-five minutes later, after baking the dessert loaves and waiting for them to cool, I did what I do best—decorate. I tied a fat, bubbly bow around each treat, tucking a small branch of artificial evergreen sprigs from my stash of Christmas decor into the center.

Madame Balleroy ambled by, peering down at my now-beautiful loaves. She closed her eyes and exhaled heavily. "This isn't arts and crafts class, Hadley. When food is cooked correctly, it doesn't need to be glamorized with…" She lifted a mini loaf and turned it in her hand, studying it. "It doesn't need frilly bows and…" Returning it to the table, she brushed a finger against the plump holly berries. "Come to think of it, I'd like you to decorate one or two loaves like this for the brunch. Place them on a cake stand and sprinkle them with powdered sugar."

I couldn't help but grin. "Loaves without bows are like a room without a rug."

"But you aren't here to decorate your food," she snapped. "If you're done baking, please use this time to work on design plans for the brunch. I'd like to review your recommendations by the end of the week."

The thought of working in the barn tonight made my skin prick with sweat. Yes, I needed to spend some time there to finish my plans. Yes, I would stay late at Madame Balleroy's if it meant avoiding Dennis and sparing my heart any temptation. But, no, I wasn't willing to roam her property in the dark by myself only days after a homicide.

My gaze drifted to Officer Butch, who was standing ramrod straight in the corner of the kitchen. I pointed to him. "Only if your security guard comes with me."

She clicked her tongue. "I hired him for my class, not as your personal bodyguard. Officer Butch stays here."

"I can join you," Hal piped up, leaning in on an elbow. "I will scare off any boogeymen."

I gulped. Unless he *was* the boogeyman. Thanks to Kinsley's superb reading skills, I'd learned the mystery brake lights I identified belonged to Hal's truck, which placed him here around the time of Seth's murder.

But, as Dennis told me last night and again this morning, that didn't mean Hal was the killer. And when I'd called Aunt Deb during work today to fill her in on the brake light discovery, she swore on her entire self-storage business that Hal had nothing to do with the homicide.

"I don't have anywhere else I need to be tonight," Hal added.

He would have to be a complete imbecile to harm me with at least two people—Madame Balleroy and Mitzi—witnessing his offer to join me in the barn. In terms of protection, Hal was twice the size of Office Butch, not to mention more intimidating.

"Um, okay…" I said tentatively. "Thank you. I will tell Aunt Deb how kind you are. In fact, I'll text her right now." I placed my dessert loaves into my plastic container, removed my phone from my pocket, and tapped out a quick text to my aunt.

> Going into the barn with Hal. Alone. Hope you were right about his innocence.

Hal chuckled. "Maybe she'll go easy on me during tomorrow's hike."

I imagined Aunt Deb watching the evening news alongside Detective Sanders, both puzzling over—and surely laughing at—my strange text message.

CHAPTER EIGHT

Kinsley practically tackled me with a hug when I got home. "Hadley, Hadley! Want to see my drawing of Razzy?"

"Sure!" I smiled widely, though I was puzzled about why she was so energetic after such a late bedtime last night. If Kinsley wasn't in bed, then Dennis must not be either. I'd taken my sweet time in Madame Balleroy's barn and only left when Hal yawned for the second time. Then I'd stopped for gas and picked up a burger. I was sure they would both be fast asleep by now.

"Don't move," she insisted. "I'll be right back!"

Quick, firm footsteps sounded on the floor in the hallway. Dennis appeared and my gaze immediately dropped—as if by looking away, I could hide from the inevitable pull of his presence.

"Hi." It was all I could manage without unraveling my carefully constructed defenses. The entire car ride home, I'd given myself a pep talk: no more flirting; no more tickle sessions; and I would cut my own darn herbs from now on. If I didn't put some serious walls around my heart, if this thing with Dennis—whatever it was—went any further, I would end up getting hurt again.

"Late night at cooking class?" he asked, stopping across from me.

I nodded, unable to trust my voice. I turned towards Kinsley as she ran back into the entry hall. The drawing she thrust into my hands was a swirl of colors, capturing the essence of Razzy in an adorable abstract form.

"It's beautiful, Kinsley," I praised, grateful for the distraction. "You chose the perfect shade of blue for her eyes." At least, I was pretty sure that's what the blue blobs were.

She beamed up at me before skipping off towards the kitchen, her little feet pattering away as she asked me to hang her artwork on the refrigerator.

With a nod, I trailed behind her through the great room, with Dennis close behind. "Absolutely. A drawing like this deserves a spot in an art gallery, but for now, my fridge will have to do."

I used a couple of magnets to pin her artwork in the middle of the fridge and then set my container of red velvet mini loaves on the counter, still debating who I should give them to.

Definitely not Dennis. If I gave him a mini loaf, he might eat it there on the spot, dropping crumbs all over the counter. He might lick his fingers clean and then decide to get a fork to avoid making more of a mess, unintentionally transferring his saliva onto the handle of my flatware drawer. If he forgot to close the drawer, I'd have to nudge it shut while touching the saliva-covered handle. By then, I might realize my stomach was growling and pluck a fallen crumb from the counter with my fingers, which were now covered with his saliva. If I licked my fingers clean, it would essentially be like swapping spit with him. And if I did that, I might as well just kiss him. But if I kissed him, he may decide to ask me to dinner, and I might disregard the very stern pep talk I gave myself and agree to join him. If we had a nice time at dinner, he might ask me out again and again and again until we were officially a couple. If we became a couple, he might run into an ex-girlfriend and then—*poof!*—suddenly disappear from my life.

I let out a slow breath, stealthily placing my coat over the container of dessert loaves. It was best to not get that ball rolling.

"So," Dennis started, leaning against the door frame, a relaxed smile on his face. *Too relaxed.* Everything about him screamed relaxed: plaid flannel pajama pants, white cotton undershirt, bare feet. It was the first night since he'd been here that he'd gotten ready for bed before closing the door to his room.

I looked away, my blood flowing faster through my veins.

"I got tickets for North Pole Night," he continued. "It's Saturday in the town square. I'm planning to take Kinsley. I got you a ticket if you'd like to come. Santa and his crew will be there."

Kinsley ran around the kitchen island like a wild bull just released from the gate. "Please come! Please, please, please, please, please—"

Dennis moved closer to me, exhaustion clear in the lines between his eyes. "I swear I didn't give her coffee with dinner," he said with a helpless shrug.

I laughed. "I can't believe she's still awake after how tired she was this morning."

"Her camp teacher told me she had a four-hour nap today. I'm jealous. I could've used one of those." He turned to Kinsley: "Don't tell your mom I let you stay up late two nights in a row. She'll never let Uncle Dennis babysit again."

Kinsley let out a peal of hysterical laughter, now jumping across the chairs like they were lily pads. "Mommy won't care! She lets me stay up until eight o'clock on special occasions!"

Dennis and I exchanged horrified looks. Uh-oh. It was already ten.

"Time for bed!" he declared.

Kinsley protested, "But Hadley hasn't said if she can come with us Saturday."

"Let's give her some time to think about it," Dennis said, but then he turned to look at me, his gaze mirroring the same unspoken question as his niece's.

"Oh! Um…thanks so much for the invitation and ticket, but I…"

I didn't have any other plans Saturday night, but I'd vowed to slow down with Dennis, to keep my guard up. His invitation scared me more than I cared to admit. It wasn't just a fun evening out; it was another opportunity for potential heartbreak.

And yet, the idea of going to North Pole Night with them sounded like fun. With Kinsley coming along, it wouldn't technically be a date with Dennis. I could just enjoy hanging out with him as friends.

"I think I would like to go," I finally said, smiling as Kinsley's joyful squeals filled the kitchen.

Dennis raised a brow, his detective skills clearly picking up on my hesitation. "You *think*? Are you sure?"

"Yes," I said, more firmly this time. "It'll be nice to see Santa, and maybe his elves, too."

Kinsley took off running around the kitchen again, leaving Dennis and me alone. Instead of chasing after her, he leaned against the counter and looked me in the eye. "Everything okay? You seem…tired. How was work today?"

I wanted to look away, but I found myself unable to break free from his sea-blue gaze. "Reid stopped by to see Vincent today." I regretted my words as soon as they left my lips. Why had I told him? I didn't want him to know Reid still affected me just with his presence.

Dennis grunted. "I'll bet ten bucks he yapped about that hideous paddlewheeler of his."

I looked down, avoiding his gaze so he wouldn't detect the churn of emotions unraveling inside me. "Actually, he did," I said as casually as possible. "He was bragging about a new varnish he's using on the deck or something."

Dennis pushed off from the counter and stepped closer, his eyes clouding with shared pain. "I shouldn't have joked about it. I know it's hard for you to see him." He reached out, gently wrapping a hand around my shoulder. "I see Akari every day at the station. Have to talk to her too. It's not easy—even though I don't care for her anymore."

I thought I'd moved past Reid, but when I'd heard his laughter rolling up from Vincent's entry hall today, it felt like I'd lost a piece of myself all over again. "How'd you guess Reid talked about his boat?"

He shrugged. "Because it's all he has. All he cares about. The guy has no clue about what really matters in life. He's a materialistic, brainless fool."

I lifted my gaze to meet his once again. "Maybe so." Even though I didn't think of Reid in those terms, it was nice to know that Dennis did.

"I have some other choice words to describe him, but not with Kinsley around."

At the mention of her name, Kinsley let out a delighted squeal. "Yummy! Are these for us?"

I turned to see her taking a dessert loaf from my container, her eyes wide with anticipation.

Dennis rushed over, his hands outstretched. "Whoa, whoa, no more sugar before bedtime."

"But are they for us?" she asked again. "Can you put one in my lunch for camp tomorrow?"

"Of course," I said. Warmth seeped back into the cold, lonely void inside my chest as I soaked up the goofy look Dennis gave Kinsley, and the gleeful squint of her pretty blue eyes as she clamped the dessert loaf even tighter.

It was absurd to think a mini loaf could lead to a doomed romantic relationship. Dennis was a good friend, and I was happy to share anything with him and his niece—my home, my loaves, or even my free time on a Saturday night. "Please help yourself, sweetie. Dennis, you too."

"Thank you. We'll save one for tomorrow," he said, emphasizing the last word. He lifted Kinsley up to sit on his shoulders, then gently took the treat from her hand, returned it to the container, and snapped its lid into place.

He stopped. Slowly, he removed the lid again, his thick brows creeping closer together as he studied the contents within.

My heart sank. From Dennis's expression, I could tell my mini loaves had either turned to mush, been damaged during the car ride home, or I'd done something terribly wrong, and they'd imploded into a sad mess.

He pointed to something inside the container. "What's this?"

"Maybe it's a note from Hadley's mommy," Kinsley guessed. "I find them in my lunchbox all the time."

"I don't think so, kiddo," Dennis said, watching me closely as I hurried over to them.

Kinsley drew her eyebrows together in concentration. "Sn... oo...p." She paused. "What does that mean?"

I froze in front of my container. Nestled among the still-beautiful loaves was a bright yellow, grease-smudged sticky note with the word "snoop" written in bold letters with a thick black marker.

Dennis's eyes swept over the note, the mini loaves, the lid... and then over to me. "It means someone here needs to stop digging around for answers before they get hurt."

"I'm not digging for anything." I lifted my chin, meeting Dennis's eyes.

"Your special note suggests otherwise," he argued, motioning to it with a flick of his wrist.

"It's not like I'm walking around with a magnifying glass,

looking for clues. I simply talked with a few people." I spoke firmly, attempting to hide the fluttering unease in my stomach. Whether it was from the threatening note or Dennis's intense, unwavering gaze, I wasn't sure.

Dennis pulled Kinsley from atop his shoulders and set her on the ground. "A *few*?"

"Yes. Or maybe a lot—I don't know. Everyone's talking about it."

"Talking about what?" Kinsley asked.

"The weather," Dennis lied. He closed his eyes and pressed his fingers into them, as though summoning patience. He looked… tired. So, so tired. Maybe he'd been staying up late in his room working on the case. "Who did you talk to, Hadley?" His voice was eerily calm. No humor, no flirtatious undertones whatsoever. He wanted answers, and he wanted them now.

I puffed out my cheeks, exhaling slowly. "Let's see," I began, ticking off on my fingers. "First, I talked to—"

"No, Kinsley, we can't eat these anymore." Dennis tugged gently on her hand, which was already halfway inside the container again, then led her away from the counter and toward the doorway leading to the dining room. "I'm gonna put you to bed and then I want to hear about all the chatting Miss Hadley's been up to lately."

Dennis paused in the doorway, turning to look back at me. "I'll need to bring the container to the station later tonight, after Kins is asleep. Will you be here in case she needs anything?"

I nodded, then gave Kinsley a reassuring smile. Her bottom lip trembled as she stared at the container of treats, clearly not understanding why her uncle was bringing them to the station instead of giving them to her as promised. "Don't worry, I'll make another batch of these," I told her.

One that didn't include a note that sent a clear message to stop asking questions about the homicide.

CHAPTER NINE

"You've been withholding information from me, Hadley. *Critical* intel that I learned from someone besides you. So start talking." Erin, my good friend and owner of the recently re-opened Whisks and Whiskers Cat Café, stood behind the coffee counter with crossed arms and an expression of mock exasperation.

"Intel?" I didn't know what she was talking about, and it didn't help that my mind was mush today. After Dennis discovered the sticky note threat in my container of loaves last night, I hadn't fallen asleep until after two in the morning. My mind was racing in endless circles, unable to rest.

Now, after a relaxed, Reid-free day at work, I'd stopped by Whisks and Whiskers for an afternoon dose of caffeine to prevent me from falling asleep during dinner. Cooking classes were canceled for the evening—hallelujah!—and postponed until tomorrow night since the police hadn't finished scouring the facility and questioning all of Madame Ballcroy's staff and students about the sticky note in my container.

"Don't play dumb with me, missy," she said. "I have the right to refuse service to any customer, especially friends who fail to tell me the town hottie is living with them."

"Oh, *that!*" I pressed a hand against my cheeks, which were now searing with heat. "It sounds so…scandalous when you phrase it like that," I whispered, my gaze darting to the customers around us. This was not something I wanted to become public knowledge. Dennis had asked me not to tell anyone that he and Kinsley were staying with me—for our safety, he'd said.

Erin handed me my usual beverage—a steaming vanilla latte with a thick layer of frothy goodness bubbling over the top. After removing her apron and placing it on a shelf below, she rounded the counter and motioned to the far side of the café. "Come on, let's go to the cat château. It's quieter in there."

The château was what Erin called the temporary room housing the dozen or so cats available for adoption, along with various plush chairs and bean bags scattered around the room for customers to sit on while they interacted with the furry inhabitants.

I followed her to the accordion-style door, closing it behind me. The room was bright and colorful, with vibrant toys scattered around the floor. The cats themselves came in a variety of colors, from sleek black to fluffy calico, and they lounged in customers' laps, at their feet, or on carpeted, tower-like structures.

The cats used to roam freely inside the café, but new, stricter health code standards forced Erin to keep them separate from food preparation areas. She was gearing up to knock down some walls and expand her restaurant with more tables for customers and a larger play area for the cats, but for now, the temporary wall partitions would suffice. Once the construction was complete, I planned to decorate the café, creating a cozy sanctuary for diners and a whimsical paradise for its four-legged inhabitants.

Erin and I made our way to an empty spot in the far corner of the room, where a fluffy white kitten waited for someone to pet her. "Who told you about Dennis?" I asked. Most likely, it was one of her baristas who worked at the Whisks and Whiskers food truck parked behind the Ladyvale Manor. Although Dennis and Kinsley left for work and day camp before Erin's crew arrived, they might have crossed paths one day.

"We discussed it in our staff meeting today, during the time set aside for Hadley-and-houseguests updates."

"Very funny," I said, but side-eyed her to make sure she was joking.

Erin sat on the floor next to the white kitten. She placed him in her lap, scratching behind his ears with her long, glossy nails. "Timmy told me. He arrived early yesterday and bumped into Dennis."

I sat across from her, tugging at the stiff fabric of my black slacks. "Your intel is half-right. Dennis *and* his niece are staying with me, and it's only until it's safe for him to return home." I filled her in on the threats Dennis had received, his initial plan to stay in a hotel, and then I asked her not to spread the news, just to be cautious.

"You're saying we need to exclude updates on your love life from our staff meetings? What a bummer!"

I laughed. "I have no love life. Not anymore, at least. Dennis and I are just friends. No dinner dates, no kissing, no physical contact—" I paused as my mind lurched back to the oh-so-close herb-cutting lesson. "—well, *limited* physical contact."

She raised an eyebrow. "Any flirting?"

"Well…"

"Okay, spill it." The half-smile forming on her lips told me she was more than ready for the kind of gossip her team would love to feast on.

I told her everything—the tickle session in the labyrinth, our park visits with Kinsley, the thyme-cutting lesson, as well as Reid's visit to Walnut Ridge yesterday afternoon. As I spoke, my emotions swung wildly, tugging my heart in a dozen different directions, leaving me reeling from the whirlwind of memories.

"I couldn't be more confused," I confessed, bringing my latte to my lips and relishing the jolt of warmth as it flowed down my throat.

"Hadley," Erin said evenly, "there's nothing complicated about this. From what I'm hearing, it sounds like he's into you. Either you like him romantically or you don't."

I lowered my latte. "It's *never* that easy. Sure, you and Rhett are happily married newlyweds now, but you had your fair share of bumps and hurdles."

She dipped her chin in silent agreement. "Okay, but you haven't answered my question—do you or do you not like him?"

"I can't...imagine myself dating him without getting hurt. I enjoy hanging out with him, the flirting and friendly banter, but the closer I get to him, the more I feel like I'm nearing the edge of a cliff, too scared to make that final jump." Setting my mug on a nearby bench, I scooped up a hefty black cat sauntering past me and hugged him against my chest, careful not to let his claws near the chunky, loopy threads of my pale pink sweater. "He asked me to join him and Kinsley at North Pole Night this Saturday. He already bought me a ticket."

"North Pole Night?" She arched an eyebrow.

"Yes. I told him I'd go. We'll be busy visiting Santa and his elves, so there won't be much time for flirting."

Erin snickered. "But plenty of time for dancing."

"*Dancing*? At the children's festival?"

"Who said it's only for children? The dance floor and live bands are the main attraction. Santa's just a fringe benefit."

The black cat must have felt my body go rigid, because he craned his neck to the right, signaling cuddle time was over. I eased him down to the tiled floor before he waddled off towards a carpeted play structure.

Dennis hadn't mentioned dancing. Was he planning to pull me onto the floor and twirl me around? Irritation coursed through me, heating my face so much that sweat prickled at my hairline. North Pole Night was one giant setup—a trap to lure me into a relationship and spit me out weeks later.

But then memories of the recent police gala flickered through my thoughts—two-stepping around the dance floor with Dennis, feeling like I was flying as he twirled me this way and that. Of course, it was different then, when both of us were dating someone else.

Still...I hadn't wanted that evening to end. I'd wanted the music to keep playing, the party to keep rolling. I'd even downloaded three of the songs we'd two-stepped to, and listened to them during my morning walks.

"Maybe it is too soon," Erin mused, her brow furrowing as she studied me. "Perhaps it would be good to give yourself more time to get over Reid before you dive into another relationship. You know, focus on yourself until you're ready to welcome another man into your life."

I nodded curtly. "This is exactly what I told myself last night. Avoid the temptation of Dennis; protect my heart. You're right, this shouldn't be complicated at all."

"I'm sure you have plenty to do this Christmas season without diving into a new relationship. Shopping, client work—"

"—cooking, buying Christmas gifts, decorating Madame Balleroy's barn," I added, "and trying to stay alive without getting a knife in my back."

"Do the police have any leads in the homicide?"

"Dennis claims they have, but he's not sharing any details with me. Oh! That reminds me...have you heard of the Knuckle-Knight?"

"Yep. We have a couple floating around the kitchen. My senior chef was flat-out insulted when I bought them, but I've caught the junior chefs using them."

I glanced around the cat château. There were half a dozen other customers in the room, all of them busy playing with the cats, scrolling through their phones, or chatting amongst themselves. I lowered my voice and asked, "Did you know Seth and his roommate invented the KnuckleKnight?"

She winced, sympathy and remorse flickering across her features. "Yes, and it's such a shame. The poor guy had just sold his invention to Winterbridge. And to think he never got to enjoy his newfound wealth before he died!"

"No," I said, shaking my head. "Seth's fiancée told me Winterbridge stole his idea without compensating either him or his roommate, Jared. All because Seth didn't make them sign a non-disclosure agreement before he met with them. Who told you Winterbridge bought his invention?"

Continuing to tickle the white kitten in her lap, Erin gave a slight shrug. "My sales rep at Winterbridge. I buy most of my kitchen equipment and supplies from her. She told me Seth struck gold with that business transaction—though she didn't mention anything about his roommate. And she wouldn't have had any reason to lie about it; they're a reputable company. Leader in the industry." Erin's expression shifted to one of concern. "What's wrong? You look a little pale."

"Something's not right. Seth or his fiancée—maybe both—lied about the theft of his invention." I spread my hands out to my sides, steadying myself as I took a deep, shaky breath. "But that's not the most troubling part. I'm wondering if the KnuckleKnight is connected to the homicide, especially since the gadget was attached to the knife found in Seth's chest."

Dennis grabbed the handle of the skillet, deftly swirling a generous dollop of butter around inside, making it sizzle and pop. Tonight, he was cooking dinner—at his insistence—and even though I enjoyed cooking alongside him, boy was I looking forward to a night away from the stove.

I'd just returned from visiting with Erin at Whisks and

Whiskers, and was lounging on a barstool by the island, attempting to read the thick book on food safety that Madame Balleroy had insisted I read.

But it was impossible to concentrate as my growling stomach succumbed to the thick aroma of garlic-laced steam seeping from the oven, in which handmade rolls were browning. They would pair nicely with the pan-seared steak and shrimp dish, fresh green beans, and homemade mashed potatoes.

I closed the book and slid it next to a cutting board piled with minced shallots, which Dennis had chopped with a swift, skilled hand. Maybe I'd read more later, after my stomach was full and I wasn't tempted to observe how small the skillet handle looked in his large hands, or the way the muscles in his forearm tensed and flexed with each tilt of the pan.

He had already changed out of his work attire and into a pair of faded black denim jeans and a snug black undershirt that showcased his wide shoulders. If the delicious aromas of the kitchen hadn't been holding me captive, I would've gone upstairs to change into something more comfortable, probably spending too much time deciding which pair of yoga pants flattered my legs the most.

Kinsley's animated voice drifted in from the formal parlor, where she was introducing her dolls to the collection of nutcrackers. It sounded like a lively party, both dolls and nutcrackers having a grand old time under Kinsley's imaginative direction. The clinks of plastic against wood and the high-pitched voices she attributed to her partygoers had me shaking my head in admiration. Her creativity knew no bounds.

"How was your day?" Dennis asked, eying the now-closed book beside me. "Better than yesterday?" What he was really asking, I was sure, was whether Reid had stopped by again.

"It was good! Much better on all fronts—less stressful, more productive, and there were no unpleasant visitors. We even wrapped up a little early, so I swung by Whisks and Whiskers to visit with Erin."

As I studied Dennis, I debated on whether to share my conversation with Erin. Would he find my discoveries about the homicide interesting, or would he be upset I'd spoken about it with her? I had made a promise not to bring up the topic during our cooking classes, but my discussion with Erin had happened outside of Madame Balleroy's. It was simply a casual chat between two friends.

I leaned an elbow on the cool granite countertop. "What about your day? Any progress on the case?" I kept my tone as light as possible, as though I was just making polite conversation.

Dennis paused, his movements with the skillet slowing as he seemed to consider his response. He glanced over at me, a wisp of a smile playing at the edges of his lips, as if he could see right through my feigned nonchalance. "I sure hope you're asking about the case of your missing nutcracker. You know I can't talk about the homicide."

"Although I am hoping for a reunion with my Prince Charming, I was asking about your...*other* case. Because I learned something today that you might want to hear."

His eyes lit up with surprise. "You talked about the case? After receiving what I can only assume is a threat less than twenty-four hours ago?" He set the skillet on the stove and turned again to face me, arms folded.

Last night, during my lengthy pow-wow with Dennis before he brought my container of loaves to the police station, I'd told him about my conversation with Seth's fiancée—Cindy—and everything she'd revealed about the KnuckleKnight invention, including how Winterbridge Supply Company had stolen Seth's idea without compensation, severely straining his relationship with his roommate, Jared.

I explained, "Today Erin told me she'd heard a different version of what happened when Seth met with the culinary supply company. Erin's Winterbridge sales rep told her they did indeed compensate Seth—and only Seth—for the kitchen gadget. She said it was a lot of money."

"Did she say how much?" he asked, with a slight edge that suggested he hadn't yet heard this version of the story.

"No, just that Seth had 'struck gold.' And it got me thinking, what if Jared found out Seth had cashed in from their invention, when Seth had initially claimed the company stole their idea?"

Dennis was quiet for a moment, the muscles in his jaw working as if he was chewing over the information. Then, as though he'd already sorted out what I'd said and come up with a game plan, he spun around to the stove, reaching for a bowl of pre-cut cubes of steak. He dropped them into the skillet, and the kitchen was again filled with the sizzle of cooking.

"It is a motive," he said. "But it proves nothing. People get greedy, but that leap from greed to murder isn't one most will take. And although I appreciate you sharing this info, it doesn't mean you should continue having conversations about the case."

"Of course," I replied, keeping my voice sweet as sugar.

He glanced over his shoulder at me, amusement brimming in his eye. "'Of course,'" he repeated, shaking his head as though this was the funniest thing he'd heard all day. "Considering this new info, I *should* make some calls after dinner. But I'd rather hang out with you and Kinsley and get to bed early. So it'll have to wait until the morning."

I looked away from him. He wanted to hang out with me? What did he have in mind?

The three of us could play a game—something like Go Fish, perhaps. And once Kinsley went to sleep, he and I could take an evening walk through the labyrinth, or just sink into the cozy sofa in the family room and watch a movie. I could find a blanket large enough to share with—

I stopped myself. *Slow down! Too fast! Do* not *imagine snuggling with Dennis on the sofa.*

The fortress I'd built around my heart had some holes, it seemed. I needed to reinforce that wall before emotions swept through like a tidal wave, washing away reason and self-preservation.

Dennis moved across the kitchen and opened the refrigerator, frowning as he removed a nearly empty carton of milk. "I thought we had more than this," he muttered to himself.

I shot to my feet. "I'll go grab some. It won't take me long." Without waiting for his response, I grabbed my bag and headed towards the kitchen door. It would be much easier to avoid any snuggle-on-the-sofa-with-Dennis thoughts if I weren't in the same room as him and his delicious black T-shirt.

"Oh, but—" he started.

"It's fine, really," I reassured him as I opened the door.

"—but I can use the cooking liquid from the boiled potatoes instead."

With one hand on the doorknob, I turned to look at Dennis, who looked more than a little puzzled by my sudden departure. "I'll need milk for my coffee tomorrow, anyway. I can't exactly pour your potato liquid in there, can I?"

CHAPTER TEN

I rolled into the parking lot for Aunt Deb's self-storage facility and cringed when I spotted the cherry-red BMW SUV in front of the leasing office.

Gayle, I seethed, now wishing I'd run by the Darlin' Mart for milk instead. It had seemed easier to borrow some from Aunt Deb, especially since I only needed a cup of it, and she was closer than the store.

Gayle Nuñez was my biggest competitor in Darlington Hills, and the number one pain in my side. The feeling was mutual; if she had her way, I would move back to Louisiana so she could have all the interior design jobs to herself.

I parked next to her SUV and glanced through the window of the leasing office, which was attached to my aunt's home. It was once a two-car garage before they converted it to office space. I couldn't recall what it looked like before.

Inside, Gayle stood with her arms crossed. She was, as always, effortlessly chic—her slim frame draped in a tailored black blouse and red leather slacks, making her seem ready for a photoshoot rather than a late-evening visit to a mini storage facility.

She appeared to be having an intense conversation with Aunt Deb, who sat behind her desk. The office typically closed at five on weekdays, but I doubted Gayle cared it was well past that time, and her sour grimace told me she was unleashing a barrage of complaints about her storage unit. She had recently leased two of the largest units on-site, so Aunt Deb would likely stay as long as Gayle wanted just to keep her happy.

Aunt Deb's storage facility had gone through a rough time last year, with multiple break-ins that prompted customers to take their business elsewhere. But with the help of Detective Sanders, she had improved security measures and there had been no incidents since early this year.

Now, her business was thriving, and Aunt Deb planned to expand by buying the empty lot next door. But one negative comment from someone as ruthless as Gayle could ruin all the hard work she put into building her reputation.

I stepped out of my car, fished through my bag for my phone, then held it up to my ear as I pushed through the door to the office. There was no such thing as a friendly encounter with Gayle, and I wasn't up for any insults she might hurl at me today.

"Sure, that sounds great," I said to the imaginary person on the other end of my phone. Giving Aunt Deb a cheerful wave, I pulled the phone away from my ear and whispered, "I need to borrow a little milk." She gave me a thumbs-up, and I redirected my attention to my phantom call as I headed toward the door leading to her home.

Once inside Aunt Deb's kitchen, I took stock of the items in her fridge. There was an unopened carton of milk and another one that was almost empty but still contained enough for Dennis's mashed potatoes. I grabbed the second carton and made my way back to the leasing office, phone pressed against my ear once again.

I breezed through the office, turning to thank Aunt Deb. My gaze landed on a waist-high figurine dressed in a red tunic with gold buttons and black pants, standing proudly in front of her desk.

"My Prince Charming!" I declared.

Aunt Deb shrugged. "You have seven other nutcrackers. I didn't think you'd miss this one. It really brightens up my office, don't you think? My customers love it!"

Gayle opened her mouth, but before she could add her opinion on the matter, I replied, "It adds a nice touch of Christmas spirit." With a polite nod to Gayle, I continued my brisk walk towards the door.

"Speaking of tacky decorations," Gayle said, "I heard Madame Balleroy hired you to decorate for this year's Christmas Eve Brunch."

I reached out and gripped the door handle tightly, suppressing any urge to retort. This was not the time or place to snap back at Gayle. I couldn't risk embarrassing Aunt Deb or giving Gayle ammunition to gossip about her storage facility. "Yes, she did," I replied, calmly.

"I've been in charge of decorating for the annual brunch for five years now, but this year, I couldn't be bothered with it. It's a waste of my time, not to mention that she doesn't pay well. I have more important clients with bigger budgets to attend to."

Something in Gayle's tone—resentment, perhaps?—put a smug smile on my face the entire drive home.

"I don't like it."

Kinsley stared at the plate in front of her, which was filled with pan-seared steak, shrimp, green beans, and mashed potatoes.

"But you haven't tried it yet," Dennis pointed out. "You'll love it, I promise. The steak and shrimp skillet is by far the most popular recipe on my YouTube channel. People say it's the best surf and turf combo they've ever made."

Confusion creased her forehead as she tried to make sense of the unfamiliar words flowing from her uncle's lips.

"Surf means it's from the sea and turf means land," I explained, pointing to the shrimp and steak bites. But this only made her eyes grow wider, more disgusted.

Dennis gathered a heaping forkful of everything on his plate and brought it to his mouth, making an exaggerated display of how delicious it was. "See? It's yummy."

I followed his lead, oohing and ahhing as I chewed. "This really *is* good, Dennis," I said after swallowing. "The butter, the garlic—all of it. No wonder this is your most popular video."

He turned his attention towards me, away from Kinsley and her untouched plate, his eyes filled with a playful twinkle. "You sound surprised."

"I am! Not because you made it, but because it was made in my kitchen. I didn't know it could produce such greatness."

He laughed. "For the record, I thoroughly enjoyed your Thanksgiving meal. The turkey was moist, the mashed potatoes were fluffier than the ones I made tonight, and you nailed the sweet potato casserole. Your stuffing was the tastiest heap of salmonella I've ever tried. Totally worth the hours of retching."

My stomach lurched at the memory. "That is *so* not funny," I scolded. "And we don't use the 's' word in this kitchen."

"Which one—stuffing, or salmonella?"

"Both are forbidden." Changing the subject, I asked, "Are you taking a break from making cooking videos while you're here? Your fans might send hate mail if you do."

He waved his hand casually. "They'll get over it. It's good to take a break now and then."

"Well, please use my kitchen if you want to record a video while you're here." Now that his cooking channel had become so popular, his videos generated a nice bit of extra cash through ad revenue. I hated to think of him missing out on that just because he was staying with me.

He seemed to consider it, but then his face relaxed into an easy smile. "Thanks, I'll keep that in mind. This one has been keeping me busy lately." He hitched a discreet thumb toward his niece, who was still giving her dinner the death stare.

"If you don't have time to produce a cooking video, you could show your fans how to harvest herbs," I suggested. "I sure enjoyed my lesson."

I could have slapped myself for that comment, which I'd blurted out before I could stop myself. And lordy, my *tone*! It couldn't have been more suggestive if I'd tried.

Dennis's eyes flickered with interest. "So you're into herb harvesting?" His voice dipped low as the corners of his mouth tilted up. "I suppose there's a lot I could demonstrate with the right assistant."

Yikes! What had I started? So much for taming my feeble heart.

I swallowed hard, trying to steady my soaring pulse. Turning my attention back to Kinsley, I pointed to her plate. "You're one of the lucky ones." My voice was tight, not as chipper as I'd planned. "There are a lot of people who wish they were eating your uncle's special dinner."

"I don't like special dinners. I like normal ones."

Dennis raised a hand to his mouth, hiding a smile. "What's a 'normal' meal?"

She shrugged. "Macaroni and cheese, peanut butter and jelly sandwiches, chicken nuggets—" Her eyes shot open wide. "Can I have nuggets instead?"

He seemed to consider it before shaking his head. "This would be the third night in a row. Why don't you just try what's on your plate?"

"You'll love it," I assured her.

Ever so slowly, Kinsley stabbed a shrimp with her fork, examining it as she brought it to her nose and sniffed. She jerked back her head so fast I thought she'd get whiplash. "Thank you, but no thank you. I want nuggets."

I gestured to her plate. "The shrimp are basically chicken nuggets of the sea. And the steak...well, it's the cousin of the chicken nugget. Every bit as tasty."

"That's right," Dennis chimed in. "They're all cousins in the great family of bite-sized foods."

Kinsley looked dubious, one eyebrow cocked in suspicion. "They don't look like cousins. Can I have a sandwich instead?"

"Sorry, Kins, but we're out of bread," Dennis said, pausing amid a bite of steak.

I glanced at the spot on the counter where I kept the bread, shocked that we'd gone through an entire loaf in several days, when it usually took me a week or more to polish it off by myself. Had I known we were out, I would've borrowed some from Aunt Deb while I was there.

"But I'm hungry," she whimpered, her quivering lip telling me tears weren't far away.

Dennis must have sensed it too, because he jumped from his chair and hustled to the refrigerator. "Let's see what else you might like." Opening the door, he peered inside. "Let's see... there's some leftover salmon from Tuesday night—" He wrinkled his nose at that one. "—Or some cranberry baked brie pastries that Hadley made during cooking class—"

"Nope."

"Okay, how about some scrambled eggs? It won't take me long to make those." He glanced at his watch and grimaced. "Don't tell your mama you stayed up late three nights in a row. I'll never hear the end of it."

Kinsley's face twisted with confusion. "Eggs? But it's not breakfast time."

Dennis put a hand on his hip. "Your mom told me you aren't a picky eater."

"I'm not. I like chicken nuggets with ketchup, ranch dressing, *or* honey."

Dennis's shoulders folded in, his head hanging in defeat. "One plate of nuggets coming up." He removed the bag from the freezer and lugged it over to the counter. "I just hope you don't turn into a chicken nugget before your parents get home. They would not be pleased."

Kinsley glanced at the value-size bag on the counter, and then looked at me, shrugging. "Hadley hasn't turned into one yet."

CHAPTER ELEVEN

I was thirty minutes late to cooking class the next night. As soon as I stepped into the kitchen, Madame Balleroy's gaze locked onto me, her mouth pinched and eyebrows knitted. She tapped the gold watch around her wrist, emphasizing how late I was, and just how much she disapproved. The rhythm of her tapping seemed to echo in the suddenly too-quiet room, drawing the attention of the other students who were busily preparing their cooking stations.

Once again, the class had dwindled in size, leaving only six other students. Hal and Mitzy had returned, now joined at our prep table by Eileen, since the rest of her group didn't return. Dennis and Detective Sanders had questioned everyone at the school and restaurant yesterday about the threatening note in my container of mini loaves. I guessed this latest incident was the final straw for some.

I'd almost skipped class tonight, but Dennis had told me two Darlington Hills police officers would patrol Madame Balleroy's tonight—one at the cooking school and another at the restaurant.

I mumbled an apology to Madame Balleroy, but it was swallowed by the clatter of pans and utensils. I hurried to my table, flustered and out of breath, and took the empty seat next to Hal. Mitzy sat across from me, and Eileen to her right. "Hey, guys," I greeted.

Hal slapped a hand across my back. "Glad you could join us, hon! Work keeping you busy?"

"I only have one more day before my vacation starts, so I've been cramming in as many to-dos as possible before then." Like my colleagues at Walnut Ridge, I was taking a full two weeks off for Christmas. We'd already finished everything for the upcoming catalog and even made some progress on the next one. Tuesday couldn't get here soon enough.

"I can't say I miss those days," Hal said with a chuckle. "Retirement is bliss, my friend. Every day is a Saturday, except there's less pressure to get all your errands done since you've got the entire week to run them." He patted my arm reassuringly. "Don't worry, kiddo. You'll get there. But for now, savor those vacation days like they're gold."

I planned to do nothing less. Sleep in, take leisurely walks to Whisks and Whiskers, and maybe even treat myself to a pedicure.

Oh, and drag myself to cooking class.

"Here." Madame Balleroy thrust a recipe card into my hand, her frustration clear in her eyes—likely directed at both me and her dwindling class size. "Read it and let me know if you have questions. Whatever you do, don't let the sugar burn on the stove. I won't have you stinking up my kitchen." Before I could respond, she spun around and walked off.

A sweet, nutty aroma taunted my senses, making my stomach growl with anticipation. Eager to find out what made the kitchen smell so heavenly, I flipped over the recipe card: chocolate-dipped hazelnut nougats. The list of ingredients was long, and the instructions were painfully detailed.

Oops. Maybe tonight hadn't been the best day to arrive late. I'd never attempted a recipe like it before, and I didn't want anyone, especially the young policewoman in the corner, to have to stay past their shift because of me.

Without delay, I preheated the oven at the empty station behind us and rounded up the ingredients and equipment. When I returned to our table, Hal, Mitzy, and Eileen were removing cookie sheets scattered with toasted hazelnuts from the oven.

With narrowed eyes, Grand-mère tracked my every movement from her throne-like chair in the center of the kitchen. I coated the baking sheet with butter, then glanced over my shoulder. She was still watching me. I spread the hazelnuts across the sheet—still watching. I slid the nuts into the oven—still, her glare was honed on *me*.

What was her deal?

Emboldened by the presence of the Darlington Hills police officer, I strolled confidently over to Grand-mère. "Yes?" I asked.

"Do you have a question?" Her tone made it clear she didn't want to be bothered answering it.

"No, but I noticed you—"

"Then get back to work, Miss Sutton," she hissed, inclining her head towards my table. "You were half an hour late."

"I came over here because you've been looking at me as though I'm doing something wrong." As though she were offended by my presence.

She let out a low laugh that contained no trace of humor. "I'm amused by your cooking methods."

I gave her a look. "What does that mean? All I've done so far is put the nuts in the oven."

"That's not all you've done. Between each step of the recipe, you pause to talk. You melt the butter—then yap, yap, yap. You place the nuts on the cookie sheet, then yap some more. You put them in the oven, then you come talk to me. I'm half-surprised you haven't reduced this kitchen to ashes. Cooking requires a deliberate mental commitment from start to finish; otherwise known as *focus*. And yours, I'm afraid, drifts in and out like the tide."

I flinched, her words hitting me like a slap of cold water. Could my habit of gabbing be the root of all my cooking woes? I *did* usually talk on the phone while preparing dinner, and I *had* been talking to my parents when I stuffed the turkey with dressing. Maybe I'd somehow missed the 'THOU SHALT NOT STUFF A TURKEY BEFORE BAKING' fine print.

I shook my head. Nah. If there was one thing I was good at, it was multitasking—especially if it involved talking. It was as instinctual as breathing.

"Well, Grand-mère," I began sheepishly, "I was simply trying to add some...personality to the process."

Instead of responding, she aimed a bony finger toward my table. "You'd better move on to the next step. You have ten more to go."

While melting the sugar, honey, and water on the stove, I kept my mouth shut for as long as humanly possible. But my silence didn't make me feel hyper-focused. I felt bored.

"Are these peaks stiff enough?" Eileen asked to no one in particular. Her lips were glossy pink, and her cheeks were colored with a generous helping of blush. It was the first time she'd worn makeup to class since the death of her future son-in-law.

"Yes," Hal said.

But Mitzy shook her head. "You need to beat the egg whites longer."

"They're fine," Hal pressed, giving Eileen a reassuring smile. "I'd bet my underpants I'm right."

"The SpongeBob ones?" I asked. Eileen let out a snort of laughter, which she quickly covered up with a pretend coughing fit.

Hal put a fist on his hip, feigning irritation. "Hey, how did you know about that, missy? Your aunt told you? That humiliating story is exclusive to my hiking club friends."

"And half of Darlington Hills," I squeaked. The tale of how Hal's pants got caught on barbed wire during a hike, exposing his SpongeBob boxers, had become a local legend. Women retold the story as though they'd witnessed it, even if they'd never hiked a day in their life.

"*All* of Darlington Hills," Eileen corrected, forcing a smile. She didn't want to be here anymore than I did, but she had come only because her devastated daughter had asked her to.

"I'm sure Mitzy hasn't heard—" I started.

"I've heard," she said dryly.

Hal tossed up his sugar-coated hands, releasing an exaggerated sigh of despair.

Eileen rolled her eyes. "Oh, Hal. Don't pretend like you mind all the attention."

I snorted. "He soaks it up like…a sponge. A certain yellow, *square* sponge."

Hal let out a hearty guffaw, making every head in the kitchen turn to see what was so funny. Grand-mère cast a warning glance at me, as though she knew who had prompted Hal's outburst. Madame Balleroy snaked towards us, her arms folded tightly.

Fighting a smile, I returned my attention to the sugary mixture in front of me, stirring it constantly to prevent it from burning. Hal had every reason to be in a good mood tonight. Someone had placed the sticky note inside my container of loaves while I was in the barn working on design plans Wednesday night. Because Hal was with me when someone slipped the note into my container, he was effectively cleared from any suspicion of writing the threat, and most likely, the homicide.

At least, that's how Aunt Deb and I saw it. We'd discussed the matter extensively during my lunch break today over the phone.

She was ecstatic that Hal was, presumably, no longer a suspect, although both Dennis and Detective Sanders had yet to confirm this. I'd told her about the KnuckleKnight invention, my conversations with Seth's former fiancée, and Erin, as well as my theory that someone had discovered Seth's lie, with which she agreed.

"So your aunt gossips about me?" Hal asked, his eyes still glazed with laughter.

I smiled but kept my eyes on my pot of sugar. "Yes, though she says your ego is healthy enough to withstand it."

He chuckled. "Well, she shares plenty about you, too."

"Oh?" I raised a brow, though I wasn't at all surprised. "What does she say?"

"She says you're quite the sleuth; that you've...assisted with several of the recent homicide investigations in town."

"Those were just lucky hunches," I said.

"You're being humble. According to your aunt, it was more than luck. She says you have an uncanny eye for detail; nothing gets past you."

"Except, unfortunately, in the kitchen," I said, studying the nougat mixture in front of me. Was it done? The recipe said to heat it until it bubbled, but the off-white mixture contained only a few tiny air bubbles, barely noticeable and smaller than the tip of a toothpick.

"What about the recent homicide?" Hal asked. "Your aunt said you have some theories on who killed the sous chef. Is it anyone we know?" Hal didn't bother lowering his voice, and I felt eyes turning on us from every direction.

Grand-mère stood and stepped towards our table, her tight-lipped gaze unreadable. Any minute now, she would make another snide comment about my inability to keep my mouth shut.

Not that I wanted to talk to Hal about the homicide. The sticky note threat made it clear that someone wasn't happy with questions I'd asked, perhaps because they knew about my involvement in solving past homicides.

Also fresh in my mind was Dennis's clear warning to me—those serious eyes when he'd cautioned me not to talk about the case at Madame Balleroy's.

"Your aunt said you learned the victim had lied about money he'd received from some sort of gadget...the KnuckleBuckle?" Hal frowned, shaking his head. "No, that's not right. The KnuckleBuddy?"

In a desperate attempt to avoid answering Hal's question, I shot my hand into the air, wiggling my fingers for emphasis. Grand-mère was only several steps away, but it was Madame Balleroy who responded to my frantic gesture.

"Yes?" she asked with an indifferent lift of her brow.

I pointed to the mixture in front of me. "Is this done?"

Madame Balleroy swept closer with the grace and menace of a hawk descending upon its prey. She leaned over the copper pot, examining the molten sugars and honey. "Mind the color, Hadley," she said in a clipped tone. "A moment too long and you'll have nothing but a pot of burnt sugar."

"Yes, but the recipe says—"

"The recipe," she began, voice tight but controlled, "is a mere guideline. It is the instincts of the chef that truly dictate when a confection is perfected."

I cleared my throat, searching the recesses of my soul for the patience and grace needed to keep from snapping back. I was tired, hungry, and ready to go home. "So the nougat doesn't have to bubble first?"

Madame Balleroy bristled at my words, as though I'd just insulted her honor as a chef. "Did you just say *nugget*?"

I pointed to my pot. "Yes, nougat."

A low, throaty laugh sounded from across the table, where Mitzy's expression twisted with disdain.

Madame Balleroy sneered. "It's pronounced 'noo-guht,' or

sometimes 'noo-gah,' but never 'nugget,' like one of those vile little chunks of poultry sold in fast food restaurants."

Now Hal was howling, pounding a fist on the table at the hilarity of my mispronunciation. Snickers sounded around me from every direction, some more discreet, others unabashed in their amusement.

I felt a blush creeping up my neck, staining my cheeks the color of a ripe cherry. Perhaps chicken nuggets were too lowbrow for Madame Balleroy and the rest of the class, but sweet, darling Kinsley sure loved them.

Refusing to be the evening's fool, I straightened in my chair and met Madame Balleroy's gaze. "Chicken nuggets aren't vile," I fired back. "My niece adores them. In fact, I like them too. People don't eat sherried lobster bisque and beef Bourguignon every night, and it would be ignorant for you to think otherwise."

I froze at the words that had just come from my mouth, my cheeks burning even hotter. I'd accidentally called Kinsley *my* niece—as though Dennis and I were married and I was her aunt.

How embarrassing! I prayed Dennis would never find out about that mistake.

But it was pointless to correct myself. No one here knew I didn't actually have a niece, and Madame Balleroy's fire-red face made it clear she had no interest in discussing the intricacies of my family tree.

"Me, *ignorant?*" she exclaimed. "No one has dared to accuse me of such a thing."

I switched off the heat on my stove and moved the 'noo-guht' to a hotplate to cool. "It was a hypothetical statement, which means it's only true if it meets the other stated conditions."

Madame Balleroy's lips curved into a wicked smile. "Very well, then. It appears as though we've identified your signature ingredient—chicken nuggets."

"But nuggets aren't really an ingredient—" I started.

"You will include them in the dish you prepare for the Christmas Eve brunch. Hand-breaded, of course."

I gaped at her. "Now I have no chance of winning," I said, though I didn't really care about taking home a trophy. I was more horrified by the thought of serving the town a dish brimming with nuggets.

Madame Balleroy's eyes narrowed. "Trust me, you wouldn't have anyway."

CHAPTER TWELVE

I stood along the right side of the enormous, hollowed-out barn, next to a stack of hay bales that stretched halfway to the lofty ceiling. With a notebook in my left hand and a pen in my right, I surveyed the cool-blue fluorescent lights suspended above. Christmas Eve was quickly approaching, and though I'd already planned most of the decor, I still needed to finalize plans for lighting elements so I could order anything Madame Balleroy didn't already have.

A steady thumping of rain pattered against the barn's metal roof. Though I usually enjoyed rainy Saturday mornings and the supreme feeling of relaxation they brought, today it compounded the overall creepiness factor of the quiet barn. There had been a few cars parked next to the restaurant, but none in the lot near the cooking school and barn.

Which was fine by me. I'd arrived early to avoid any chance encounters with whoever had slipped the note into my container and, who, most likely, killed Seth. I'd even brought my canister of pepper spray, which was clipped over the hem of my jeans, ready to grab if needed.

In just ten days, thirty-five round tables, each big enough to seat twelve guests, would sit in the center of the barn. The cluster of tables would stretch from the small stage in the front all the way to the barn door entrance.

If Madame Balleroy sold out of tickets for inside seating, there were another dozen tables available to set up just outside the entrance to the barn. So far, she had sold only half of the tickets available. Given the recent homicide, I doubted she would sell too many more.

Though I dreaded the embarrassment of entering a chicken nugget dish into the cooking competition, I couldn't wait to see the decorations I'd planned come alive. Madame Balleroy had given her stamp of approval on my idea for a rustic woodland wonderland theme, which differed greatly from Gayle's usually lavish decorating style, with luxurious fabric, gilded accents, and opulent floral arrangements. Thankfully, Madame Balleroy was open to trying something different.

My theme incorporated natural elements and earthy colors like moss green, terracotta red, and cozy neutrals. Decorations like pine garlands, birch log candle holders, miniature evergreen trees, and wooden snowflakes would create a welcoming environment, while the enchanted forest photo backdrop, complete with a painted mural, artificial moss mats, colorful mushroom stools, and faux tree stumps would add an element of fun for all the kids in attendance.

Now, I just needed to finalize the lighting for the event.

Popping off the cap to my pen, I sketched the basic layout of the space, noting where natural light would stream in through the windows behind the stage and near the entrance. I would recreate these plans on my computer later, but the feel of a pen scratching against paper always got my ideas flowing.

For a space this large, I'd need to use a combination of lighting techniques. The cool-toned fluorescent lights suspended from the ceiling, though not my favorite form of ambient lighting, offered a soft, diffused glow throughout the barn. Twinkling fairy lights, strung throughout the rafters, added an idyllic charm, but offered little in the way of light.

I backed up as far as I could against the stacks of hay, taking in the barn's enormity. Edison bulb string lights, wrapped around free-standing wooden poles, would add warmth and help to offset the harsh fluorescent lighting. I sketched it out in my notebook: twelve free-standing poles positioned around the perimeter of the tables, with string lights strung across them, low enough to cast amber glows below but high enough so children wouldn't tug on them.

LED candles in old-fashioned lanterns would also be a nice touch. Walnut Ridge carried a line of them that would look amazing.

I stood up straighter, a new idea forming in my mind. Maybe I could order some decorations from Vincent. The lanterns weren't the only decorations in Walnut Ridge's catalog that would complement the theme. There were the wood-slab chargers—new this season—burlap table runners for the buffet tables, and faux fur throws we could drape over the wooden benches near the photo backdrop.

Only problem was, Walnut Ridge decor was on the pricier side, which was why I hadn't bought a ton of stuff for my own home from the company.

I sighed, returning my attention to the question of string lights. With that many lights, I would need multiple electrical outlets, and I'd need to run extension cords to...where?

Ideally, there would be outlets along the side walls I could use, but I didn't know if I could access them with the stacks of hay. Madame Balleroy probably had the answer, but I wasn't in the mood to talk to her this morning. I was still reeling from my chicken nugget dish assignment.

Heading toward the entrance, I ran my hand along the hay, feeling for a gap that would allow me to reach the wall behind the stacks. I found one toward the front of the barn, where the bales were stacked only four units high, making for an easy climb over to the other side.

Or so I thought it would be easy.

After stuffing my notebook and pen into my tote bag, I leaned it against the base of the hay bale and started my climb.

Struggling against the uneven surface, I gripped handfuls of the prickly hay, using them as makeshift handholds to pull myself up. But my no-tread sneakers, not optimal for scaling walls of hay, kept slipping on the dry, weathered straw. After several attempts, I finally hoisted myself up and over the top of the stack, collapsing momentarily onto highest bale, where I used my phone's weak flashlight to survey the other side of the haystack.

Despite the beam of light, the darkness was too thick to make out any electrical outlets. There was, however, enough room for me to squeeze between the haystack and the wall if I wanted to jump down to the other side. *If* I wanted to.

Question was, would I be able to get back up? And more importantly, what sorts of critters lurked behind the hay?

I swept my flashlight up and down the dark wall, hoping to scare away anything before I descended. Rain rippled against the wall next to me, but it sounded softer now, its tapping less frequent.

Something inside me stirred as I imagined the storm clouds passing by and giving way to clear skies. Better weather meant dry streets, which meant North Pole Night would continue as planned.

This morning, when I went downstairs, I spotted Dennis sprawled across an armchair in the family room, engrossed in a book, with only the dim light of a desk lamp illuminating the room. One hand held the book, the other rested gently on Razzy, who lay next to him. He'd gestured towards the window when he saw me, where heavy sheets of rain thrashed against the glass, and said if the rain didn't let up soon, the town would have to cancel North Pole Night. The disappointment was as clear in

Dennis's voice as his tired blue eyes. Poor Kinsley would be even more upset if the event was canceled.

But now, with the rain subsiding, the possibility of North Pole Night seemed within reach. I smiled as I swung my legs over the haystack and jumped into the darkness below. I needed to finish my work in the barn quickly so I could get on with the rest of my day, and then have plenty of time to get ready for tonight. Shower, hair, makeup—my typical pre-date routine. Except, of course, it wasn't really a date.

Considering the number of cobwebs I walked through during my search, I'd need to triple the time it would take me to wash my hair.

I found an electrical outlet twenty feet from where I'd descended the haystack, and then another one twenty feet from that, approximately in the middle of the barn.

Thank goodness. I could run an extension from there to the Edison bulb string lights and—voilà!—we would dine under a canopy of twinkling stars.

I turned around, ready to climb the haystack again, when something moved across my cheek. With a panicked yelp and swipe of my hand, I brushed off what felt like the tickle of spindly legs. A small black insect sailed away from me, into the blackness beyond the beam of my flashlight.

My heart thudded as I imagined how many more creepy-crawlies lurked between me and my exit. I took off running.

No more behind-the-haystack exploring; I wasn't getting paid enough to tear down spider webs with my face.

Technically, I wasn't volunteering my time, but it sure felt like it since I wouldn't normally exchange my services for cooking classes. Were they even helping me? Would they atone for my past kitchen sins? Absolve me from the guilt of serving my guests salmonella?

I regretted not bargaining more aggressively before accepting Aunt Deb's plan—I should have demanded that Madame Balleroy include my name in the brunch program and all promotional materials. I'd been so humiliated by my Thanksgiving mishap that I hadn't considered whether the agreement was truly beneficial for me.

Sweeping the flashlight against the wall of hay to my right, I searched for the exit point. It had to be somewhere nearby. When I found it, I'd catapult myself over and march directly to Madame Balleroy's restaurant and re-negotiate the terms of our agreement.

First, I would ensure she listed me as her designer in the event program. Then, I would suggest using decor from Walnut Ridge instead of the other vendors we had planned on. It would be a fantastic marketing opportunity for Vincent and would reflect positively on me if I successfully negotiated this deal.

The cramped space around me brightened and the barn doors groaned as they swung open. A man spoke, his voice tight and unsteady, "I told you, I'll do what I can. But no promises."

I wracked my brain, trying to place the face that went along with the voice, whose intensity sent chills crawling down my neck. I turned off my phone's flashlight just as the doors closed, darkness enveloping my tiny space once again.

"I swear, I had nothing to do with it," the man continued. "Seth was the one who arranged it."

"Don't *lie* to me," a second voice seethed, this one clearly belonging to Madame Balleroy. "You continue to disappoint me, time and time—" She paused, then called out, "Hadley, dear, are you in here?" Her voice had turned saccharine, dripping with artificial politeness.

Now it would be just plain weird for me to call out, "Here I am!" from behind the haystack. Not only that, but the icy tension in their voices told me their conversation was not meant to be overheard.

I listened to the strained silence that followed Madame Balleroy's sugary call to me, praying no spiders or other bugs would crawl across my face again, or else I would reveal my location with a scream.

The silence lasted for several more roaring heartbeats, until Madame Balleroy continued, "You are my program director—though not a very effective one lately. I am paying *you* to handle these matters."

So it was Jared that Madame Balleroy was lambasting. Seth's former roommate, former friend.

"You *will* make her comply," she said. "Because if you don't—"

"I'll take care of it."

"Seth got the Roma, and you will too if you don't—"

"I said I'll do my best," he snapped.

"Good. Now come help me with the table. We need it to accommodate tonight's surge in reservations."

Two pairs of feet shuffled across the smooth concrete flooring towards the storage area behind the curtain. A couple of minutes later, they left with a table, Madam Balleroy snipping commands at Jared the entire time.

After counting to sixty to make sure they were beyond earshot, I found a stable spot to place my foot and grabbed onto a dense clump of straw. It was time to skedaddle. Using the wall behind me for support, I shimmied back up the haystack, reaching the top much faster than the first time.

With my heart beating at a steady clip, I grabbed my bag and made my way towards the massive barn doors. The rustic iron handle was cold against my bare palms as I pulled it open and peeked outside. Madame Balleroy and Jared were at the far end of the sidewalk, rounding the turn towards the restaurant.

After they disappeared from sight, I slipped through the door, speed walking toward my car. The rain had stopped, and the sidewalk glistened with the early morning sunlight.

My mind raced in a dozen different directions, overwhelmed by everything I'd overheard. What had Seth arranged, and what—or *who*—was Jared supposed to "take care of"?

Most concerning, perhaps, was Madame Balleroy's threat—that Jared would "get the Roma," just as Seth had. Was that a culinary euphemism for a knife through the chest?

My feet hit the black asphalt parking lot, and I relaxed a little, taking a deep breath and filling my lungs with cool fresh air as I reached for the handle of my car.

"Oh, Hadley!" Madame Balleroy called from outside her restaurant. "I need to have a word with you before you leave."

CHAPTER THIRTEEN

Madame Balleroy stood outside her restaurant, tapping her foot against the pavement. As I neared, her dark eyes landed on the tote bag hanging from my shoulder, a glimmer of suspicion crossing her expression.

Had she seen my bag leaning against the haystack? Did she know I'd overheard her conversation?

"Leaving so soon?" she asked.

"Yep!" I kept my tone warm and cheery, as though I hadn't just heard her chilling conversation with Jared. "I got here early, worked a while, then, um...stepped outside to take a call from my boss at Walnut Ridge."

"Why didn't you take the call from inside the barn? Where it wasn't raining?"

My throat tightened. She *was* wondering if I had heard her conversation.

"I get better reception outside," I said with a shrug. "If you knew my boss, you'd understand how frustrated he gets with poor cell signals. I do my best to avoid irritating him."

"Such a demanding boss," she drawled. "Does he usually call you so early on the weekend?"

She wasn't letting this go. Madam Balleroy didn't care if Vincent bothered me on a Saturday morning; she wanted to make sure I hadn't heard her and Jared.

"Actually, he was returning my call. We were discussing an idea I had about decor for the brunch, one that would benefit you as much as him."

She raised her brows, prompting me to continue.

"Walnut Ridge carries several decorations that would harmonize beautifully with the rustic woodland wonderland theme: table runners, lanterns, and wood-slab chargers. Instead of purchasing these items, I was thinking he could loan them to you for the brunch in exchange for recognition in the event program."

I held my breath as she studied me, praying that she would believe my explanation about the call from Vincent. I also hoped she would agree to my idea; it was a good one, even if it had been created on the spur of the moment.

"Very well," she said at last. "As long as I don't owe him anything more than a spot on the sponsors' page." She gave a definitive nod, as though it were already a done deal, then walked back into her restaurant without another word.

I gulped. Now I just had to pray that Vincent would go along with the idea.

By the time I got home, Dennis and Kinsley were gone, getting an early start to what he'd claimed to be an endless list of errands. I would have to wait to share what I'd overheard in the barn.

After sneaking in a too-short workout on my treadmill and downing another cup of coffee, I'd called Vincent and pitched my idea to him, leaving out the minor detail that Madame Balleroy thought he'd already agreed to it. Thankfully, *mercifully*, he not only approved it, but praised me for such a fantastic idea.

Then I'd set out on my long list of errands, stopping only when my stomach threatened to implode if I didn't eat. After placing an order for Edison bulb string lights at the hardware super center, I drove towards the town square.

It was Whisks and Whiskers' grand reopening event today, and Erin was offering half-off coffees and desserts, as well as free samples of her new Yuletide mocha drink. She'd scheduled the event to coincide with North Pole Night, when the town square would be packed with people.

I didn't want to miss her celebration; she deserved a strong show of support after everything her business had been through lately. When it had closed last month, the entire town felt the pinch of losing their favorite gathering spot—humans and rescue cats alike.

The chime above the door rang merrily as I pushed it open, and a warm blast of air scented with coffee and cinnamon greeted me, along with a vibrant buzz of excitement from the throng of customers inside.

It was a little past three o'clock, but the café was packed. I was lucky to find an empty stool at the coffee bar, where I ordered the daily lunch special: turkey avocado club and tomato basil soup. Halfway through my sandwich, I removed my phone from my bag and texted Dennis.

> Great news—I'm at W&W and the town square is already packed with people setting up for the event. Looks like North Pole Night is still a go! :)

I'd parked five blocks away, since the streets near the town square were already lined with cars. But I hadn't minded the walk; it felt good to stretch my legs and turn my face to the sky, catching the dim rays of sunlight filtering through the thick clouds. If it hadn't been for the promising weather forecast for the evening, I would've worried the rain might return.

DENNIS

Kins just squealed when I read your text aloud.
I'm looking forward to tonight. Want to leave the
house at 7:00?

I'll be ready.

Good. Kins is ready to charm the socks off
Santa.

Maybe she can put in a good word for me.
Convince him to put me on the nice list this year.

That's doubtful. Santa's pretty strict about his
lists, you know.

I tossed the last bite of sandwich into my mouth, giggling as I chewed. Seven o'clock could not get here fast enough. It was only four now; what was I going to do for three more hours? I didn't need *that* long to get ready.

Erin strode by me, balancing a heavy tray of cake slices and frothy cups of coffee. She attempted to give me a smile, but it came across as more frazzled than anything, bordering on panic.

I hopped off my stool and caught up with her, matching my strides with hers as she headed for the cat château. "What's wrong?"

Her long blonde hair was tied back into a ponytail, covered with a turquoise Whisks and Whiskers baseball hat that made her green eyes shine even brighter. "Well, there are a lot more people than I'd planned, and I'm not fully staffed yet." She balanced the tray in one hand to open the door, but I reached in front of her and pulled it open as she walked into the room. With all the grace and ease of an experienced restaurant owner, she delivered the plates and mugs to a group of five sitting around a low table, each with a cat on their lap.

She turned away from the customers to face me, this time

with a wide grin on her face. "But I couldn't be happier about today's turnout."

"It *is* packed," I agreed as we walked back inside. "What can I do to help?"

Erin gave me an amused smile, almost as if my question was absurd. "You're not an employee, you're a customer. Just sit back and enjoy."

"I might not work here, but I'm your friend. How can I help?" I asked again.

Erin looked toward the entrance, where the door was propped open by customers waiting in line. "Well, I could really use your help handing out Yuletide mocha samples to people passing by outside. Today's a golden opportunity to get them hooked on my coffee again." She winced. "But only if you have nothing better to—"

"I'm all yours for the next forty-five minutes." After that, I had one last errand to run before I started getting ready for North Pole Night.

Erin thanked me profusely, then gave me a Whisks and Whiskers apron and plastic gloves. She led me outside to the front patio of her café, which held a dozen white metal bistro tables, each surrounded by four matching chairs.

It was colder outside than when I'd arrived, but my sweatshirt and fleece-lined coat would keep my core warm. My legs, however, clad only in thin black leggings, might turn to popsicles while I hawked Erin's coffee samples.

Timmy, the café's manager, stood near the front of the patio, handing out small paper cups to anyone strolling by.

"Timmy lost his voice," Erin explained. "He's done so much talking out here today that it quit on him."

Timmy confirmed this with a helpless shrug, then lifted an already filled cup from the table next to him, holding it out to me.

"Thanks, but I'm here to help you, not drink your samples—at least, not *too* many of them," I joked.

He returned the cup to the table, then placed his palms together and gave a silent bow of gratitude.

"I'm happy to help! Why don't you fill them, and I'll do the talking."

Timmy gave me a double thumbs-up, then retrieved two samples from the table and handed them to me, along with a couple of napkins.

"Oh, my…" I began, as I studied the words printed on each napkin. Just below the café's logo was a simple sketch of a cat, along with a note in a messy, child-like font: *Hey, human, are you a Wi-Fi signal? Because I'm feeling a strong connection here. Adopt me, and I'll spend all my nine lives with you.*

"These are freakin' adorable," I told him before turning towards a man and woman about my age, their hands interlaced as they approached the café. "Come try the best coffee this side of the North Pole!"

They briefly tore their eyes away from each other to accept a cup, then resumed their conversation. I took a napkin from the top of the stack and slid it into my coat pocket, my lips frozen with a smile as I imagined Dennis's booming laugh when I showed it to him later. He was a cat person through and through, and Razzy knew it. She didn't cuddle up beside just anyone; they had to earn her love.

I helped Timmy for another forty minutes, watching with building excitement as food vendors set up their stalls in the town square, arranging them with festive decorations while firing up their stoves, ovens, and grills. The smell of candied pecans now filled the air, mingling with the coffee aroma surrounding Whisks and Whiskers.

I'd given Timmy a parting hug and was about to head to the florist on Orchard Road to confirm the order for floral arrangements at the brunch when I spotted Natasha sipping on a large mug in the far corner of the patio. I took one step toward her, then hesitated. It was already a quarter 'till five, and the clock was ticking at warp speed towards seven o'clock. I *had* to swing by the florist since they were closed on Sundays, and I *had* to give myself enough time to get ready.

I would need to make this a quick conversation with Natasha.

"Thank goodness the café reopened," I said, by way of greeting.

"You know it." She gave me a subtle smile, as though she didn't want to be rude, but had been savoring her solitude before I walked up.

I continued anyway, "Do you have the night off at Balleroy's?"

"I wouldn't be here if I didn't," she pointed out. "I'm taking my kids to North Pole Night a little later. Just soaking up some me-time first while my husband drags them on errands."

"Great sweater," I said, pointing to it. "It's perfect for the event." It was colorful—a tennis ball shade of green—and whimsical, featuring pink snowmen on roller-skates holding colorful gift boxes. A thick red bow kept her hair tied back, while chunky gold hoop earrings brought a touch of glamour to her holiday ensemble.

A goofy grin crossed her pretty face. "Seriously? This thing is *hideous*. Pink snowmen? Roller-skates? I wouldn't wear it if it didn't make my little ones so darn happy. The things we do for our children, right? They gave it to me last year for Christmas and now they fully expect me to wear it," she laughed. "I hope your kids aren't as cruel to you."

I shook my head. "No, I don't have children yet. Just a niece...well, not really." I took a sharp breath, realizing it was the second time I'd accidentally referred to Kinsley as my niece. Instead of explaining the situation, I simply told Natasha, "This is a good night to take off. Madame Balleroy was in a rotten mood this morning."

"Madame Balleroy in a bad mood?" she scoffed. "I have a hard time believing that." Her tone was thick with sarcasm, her expressive eyes rolling dramatically. "You were there working on brunch decorations?"

I nodded. "I heard her say the restaurant is booked tonight. You'd think that would've put her in a good mood."

"We've been booked for the past two nights." She raised a palm, her face a twist of confusion. "No one can figure out why. After the homicide, we struggled to fill even a quarter of our tables."

Slowly, deliberately, I scanned the surrounding crowd, searching in every direction for anyone who I wouldn't want to hear what I was about to say. I knew it was a risk to talk to people about Seth, but I trusted Natasha. Maybe it was because she was married with kids, or because her wide, expressive eyes radiated honesty. Whatever it was, my gut told me I could trust her.

"Do not tell anyone I told you this—please—but I overheard a conversation I wasn't supposed to while I worked in the barn this morning." I waited for her to nod before continuing, "Madame Balleroy was mad at Jared—*really* mad. Apparently, he hadn't done something she'd asked him to, and she demanded that he take care of it. That he needed to 'make' some woman comply."

"She's mad about the article," Natasha said without hesitation. "The *Darlington Hills Dispatch* reporter called her yesterday afternoon and said the story about the restaurant and cooking school is on hold indefinitely. Most likely, in my opinion, because of the homicide. I was in the kitchen with Madame Balleroy when she got the call. She launched into a tirade, first blaming all of us for cooking food unworthy of the reporter's time, and then blaming Jared behind his back, who was off yesterday. I'm sure that's why she got mad at him this morning."

"Why would she blame Jared?" I asked.

Natasha's gaze swept around the patio before she leaned in closer. "He's her program manager. Madame Balleroy hired him to not only coordinate special events but also to promote the restaurant and, more importantly, *her*."

I recalled my previous conversation with Natasha, where she'd told me Seth's popularity and charming personality were a big reason Madame Balleroy's restaurant was so successful. "Do you think Madame Balleroy was jealous of Seth's fame?"

"Probably," she muttered. "It would explain why she pushed Jared so hard to secure her more media coverage and social media attention. I'd even dare to say it had become an obsession of hers."

Natasha's eyes shifted to her coffee. Tendrils of steam still swirled above it, casually mixing with the chilly afternoon air. She grabbed it by the handle and lifted it in a toast-like gesture. "Have a good rest of the weekend, and don't work too hard."

It was her polite way of dismissing me, of telling me she wanted to resume her peaceful me-time before her family returned.

"Have fun at North Pole Night," I said, turning away from her table. "Maybe I'll see you there—" I stopped, spinning around again to face her. "Actually, one more question...Madame Balleroy told Jared that Seth 'got the Roma' and said he would too if he didn't take care of business."

Her back stiffened. "*Seth* got the Roma?"

I nodded. "What does it mean?"

Natasha's eyes darted across the small table, and I could see the gears turning in her mind. "Grand-mère must have blamed Seth for the beetle."

"The one that a customer found in their short rib bourguignon?" I confirmed. After she gave a faint nod, I pressed, "But what is the Roma?"

She whispered, "It's a peculiar tradition of Grand-mère's. Instead of throwing out unused tomatoes, she keeps them in a pile out back—for composting, she claims. But if someone screws up in the kitchen—like, really screws up—then she gives them a rotten Roma tomato. It's the kiss of death; an unequivocal signal that they no longer work at the restaurant." Natasha's eyes rose, connecting with mine. "Grand-mère must have fired Seth shortly before he was murdered."

The sun retired early tonight. Normally, at this time of year, it would dip below the horizon around five o'clock and leave us with another forty-five minutes of fading light. Tonight, with dark clouds shrouding the sky, it felt much later than it was.

Streetlights buzzed to life, casting a warm glow onto the stone-paved town square. Children bundled up in thick coats ran around, their breath visible in the chilly air.

I kept to the western side of the square as I headed towards the florist on Orchard Road, only a few blocks away. A group of men with ponytails, leather jackets, and ripped jeans strummed guitars on the stage as they warmed up to play.

My eyes fell on the dance floor in front of them, and I picked up my pace, walking so fast I probably looked ridiculous. But I was too excited to care.

I veered left onto Orchard Road, heading farther away from the town square. The cheerful sounds grew fainter, replaced by the steady rhythm of my sneakers on the pavement.

Except for the pizza parlor on the southwest corner of the intersection, most of the other shops and restaurants had closed early for North Pole Night, and without the warm glows from their windows, the street lamps struggled to fight against the encroaching shadows. Cars were parked tightly along the curb, showcasing the impressive parallel parking skills of locals.

Following the sidewalk, I headed towards the florist, guided by its bright pink sign at the end of the street. To my left, a line of trimmed hedges stretched up to my waist, separating the sidewalk from the different businesses along the street.

I wrapped my coat closer around me. It wasn't just the chilly air sending a fresh wave of shivers across my skin; it was also a growing sensation of being watched. I tried to brush off the feeling; after all, how could I possibly sense if someone's eyes were on me? I wasn't an animal with heightened awareness.

And yet, the feeling persisted. It was as real as the blood hammering through my veins. If it weren't for the occasional person walking past me towards the town square, I might have postponed my errand until Monday.

Most likely, the feeling of paranoia stemmed from my conversation with Natasha—the revelation that Grand-mère had, after all, blamed Seth for the beetle-in-the-bourguignon atrocity.

I mulled over Natasha's words while recalling the evening of Seth's death. Grand-mère had come into the kitchen, demanding that Madame Balleroy go "frost the cake" in the restaurant's kitchen. It was a secret way of telling her something horrible had happened that she needed to address.

But Madame Balleroy had ignored her grandmother's coded plea, and instead gave Chloe and me a tour of the grounds, staying with us the entire time, except for a brief solo trip to cut —or rather, hastily uproot—herbs for Chloe's dinner. Where *had* Madame Balleroy gone during those five minutes she left us in the barn? She'd received a text moments before she excused herself. Was it Grand-mère, beckoning her to witness the Seth's firing—or something worse?

Despite their constant bickering, it was clear Grand-mère and Madame Balleroy shared a common goal: to do everything in their power to make their restaurant a success. But to what lengths would they go to protect their business and its reputation?

I needed to talk to Dennis about the conversation I'd overheard in the barn and Natasha's revelation about the tomato. But the big question swirling through my mind was *when* I'd tell him. If I spilled everything before North Pole Night, he might have to ditch our plans altogether and head to the station, as he had several times before. Kinsley would be so disappointed.

I would be disappointed.

I'd fill him in later, I decided. Either tonight or, more likely, tomorrow. One day wouldn't matter.

I walked past the entrance to a children's playground, which was bordered by an even denser perimeter of hedges. I smiled at the thought of returning here tomorrow with Dennis and Kinsley. The play structure, tall enough to see over the hedges, was a massive and intricate maze of slides and tunnels that promised fun for any child.

The florist's sign loomed larger with each step, casting a soft pink glow over the street. Although my senses still tingled with unease, I sighed with relief when I finally reached the shop's front door.

Kathy Fermido, the owner of Hill's Blossoms, greeted me with a glance at her watch when I entered.

"I'll make this quick," I promised. "You're probably heading to the town square, just like everyone else. I'm Hadley Sutton; I spoke with you on the phone earlier this week about flower arrangements for Madame Balleroy's Christmas Eve brunch. I'm here to confirm the order and go over a few details."

She brightened. "Ah, yes! I'm glad you stopped by. I'd like to show you my recommendations for flowers that will complement the rustic woodland theme for the brunch, which I attend every year with my family. I'm thrilled to provide flowers at this year's event. They've been so *drab* in previous years."

She had Gayle to thank for the "drab" flower arrangements, but I kept the snide thought to myself. It would be unprofessional and catty to say nasty things about Gayle, even though she was my competitor.

Kathy ushered me into her tiny office, which had two large bookcases containing binders and photo albums. Knowing exactly which one she wanted to show me, she plucked an album on the top shelf and flipped to a series of photos of flower arrangements she'd once prepared for a western-themed wedding.

I selected my favorite three, all of which featured a mix of wildflowers with more traditional blooms, and asked her to include poinsettias and fir branches to give it a Christmasy feel.

Kathy pulled the photos from the album and set them on a desk next to the far wall. As she jotted notes in a spiral notebook, I swept my eyes across her tidy little space. A simple acrylic painting of sunflowers hung on the wall opposite the bookshelves, and a jumbo-sized calendar hung above her desk.

From the looks of her calendar, Kathy had a busy December. She had at least one, sometimes two or three events every day of the month. Except for December 29. There was a large red X drawn over her loopy handwriting. I stepped closer, narrowing my eyes to read it.

I gasped. Under the X, she'd written Riggs-O'Boyle wedding.

Kathy looked up from her desk. "Is something wrong, dear?"

I motioned to her calendar. "I just saw that you were supposed to do flowers for Cindy and Seth's wedding this month."

She nodded, her smile shifting slightly. "I was disappointed when they canceled their order. They had selected my Premium Plus package, and I don't get too many of those orders. Do you know them?"

Know them. Not *knew* them. Kathy didn't know Seth was dead.

"I met them recently," I said, but before I could share the devastating news about Seth, Kathy started talking.

"I spent days planning all the arrangements for their special day, so I was quite disappointed when Cindy's mother called to cancel the order."

"She...didn't tell you why she canceled it?"

"No, but I presume the wedding was called off. It happens

from time to time, but usually not so close to the big day. But as disappointed as I was, the bride's mother was likely relieved. Mrs. Riggs wasn't happy about the wedding in the first place."

"Why not?" I pressed.

Kathy shrugged, then handed me an invoice for the floral arrangements. "She said her daughter had already broken off the engagement once due to a disagreement over money she lent him. She used up all her savings, so Mrs. Riggs had to pay for most of the wedding."

"What made her daughter decide to get back together with him?"

"I don't know. I try not to ask too many questions, dear." Kathy turned and retrieved a pink leather purse from a cabinet in her desk. "I need to meet my family at the town square now, but please call me this week if you have questions about your order."

By the time Kathy closed her door behind me, it was almost five-thirty—time to head home and get ready. Stepping out into the chilly evening, the cheery sounds from the town square were louder now, drowning out any lingering feelings of paranoia. The energetic beat of the drums echoed through the streets, beckoning me to the dance floor.

But first, I had to retrieve my dance partner.

At the end of the florist's walkway, I turned right and began the trek back to my car, humming along with the band's folksy version of *Jingle Bells*. It was lively, cheerful, and perfect for dancing.

I stopped next to a hedge to snap a quick photo of the giant play structure and texted it to Dennis.

> Playdate at this park tomorrow? It's got more slides than a PowerPoint presentation.

> Only if you'll ride on my lap down the tall one.

That *flirt*! I pounded my fingers against the screen, accusing him of just that, then hit send as I resumed walking.

My gaze was drawn to a sudden glint of light under the hedge. An instant later, a sharp pain shot through my right ankle. I cried out and stumbled backwards, clutching my hand to my leg. With a quick glance, I saw the torn skin and the blood flowing down onto my white sock.

Something darted out from under the hedges and raced off towards the playground, and I sprinted like a maniac in the opposite direction.

CHAPTER FOURTEEN

I didn't stop running until I reached my car. Flinging open the door, I nearly collapsed into the driver's seat. My breaths came in ragged gasps as I fought off the intense nausea, feeling just as sick as I did when I had food poisoning.

What. Just. Happened?

My slashed ankle. The glint of light under the hedge. The thing that ran away after cutting me.

It was a branch, I told myself as I sucked in one rapid breath after another. Merely a long, sharp branch protruding from the underside of the hedges.

But the glint of light. What was *that?*

I didn't spend any longer considering all the possible explanations, and instead peeled out of my parking spot, cringing from the pain of pressing the gas pedal.

Instead of turning left onto Picket Lane, towards home, I cranked the steering wheel to the right and sped off.

"Call Carmella," I told Siri.

My friend answered after two rings. "Hey girl! How's it—"

"Are you home?"

"Yes, what's wrong?" Her tone shifted, now mirroring the urgency in my own.

"I cut myself. I need…a Band-Aid, I think." At least I hoped I didn't need anything more than that. I'd already gotten stitches once this year; I couldn't handle another needle-through-the skin session.

"What's really going on?" she demanded. "You sound upset. Are you crying?"

"I need a Band-Aid," I repeated. "Probably a big one. I can't go home yet. Dennis is there and I don't want him to see it—not yet, anyway."

"Oh, sweet Lord. What sort of trouble are you in?"

"A giant heap of it. I'll explain when I get there."

Three minutes later, I banged on Carmella's door.

"Hey," I said, panting. As she ushered me into her apartment, she scanned my face, my hands, my legs—

"Oh!" Carmella's palms flew up in surprise and she quickly looked away from my injured ankle. She fanned herself with one hand while the other covered her mouth. "I can't…I don't do blood. And that's a lot. Come with me."

Grasping my arm, she dragged me through her family room, down the short hallway, into her bedroom and adjoining bathroom, where she removed a clear purple plastic bin from under her sink.

"This should have everything you need," she said. "If not, I'll drive you to the emergency room—again." She backed away slowly, cautiously, her once vibrant brown skin turning paler with each step. "I'll be on the other side of this door while you patch yourself up and explain why your leg is flowing like a faucet."

I rolled my eyes and hiked my leg onto the counter for a closer look. "Come on, it's not that bad—" The lightbulbs above the mirror shone on my fresh wound, and I recoiled in disgust. "It *is* bad! Oh, God, Carmella, there's a flap—"

"Do *not* say that word," she hissed. "Unless you want to scrape me off the floor when I pass out, don't give me a play-by-play of your patch-up job."

I opened the purple bin, which turned out to be the most organized first-aid kit I'd ever seen. "How'd you cram an entire pharmacy into this tiny container?" I joked, trying to lighten the mood for both Carmella and myself.

"I have good spatial-relations skills. Just call me Queen Tetris."

I forced out a laugh, despite the constant pain gnawing at my ankle. My shaking hands landed on a bottle of hydrogen peroxide. Regardless of what type of sharp object cut me, I needed to clean it before bandaging it.

With a twist, I unscrewed the top and braced myself. This would hurt.

I closed my eyes and poured.

"Yeow!" I screamed as the bubbly fizz of the peroxide consumed my wound, making my entire leg feel like it was submerged in fire. Like an echo on the other side of the door, Carmella's scream joined mine, only louder and more panicked.

"Everything's fine," I panted. "Nothing to worry about."

"*What* happened tonight?" she demanded.

I blew on my leg, desperately trying to ease the searing pain. It was so intense, it felt as though I had poured acid on the wound. "I don't know. Something cut me when I was walking back to my car…something from under those hedges near the playground on Orchard Road. A sharp branch, most likely, or possibly a feral cat. Except…"

"Except *what*?" she insisted.

I rummaged through the container and settled on a roll of gauze. "Right before the…branch, or whatever, cut me, I saw a glint of light from under the hedge."

There was a low moan on the other side of the door. "I don't like where this is going, Hadley. Branches don't glint. Neither do cats."

"It was a branch. It *had* to have been. I don't want to consider any other possibilities right now." I quickly tore open the plastic wrapper and pressed the gauze against my cut.

The bathroom door creaked as Carmella pushed it open, just enough for her to peer inside. "If you're so sure it was a branch, then why don't you want to tell Dennis?" she asked, her gaze as piercing as the object that cut me.

"Because Dennis likes to ask questions, and I don't have time for that right now. I'm going to North Pole Night with him and Kinsley at seven o'clock, which leaves me one hour to stop the bleeding, drive home, take the fastest shower in the history of Hadley, blow-dry and curl my hair, put on makeup, and decide what to wear. If I tell him what happened"—I gestured to my still-bleeding cut, which Carmella blocked from her view with an outstretched hand—"then it'll blow our fun plans. He'll spend the night dealing with this instead."

Carmella stepped completely inside the bathroom, eying me suspiciously. She folded her arms. "What's so important about North Pole Night?"

"Do you know how many times Reid canceled our plans because he had to deal with something on his boat? It happened so many times that I lost track. I'm *tired* of looking forward to a date, thinking about it incessantly all week, and then getting ditched for something more pressing. And," I added, softening my voice, "I want to dance with Dennis again. I didn't get enough of it at the police gala, and I want *more*. Sure, I'm probably setting myself up to get hurt again, and I don't know if he feels anything for me, but I just want to have some fun with him tonight. I'll tell him about my cut later—after Kinsley has seen Santa, after I've dragged Dennis onto the dance floor."

I peeked under the gauze once again, relieved to find the bleeding had slowed. The cut didn't look nearly as deep as when I'd cut my hand and needed stitches, but it stung every bit as much.

Carmella unfolded her arms, then placed a reassuring hand on my shoulder. "Dennis isn't Reid, hon. Maybe he wouldn't bail on your plans if he knew how important they are to you."

"Maybe, but I don't want to take that chance. It won't hurt anything to wait a few hours to tell him."

My thoughts were fixated on the empty dance floor in the heart of the town square, as if some invisible magnet were drawing me towards it. Nothing would stop me from following through with our plans tonight, not even my throbbing ankle or the inevitable barrage of questions from Dennis.

I pursed my lips and shook my head, conflicted. "What's wrong with me? Why am I setting myself up for disappointment? I *promised* myself a break from dating, and yet I still want to go out with him tonight."

Carmella scowled. "Breaks are overrated. I took one after Neil; I turned down two dates with perfectly decent men, and now I can't help but wonder what I might have missed by over-indulging in avoidance."

"Avoidance?"

"Trying to protect myself from getting hurt." Carmella leaned a shoulder against the wall. "I finally decided that heartbreak is unavoidable, whether I take a two-month or two-year dating hiatus. Because all relationships are doomed to fail...except for the one that isn't. And that's the one we need to be ready for and open to—which is hard to do if you're taking a break."

I played with the frayed edges of the gauze pad, mulling over her words. "Your advice is the exact opposite of Erin's. She suggested taking time to get over Reid before jumping into another relationship."

"Well then, you'll just have to decide for yourself which option feels right." She wrinkled her nose, as though reconsidering her words. "Besides, Erin's a married woman now. She's rusty when it comes to dating advice."

I laughed. "She got married a month ago. She's not *that* rusty."

"You won't see me asking Erin for dating advice, and Lord knows I need it. Case in point, I had a dinner date planned for tonight—a friend of the head football coach at my school—but he called an hour ago to ask if I would instead join him and his buddies at the bar to watch the big hockey game that's on. I said no, and he 'postponed' our date for a week. I'm sure I won't hear from him again."

"I'm sorry," I said quietly. "But he sounds like a jerk, so at least you didn't have to suffer through an entire meal with him."

Carmella waved off my condolences, acting like getting ditched for a sports game wasn't a big deal. "Dennis cares about you, Hadley. How are you so blind to it?"

"Dennis is a hopeless flirt," I clarified. "Has been since the day I met him."

"With *you* he is, but I've never seen him act that way around other women, not even with his ex-girlfriend," she said, gesturing to Akari's apartment below hers. "There was no spark like the one I've seen with you two. You should take a chance on him."

"Well then, I need to get ready for North Pole Night." Visions of Dennis's strong arms wrapped around my waist, pulling me closer with each turn, made my stomach flutter with nervous anticipation. With a swift glance at my watch, I grabbed a bandage and a fresh roll of gauze, then wrapped it around my wound. "I owe you a roll."

"Don't worry about it; I have four left, and I don't expect to use all of them."

"Then I'll make it up to you with a coffee—or, better yet, since you're staying in town for the holidays, why don't you join my table at Madame Balleroy's Christmas Eve brunch?"

She lifted her brows, considering the invitation. "You're sure there's room for me?"

"Of course! The table is enormous—it seats twelve—and we

still have two open seats. It'll be Aunt Deb, Roy, Michael, and me, along with Dennis and his family, since they'll be here over Christmas."

"I'd love to join. And I'll point out every time Dennis flirts with you, just in case you fail to notice."

CHAPTER FIFTEEN

After hobbling from Carmella's apartment to my car, then from my car to my house, and pretending not to hobble past Dennis and Kinsley—both already dressed and ready to go—I took a lightning-fast shower and refreshed my makeup.

I had grabbed the first red sweater I found in my closet and paired it with slim-fitting jeans, then sat on the floor and took my sweet time putting on socks. It was a festive pair, emblazoned with colorful, laughing Santas. They were laughing at *me*, I'd decided as I slid the sock over my bandage. Laughing at my stupidity for planning to traipse all over the town square with a throbbing ankle.

Now, as I waited in line with Dennis and Kinsley to see Ol' Saint Nick himself, it took everything in me not to sling an arm around Dennis and use his wide shoulders for support as we shuffled forward. The walk from his car had been a grueling one, and now my ankle was reeling from the abuse.

But I did my best to ignore the fiery pain underneath the happy little Santas. I refused to let it ruin the night. I wanted to soak up every drop of this enchanting Christmas wonderland. Every gingerbread-laced aroma teasing my tastebuds, every drumbeat that lured me to the dance floor, and every stolen glance at the stunning sandy-blonde man by my side.

"Santa's looking a little thin these days," Dennis whispered, his soft breath suddenly warming my ear. "They couldn't find a larger man for the role?"

Laughing, I glanced at Kinsley before whispering into his ear, "Talk to Michael about that. This Santa is from the community theater."

He grunted. "Tell your cousin he needs to improve his casting skills." Dennis shook his head playfully, but his cooler-than-usual tone made me wonder just how much he still resented Michael for stealing his girlfriend.

My heart sank a little, suddenly flustered and confused. Had Dennis gotten over Akari, or was he still bitter? And all our recent flirting—I couldn't figure it out. Was it genuine, or simply habitual? How did he feel about *me*? Was he content being friends who flirted, or did he want it to be something more?

It was a puzzle, one more frustrating than any mystery I'd ever sought to unravel.

A spirited breeze peppered my neck with chill bumps as it filtered through my wet hair. I hadn't had the time to blow-dry it, so rather than being late, I'd pulled a fluffy pink Santa hat over my hair before heading downstairs.

I'd felt self-conscious in it, to say the least...until Dennis's eyes widened with surprise when he spotted me on the stairs. Then, to my bewilderment, he removed a green elf hat—complete with attached pointy ears—from his back pocket and slid it over his head. At least we would look silly together.

Kinsley, bouncing on the balls of her feet, tugged on the sleeve of Dennis's black leather coat. Its sleek design accentuated his strong build, and combined with his indigo jeans and black boots, he looked irresistibly attractive. I had to clasp my hands in front of me and interlock my fingers to resist the urge to reach out and touch the thickest part of his arms, where the soft leather hugged tightly.

"Look! We're getting close to Santa!" she said, with a squeal.

Dennis turned his attention to Kinsley as she counted exactly how many people were in front of us. I kept my eyes on him—on those warm eyes that crinkled with amusement at his nieces' bubbling excitement; on those thick, dark eyebrows that rose in admiration of her counting skills; and on his deep-set dimples that dug even deeper into his cheeks as he offered an encouraging smile to Kinsley, who was now on her tiptoes, straining to see over the crowd.

"Only twelve more people!" Kinsley chirped, her voice rising above the chatter in the area.

Dennis hoisted her onto his shoulders. "But only three more families. I sure hope you have your list ready for Santa."

Kinsley giggled. "I know *exactly* what I want this year," she said, reaching down to pat her uncle's head as though he were her noble steed.

Dennis placed his hand on the small of my back, guiding me forward in line. His gaze fell on my feet, his eyebrows furrowing. "Are you okay? Looks like you're limping."

I closed my eyes for a heartbeat, hating that he'd asked me that question. Because now I either had to tell him everything or lie.

How would he react? Would he turn on a heel and leave North Pole Night to investigate what had happened? Would he assume the worst, as he sometimes did, and say my slashed ankle was another threat tied to the homicide?

But Kinsley hadn't seen Santa yet, and I hadn't spun around the dance floor with him.

So I lied.

"I'm fine," I laughed, giving a small shrug. "It's just a minor cut."

Too many details! I scolded myself when the words fell from my mouth. Now it would be hard, if not impossible, to later explain why 'just a minor cut' required a wrap-around bandage.

His eyes narrowed ever so slightly, as though he had seen through the flimsy veil of my cheery explanation. But instead of pressing the issue, Dennis simply nodded.

"What *I* want to know," I began, changing the subject, "is where you got your elf hat. I'm not sure which set of ears I should talk to."

He gestured to the tall, pointy ones on his hat. "Tonight, you can whisper into these," he said, his voice a flirtatious whisper. "I bought it online before last year's North Pole Night."

His statement sparked a series of new questions to ponder as we drew closer to Saint Nick. Who did Dennis go with last year? It wasn't Kinsley, since this was the first time she'd been to Darlington Hills. Surely he hadn't gone alone...but I couldn't imagine him hanging out here with his guy friends. Had he gone with another woman? Danced with her beneath the snowflake-shaped string lights?

The family in front of us said their goodbyes to Santa as their little ones hopped down from his lap. Kinsley grew quiet and serious, with no trace of her earlier excitement.

"Your turn, Kins," Dennis said, removing her from his shoulders, then gesturing to Santa's outstretched arms. "And put in a good word for Hadley while you're up there."

She didn't budge. With a low chuckle, Dennis grabbed her hand and walked her over to the not-so-big-man in red. I stayed put, snapping a round of photos of Kinsley's wide-eyed, frozen stare as she sat on Santa's lap. Then, moving my phone ever so slightly to the right, I took even more pictures of Dennis's light-the-night smile as he watched his horrified niece rattle off the items on her wish list.

Kinsley relaxed after some time, and Dennis walked away from her to join me. "She's an awesome little squirt, isn't she?" I nodded enthusiastically, and he continued, "And I can't thank you enough for letting us stay with you."

"I don't mind at all. It's been fun." Gritting my teeth, I mentally slapped myself for such an aloof response. I could do better than that. I *should* do better—should take a chance on Dennis, as Carmella had suggested. "Actually, I've enjoyed it more than you can imagine," I admitted. "I look forward to coming home after work. Coming home to…you."

"Yeah?" he said, his eyes creasing with a grin. "Well, I feel the same. You have a way of brightening the darkest month of the year."

He didn't have to explain what a "dark December" meant; I already knew. It was the month his childhood best friend, Alex, was killed in a drive-by shooting when Dennis was a freshman in college. It was easy to understand why this time of year was anything but merry and bright for him.

"But don't worry," Dennis hurried to add, "Even though you've reassured me we aren't imposing, we won't over-stay our welcome. I'm getting close on the money laundering case, so we should be out of your way soon enough."

That wasn't what I wanted to hear. If he'd said it to make me feel better, it did anything but.

Disappointed gnawed at me as I watched Kinsley, who was now as talkative as ever, chat with Santa. I didn't want to think about coming home to a quiet house or cooking in my spacious, beautiful kitchen by myself. The Christmas season wouldn't be the same without them.

A stronger gust of wind blew, making me shiver in the cold air.

"We'll warm up once we walk around again." He rubbed his hand against my back, instantly warming my core—not from the heat of his touch, but from the nervous energy now buzzing through my veins. Soon enough, if I worked up the nerve, I'd casually ask if he wanted to check out the dance floor.

Kinsley bounded off Santa's lap, waving a spirited goodbye to him before grasping Dennis's hand once again. "Can we go see the elves now? Santa said we get to make our own wooden airplane at their workshop."

Dennis nodded. "Absolutely. But there's something I'd like to do first, kiddo." He found my hand and pulled the both of us along. "First, I want to dance with Hadley."

The pain in my ankle vanished as blissful adrenaline fueled my dash towards the band—past the row of food carts lining the edge of the square, past the heap of artificial snow in which children played, and around the side of the fountain. The entire town seemed to be here, everyone's faces rosy from the cold. Children bundled in colorful hats and coats posed in front of the giant Christmas tree near the fountain as their parents snapped endless photos of them. All around us, excitement pulsed through the air in anticipation of Christmas, which was now only eleven days away.

As we neared the edge of the dance floor, the band finished playing "Jingle Bell Rock" and immediately launched into another upbeat song that was impossible not to dance to.

Putting both hands on his knees, Dennis leaned over until he was eye level with Kinsley. "Do you mind waiting here while I dance with Hadley? We'll stay close by, I promise."

Beaming, Kinsley looked between Dennis and me. "Don't step on her toes!"

"You are just like your mama," he teased, then turning to me, Dennis held out his hand. "Want to dance?"

I grasped it, and he tugged me closer, his other arm wrapping around my waist. My pulse ratcheted up to sprint mode. "I've wanted to since I heard there would be a band tonight."

That was another lie. I'd wanted to since we'd left the police gala several weeks ago.

String lights crisscrossing overhead cast a warm glow on the near-empty dance floor. Only three other couples swayed alongside us, giving us plenty of room to move. Dennis and I spun in circles, our footsteps pounding the dance floor in-time with the lively beat.

"I've never heard this Christmas song before," I told him. "I like it."

He glanced over to where Kinsley stood watching us. "You won't hear it on the radio. The lead guitarist, Rocky Moore, wrote it himself before last year's North Pole Night."

"How does tonight compare to last year's event?" I asked, casually.

"It's every bit as packed. This morning's rain didn't stop people from coming. And last year, I was assigned to patrol the event, so I didn't enjoy it nearly as much as I am tonight."

"That's a sight I'd like to see—you in your patrol uniform and elf hat." A bubble of laughter escaped me as Dennis dipped me low, his eyes glowing with mischief. The music was a rolling wave of notes that seemed to carry us away from the world and all its worries. As he lifted me back up, I caught the familiar shower-fresh scent of him—soft, warm, and inviting.

"I'll model it for you anytime," he offered.

"I might just take you up on that," I giggled, finding his smiling eyes once again. He was steering us backwards, and it took every ounce of faith to not look behind me as we moved. "Do you always stay here for Christmas, or do you ever travel home for the holidays?"

Dennis looked away. "I haven't been home for Christmas since...well, since Alex's death. I still fly home to visit—usually twice a year—just not in December."

"Is that why you moved to Darlington Hills when you completed your service in the Army? Because of the memories in Texas?"

His eyes widened slightly, as though he were surprised by the question. "No...not exactly. That's a long story for another day.

Because right now"—he lifted our hands and gave me a gentle nudge to twirl under his arm—"I just want to dance."

As did I. Dennis pulled me even closer, and I felt the heat from his body as we moved in sync with the music. Every few seconds we glanced at Kinsley, who was clapping energetically, as though cheering us on. As more couples filed onto the dance floor, Dennis steered us closer to her.

My ankle burned as I pounded my feet against the dance floor. I would regret it, no doubt, but the song wasn't over, and I wouldn't stop until I had to. It was as if the music had cast a spell over me, each note twining around my heart, knocking at the wall I'd built around it.

I felt myself falling for Dennis more and more with each shuffled step and under-the-arm twirl. Falling into those sea-blue eyes that seemed to run so deep. It was a feeling unlike any I'd experienced—not with Reid or anyone else before him. Dennis was kind, incredibly intelligent, gorgeous, and always a joy to be around. More than that, there was an undeniable sense of familiarity about him—as though I was right where I was meant to be. Where I wanted to be.

And if his wide smile was any indication, I'd say he was enjoying our dance every bit as much—which made me feel even more guilty for not telling him about my slashed ankle, and then lying about it when he noticed my limping.

I would tell him about it...eventually. But when I did, would it change anything between us? Would it wipe away his smile or turn his soft eyes hard?

What a mess. A complicated, crazy mess driven by my selfish desire to dance with him again. And here I was, hand-in-hand with him, our bodies closer than ever...and enjoying every second. I hoped it was worth whatever fallout would surely come of my selfish lie.

Unless, perhaps...I didn't mention it to him. There was no

reason to make a big deal out of it if it was merely a branch or an angry cat.

The band cranked up their energy, strumming their guitars and pounding their drums, their crescendo summoning a fresh wave of couples onto the dance floor.

A teenage girl, struggling to drag her date to the dance floor, accidentally bumped into Kinsley, who tumbled to the ground, her eyes wide with surprise. Dennis and I stopped mid-twirl and ran over to her.

"I'm so sorry," the teenage girl told Kinsley, dropping to a knee. "Are you okay?"

Dennis swooped Kinsley off the ground and hauled her up into his arms. "Don't worry, she's a tough cookie, aren't you, Kins?" When her eyes brightened at the word "cookie," he added, "that's right—like a big, yummy chocolate chip cookie."

Bouncing Kinsley in his arm to the cheerful beat of the song, Dennis found my hand with his free one and pulled me back onto the dance floor. Within seconds, Kinsley was smiling again, clapping and bopping her head with unabashed giggles.

Our bodies no longer moved in sync, the tempo no longer guided our steps, but we were in our own little world where only laughter, music, and joy existed. Dennis's eyes locked with mine, and for a moment, the loud, festive chaos around us faded into a hazy blur of happiness.

CHAPTER SIXTEEN

The three of us danced together for two more songs until my ankle screamed at me to give it a break. The bandage now felt damp, and the last thing I wanted was for blood to soak through my Santa socks or worse, seep down to my white sneakers. I wasn't ready to confess that it was more than "just a minor cut."

The song ended, and Dennis let go of my hand with an obvious hesitation before gently placing Kinsley back on the ground.

"I hate to be a party pooper," I said when the band started playing another song, "but I'm going to skip this next dance. I'll be right back."

"Where are you going?" Kinsley asked.

"Kins—" Dennis started.

"It's okay," I laughed. "She's full of questions. I bet I know where she picked up that habit." I gave him a playful wink, then turned to Kinsley. "I'm going to Whisks and Whiskers to use the restroom." *To tape my leg back together*, I thought wryly.

"Take your time," Dennis said. "We'll be waiting here—or dancing—if Kins doesn't give me a break." He tugged at the light-brown hair flowing from under Kinsley's purple knitted hat.

"Save one more dance for me," I said, touching Dennis's arm lightly before walking away, doing my best not to limp.

Navigating through the bustling town square, I finally opened the door to Whisks and Whiskers, where a large crowd was seeking warmth and coffee. I maintained my composure until I reached the privacy of the restroom. Once inside, I locked the door behind me and leaned heavily against it, letting out a shaky breath I didn't realize I'd been holding. The *pain*. I was now paying the price for every step I'd taken on the dance floor.

Wincing, I rolled down my Santa sock, which now sported a wide crimson stain. It wasn't as much blood as I'd feared, but I removed a new bandage from my tiny crossbody handbag and replaced it anyway, confident it would last until we got home.

I made my way through the crowded coffee shop once again, catching Erin's eye and giving her a friendly wave as she hurried around behind the counter. Then I stepped back out into the town square and grinned the instant I spotted Dennis and Kinsley. They were still on the dance floor, Kinsley's movements wild and spastic, and Dennis's a more reserved bounce. I headed for them, picking up my pace as I drew closer.

Less than twenty feet away from them, I spotted Chloe Johnson, the *Darlington Hills Dispatch* reporter I'd met the night of Seth's death. She sat next to a man on the wide stone rim of the fountain. Both gazed lazily around the square, looking like they'd rather be anywhere than here.

Chloe caught my eye and waved, brightening a little. I hesitated. Though I'd normally stop and say hi, Dennis and Kinsley were still dancing, and I didn't want to miss out. The music lured me closer, each note a steppingstone towards the dance floor.

I returned Chloe's greeting with a friendly wave of my own before continuing towards Dennis and Kinsley. Then I stopped. Slowly, I turned to look back at a glimmer of red that had caught my attention.

Dangling from a braided hemp necklace, nestled in the Vneck of Chloe's thick sweater, was a pomegranate seed pendant encased in a ruby-colored resin.

No way. It was just like the bracelet Seth's grieving fiancée, Cindy, wore the night I met her during my cooking class.

The cold and pain faded away, leaving only the deep thrumming of my pulse in my ears as I fixated on the pomegranate pendant—Seth's signature ingredient. My feet moved towards her, as though acting of their own accord.

"Chloe!" I said, shocked by the light, cheerful tone of my voice. "It's so good to see you. Have you been here long? Isn't this event amazing?"

Dang. I was *good* at faking my enthusiasm. Even Michael would be proud of his cousin's acting skills.

"We've been here about an hour, but I doubt we'll stay much longer," she said. "It's colder than I thought it would be." As she spoke, the man sitting to her left eyed me in a way that made me wish I were wearing even more layers of clothing. He looked to be in his late twenties, with auburn-brown hair that peeked out from under a blue knit beanie.

"Chloe has a habit of not checking the weather before heading out," he said. In a thick, woolen overcoat and chunky scarf wrapped snugly around his neck, he was dressed far more appropriate for the weather than Chloe—and he looked to be proud of it.

Chloe grunted and rolled her eyes. "I thought this sweater would be warmer. It's *wool*, Kraig." She gestured hastily to the man. "Hadley, this is my husband."

Ah. So, this was the husband Chloe had mentioned during our tour the night of Seth's murder. What she'd failed to mention was that he was quite unpleasant—at least based on my first interaction with him.

Kraig dipped his head slightly but kept his hands in his pockets. "Nice to meet you, Hadley." His deep-set hazel eyes traveled over my body once again, making me shiver with disgust.

"Nice meeting you," I lied, then turned my full attention to Chloe. "So, how's your article on Madame Balleroy coming along?" I assumed she wouldn't know I'd found out she'd killed the story.

Chloe bristled at the mention of Madame Balleroy. "I'm not writing the article anymore."

"Oh?" I raised my eyebrows in mock surprise.

"Considering the ongoing homicide investigation, now's not the best time for a fluff piece about her restaurant," she explained. Though her face remained stoic, I sensed something like sadness hidden behind her words. "And even if the cops do find Seth's killer, I doubt I'll run the story. Madame Balleroy and her staff have been *hounding* me about it. Her program director even went over my head and complained to my editor, who backed me up, of course." Chloe scrunched up her nose, eyeing me quizzically. "I don't understand why you would pay money to take cooking lessons from that woman."

"I didn't sign up voluntarily," I admitted. "My aunt made me go after I accidentally served Thanksgiving guests a turkey stuffed with salmonella."

She barked out a laugh. "That sounds like a better story than the one I was planning to write."

My mind raced to piece together why Chloe wore a necklace so similar to the bracelet Seth had made for his fiancée. Perhaps they were friends and had bonded over a shared appreciation for good food?

It was possible, though not likely. When Chloe had stepped into the cooking school's kitchen, she and Seth hadn't greeted each other as friends would. They didn't talk to each other during the tour, except for when Seth described the Christmas Eve brunch menu at Madame Balleroy's request. *So strange.*

I widened my eyes, molding my expression into one of pure delight. "Oh, my goodness, I love your necklace!" I exclaimed, pretending to notice it for the first time. "My friend is obsessed with pomegranate seeds. She uses them in everything. Salads, smoothies, even cocktails. Mind if I ask where you got it? It would make the perfect Christmas gift for her." The plastic pomegranate seed pendant dangled in the center of the necklace, surrounded by heart-shaped beads on either side.

Interesting. I didn't remember seeing heart beads on Cindy's bracelet.

Chloe ran her fingers over the smooth beads of her necklace. "I got it, um…"

"Her grandma sent it to her last week," Kraig interrupted, rolling his eyes. "Jeez, Chloe, have you already forgotten?"

"Yes, that's right. My grandmother sent it to me for my…for an early Christmas gift. It's a…souvenir from her recent trip to Mexico."

Kraig snorted. "It's not much of a gift, if you ask me. From the looks of it, I doubt it cost more than five bucks."

"Well, your grandma has excellent taste," I told Chloe, then turned my eyes out to the crowd, inhaling deeply. "The aromas from all these food stalls are driving my stomach mad. I wouldn't be surprised if you could hear it growling over the music. Have you guys sampled any of the food tonight?"

Chloe shook her head, her hand still on her necklace.

It was obvious her mind was elsewhere as she gazed out at the bumping dance floor, her eyes distant and lost in thought. I spotted Dennis; his questioning gaze met mine, his mind likely churning with curiosity. This was yet another conversation to add to the list of things I needed to tell him.

I faced Kraig and plastered on a smile. "This is my first time at North Pole Night, so I'm not familiar with the popular food options here. There's so much to choose from: barbecue sandwiches, burritos, hamburgers, hotdogs, loaded potatoes. And they even have a fish taco stand, which is what I'm leaning towards."

"*Fish?*" he practically spat. "That's the last thing I would eat from a food stall."

"Seriously? I thought you liked fish. If I remember correctly, you made salmon for Chloe last Thursday, the night of—"

"I'm cold, Kraig," Chloe interrupted, jumping to her feet. "Let's go."

He laughed as he got to his feet, giving me a look that implied I was clueless. "What makes you think I cooked fish for my wife? It's disgusting, and it smells terrible. Real men eat meat, and lots of it."

Without even looking at me, Chloe grabbed Kraig's arm and pulled him into the middle of the lively crowd.

"What did the reporter have to say?" Dennis asked the minute I joined him and Kinsley on the dance floor again. "She didn't look too happy when she left."

Whew! He didn't miss a thing. I'd greedily hoped to dance with him before talking to him about Chloe, but his too-serious expression told me he didn't want to wait.

"You probably already know this, but I'm pretty sure Chloe was—" I paused, wanting to choose my words carefully in case Kinsley overheard, though I doubted she would since she was busy spinning in circles to listen to a boring adult conversation. "—Chloe was *involved* with Seth."

Dennis blinked, his subtle smile gone. "How so?"

I glanced at Kinsley, hesitating for a moment to make sure she was still lost in her whirlwind of excitement. "Her necklace...it's nearly identical to the bracelet Seth's fiancée wore when I met her a few days ago. The one-of-a-kind bracelet Seth *made* for her."

Dennis jerked his head to the right, searching the crowd into which Chloe and Kraig had disappeared. "A similar piece of jewelry doesn't mean they were involved."

"True, but when I asked Chloe where she got it, she stumbled around a bit before her husband reminded her that her grand-mother gave it to her last week."

"And you're thinking that's the story Chloe told her husband?" he said.

"Yes. She claimed her grandma bought it in Mexico. I'm telling you, it was exactly like Cindy's bracelet." I explained that pomegranate seeds were Seth's signature ingredient, then detailed how the beads were shaped to resemble those tiny seeds.

"So, either Seth had started selling his jewelry in Mexico, or Chloe lied about who gave it to her."

He nodded, looking thoughtful. "There are usually more than two explanations. Chloe's grandmother could have bought the necklace in Mexico, and then Seth could have ordered his fiancée's bracelet online and claimed he made it himself. Or maybe Seth went to Mexico recently and found it there."

"Maybe, but his fiancée said Seth learned how to make the beads after watching a YouTube video." I looked over to the fountain where she'd stood, and recalled her nervous, jumbled answers to my questions about the necklace. "Though I think she lied about who gave it to her, I do believe she got it last week. When Detective Sanders questioned Chloe in the classroom, I noticed she was playing with what I thought was a piece of twine. Now I realize it was her necklace. It's possible Seth tied it around her purse while Chloe and I were on the tour."

"It's possible they were just friends," he said.

"I doubt it. They didn't interact much during the tour. It was as if they were intentionally avoiding each other."

Dennis seemed to consider this, his eyes narrowing as though considering what all this meant. He checked his watch, then stopped Kinsley mid-twirl. "Come on, kiddo, let's go visit Santa's elves. Looks like we'll need to head back to Hadley's earlier than I'd hoped. I have some calls to make."

My heart sank a little as we walked away from the dance floor —away from the opportunity to dance with him again.

"That *is* interesting," he commented, his voice low and thoughtful. "Anything else?"

I cringed. The list was long. Telling him about my ankle would have been a good place to start, but now I felt foolish for not mentioning it earlier.

"Well," I began, "when Detective Sanders questioned Chloe the night of Seth's death, did she mention the phone call she received during our tour with Madame Balleroy?"

He raised his brows. "Why do you ask?"

"Did she tell Sanders *who* called her?"

"Did she tell *you* who called?"

I tossed up my hands. "We can't both keep asking each other questions. One of us needs to answer them."

He gave me a playful nudge with his elbow. "Which one of us is the detective?"

"Fine, I'll answer," I groaned, reciprocating his nudge. "Towards the end of our tour the night of the homicide, Chloe got a call from her husband—or so she claimed. Madame Balleroy insisted she invite her husband to an on-the-house dinner after the tour but Chloe declined, saying her husband had already started cooking salmon."

As he listened to me, Dennis guided Kinsley towards a line of tables pushed together, each one covered in materials like wood, paper, paint, and other supplies for building toy airplanes. "Go ahead and get started, and ask a friendly elf for help if you need it," he suggested before turning back to me. "What makes you think Chloe lied?"

"She was all lovey-dovey with whomever she talked to that night, calling him sweetheart and such—which was completely different from how she interacted with her husband just now. After only two minutes of watching them snip at each other, I questioned if it was really Kraig who called her that night. To confirm my suspicions, I asked Kraig about the salmon dish he supposedly made last week.

He said I was crazy to think he would ever cook fish. He hates it."

Dennis stepped back, his eyes going wide. "You fact-checked Chloe's story *right in front of her*? I'm surprised you didn't ask if he suspects his wife is cheating on him."

"Oh, hush!" I laughed. "Give me some credit. I was subtle with my questions."

"Right," he said, laying the sarcasm on thick. "That's why they bolted from you faster than a cat with its tail on fire."

"Okay, okay, maybe so," I admitted with a giant eye roll. "But don't you think it's strange? That Chloe lied about her phone call and dinner plans with her husband? That she wore a necklace just like Seth's fiancée?"

Dennis raised a brow at me. "Your instincts are good, Hadley. I can't say much, but we are aware of the call Chloe took while in the barn with you. It was indeed with Seth, and phone records show—"

"Wait. If you confirmed Seth called Chloe, then that means he was stabbed soon afterwards."

"Estimated time of death was five minutes past nine," he confirmed. "Only about five minutes before you found his body."

I shuddered at the memory. If only we'd returned sooner from our tour, Seth might still be alive. "What were you saying about phone records?"

"The records indicated that Seth and Chloe had been in contact multiple times during the two weeks leading up to his murder. However, Chloe insisted it was a strictly professional relationship and that their discussions were focused solely on the news article she was writing about the restaurant."

I snorted. "There was nothing professional about her phone conversation with him."

"I'll look into it," he said simply. "Anything else I should know?"

"Actually...yes."

"You're kidding." He didn't look particularly pleased.

I shrugged, smiling innocently. "I had a busy day—bumped into some people, had some conversations."

He shook his head, a subtle grin creeping across his expression as he sized me up. "How did you manage to get yourself so tangled up in this investigation? And why am I surprised? I should have known you'd find your way into the thick of it."

As we watched Kinsley finish making the wooden airplane, I told Dennis about the heated conversation I'd overheard in the barn this morning between Madame Balleroy and Jared, recounting every detail I could remember.

Then, as we waited in line for corn dogs (Kinsley's choice), I told him about my conversation with Natasha—how she said Madame Balleroy was upset with Jared because Chloe canceled the feature article on the cooking school and restaurant. I also mentioned Madame Balleroy's apparent obsession with gaining social media followers, and the florist's comment about Eileen's lack of enthusiasm about her daughter's marriage to Seth.

When we then washed down the corn dogs with hot apple cider (my choice), I told him about Grand-mère's firing of Seth the night he was murdered, and the ceremonious Roma tomato that went along with it.

Dennis had groaned upon hearing that, muttering that he could solve the case a lot sooner if people were more upfront when he questioned them. He sent off a flurry of texts to Detective Sanders and the police chief before informing Kinsley she had time for one more activity before we had to leave.

I almost told him about my ankle while we watched Kinsley play in the dwindling pile of fake snow, but then she gleefully threw a snowball at my face, and the three of us didn't stop laughing for a full five minutes.

I was so close—so very close—to telling him during our walk

to his car, during the drive back home, and even as we strolled along the tree-lined path towards the Ladyvale Manor.

But as soon as we stepped inside, he declared it was time for Kinsley to go to bed. "Uncle Dennis has some work to do," he told her before turning to me with his arm extended.

I frowned at it. Did he want to shake my hand? Or…

Slowly, I reached out and took his hand. His gaze, as intense as ever, bore into me as he squeezed it. "Thank you for coming tonight. You made Kinsley's day for sure…and mine."

A little part of me melted. Something about the way he said it, the simple vulnerability in his eyes, stirred emotions within me that I couldn't quite define. I wanted to dance with him again—in the town square, in my backyard under the hazy moonlight, or in my shiny, marble-tiled entry hall. It didn't matter where; I just wanted to be close enough to him to feel the warmth from his body and to catch that subtle shower-fresh scent that seemed to cling to him.

But I'd seen eyes like his before. Hopeful, yearning, passion-filled eyes that had promised forever, only to fade into nothingness in the end. I'd seen it with Reid, Ricky, and every other man I'd cared about before.

"Anytime," I finally said, my tone soft but cool. I wanted to say more—wanted to tell him it was probably the best "date" I'd ever been on, and that I wanted endless more just like it—but I couldn't. I wasn't ready to get caught up in yet another whirlwind of love and heartbreak.

His fingers lingered a moment longer before he released my hand and scooped up Kinsley in his arms. Her head rested on his shoulder as she opened her mouth to yawn.

"I know it's late, but I need to go to the station for a bit to look into the new info you shared," he told me. "Will you be here while I'm gone?"

"Absolutely," I reassured him. "I'll be here if she needs anything."

He thanked me with a smile, then turned around and carried her up the stairs, murmuring to her in a soothing tone that would surely lull her to sleep. "Whatever you do, Kins, don't tell your mama I let you stay up late five nights in a row. Your Uncle Dennis will be in all sorts of trouble if she finds out."

CHAPTER SEVENTEEN

An hour later, I sat at the desk in my upstairs office, struggling to stay awake as I drafted an email to the lighting rental company for our Christmas Eve brunch. With each sentence, I drifted off, only to wake with a start when my head rolled.

This went on for at least five minutes, all while Razzy watched me, probably laughing to herself from atop a stack of papers by my computer. Her aqua-blue eyes seemed to narrow with each glance I gave her, almost as if she were rebuking me for not allowing her to sit directly on my keyboard.

I leaned back in my chair, wondering if perhaps I could take a quick nap at my desk and then finish the emails I needed to send. Switching off the small brass lamp next to my computer, I stroked my hand down her back. "You would like that, wouldn't you, Razzy girl? If I nod off, then you could claim your spot on my keyboard."

She whipped her head toward the open doorway, her ears flattening against her head. Without the desk lamp, only the muted light from the window illuminated the room in a soft, bluish hue. I followed her gaze and listened for any sound that might have caught Razzy's attention.

With my heart thumping a little faster, I strained my ears against the silence of the Ladyvale Manor. The old home was prone to all sorts of creaks and groans, but tonight, it seemed to hold its breath with me.

Then there it was—a faint shuffle of footsteps. They were hesitant, as though whoever it was didn't want to be heard.

"Hello?" I called out.

"Hadley?" came a small voice from outside my office.

I bolted from my chair, hearing the fear in Kinsley's voice. "I'm here, sweetie," I said as I stepped into the hallway. "Is everything okay?"

"Uncle Dennis isn't in his room, and I had a bad dream." She hugged herself tightly, her bottom lip quivering as she spoke.

"Don't worry, he'll be back soon. But I can tuck you in again. It's almost midnight, so you should try to go back to sleep."

Her tousled locks fell into her eyes as she shook her head with determination. "I don't want to sleep. I'm scared."

"Do you want to tell me about it?" I said, gently.

She shook her head again, her eyes widening. "I'm too scared to say it out loud. And I miss my mommy."

"I know you do, hon, and she misses you, too. But think about all the adventures she's having right now on the safari. She's going to have so many exciting stories to tell you when she gets home."

Kinsley seemed to consider this, then nodded. "I hope she sees a lion. They're like Razzy, but bigger."

At the mention of her name, Razzy sauntered out of the office and into the hallway, then snaked her way between my legs. I reached down and picked her up. "Why don't we see if she'll cuddle with you in bed? She always seems to keep the bad dreams away." I gave her a reassuring smile as I stroked Razzy's soft fur.

"Okay," she whispered, a hint of relief seeming to break through her fear.

Balancing Razzy in one arm, I took Kinsley's hand with the

other and led her back to her room. The moon spilled silver light across her small bed as we entered, illuminating the collection of stuffed animals gathered at the headboard, including the teddy bear I'd given her. I set Razzy down on the purple blanket, and she immediately began kneading it with her paws, purring louder as she settled into a comfortable position.

Kinsley took her time climbing onto the bed, being extra careful not to disturb Razzy. I tucked the covers around Kinsley and her entourage of stuffed animals. "There," I whispered. "Razzy will keep watch over you while you sleep. I'll be down the hall if you need anything, but you'll go to sleep sooner if you think happy thoughts. Remember the elves we saw tonight, sweetie. And all those snowballs you threw," I chuckled, and she giggled along with me.

I was halfway to the door when Kinsley called out to me, "Hadley, is it true that Darlington Hills is haunted? Bobby Watson told me it is."

"Who's Bobby Watson?" I asked.

"He's in my camp group and he's five, like me. Yesterday he said there are ghosts in a creek, and they come out at night to eat people."

I wrapped a hand around my mouth, holding back a smile as I remembered all the times my cousin Michael had terrorized me with similar ghost stories about Bonn Creek—or Bone Creek, as the superstitious locals called it—when we visited Darlington Hills at Christmastime.

What was it with little boys trying to scare girls? Most likely, they just want someone to be scared alongside them.

Returning to the edge of her bed, I placed a reassuring hand on top of her head. "Bobby Watson doesn't know what he's talking about. Yes, people around here like to tell stories about what happened in this town a long time ago, but there aren't any ghosts. You should ask your Uncle Dennis about it tomorrow."

"I already asked him last night."

"Well then, you should trust what he told you. He's patrolled this town plenty of times at night, so he knows Darlington Hills better than anyone."

"But he said it *probably* isn't haunted," she whimpered.

Well, no wonder poor Kinsley couldn't sleep. I would have to talk to Dennis about scaring small children with his 'probablies.'

I brushed a stray hair from her forehead. "I promise, there isn't anything spooky around here. Your uncle just likes to keep a little mystery in the air. It makes his job as a detective more exciting."

She nodded, but her wide eyes told me she still wasn't convinced. I sat on the edge of the bed, careful not to jostle Razzy and prompt her to run from the room. "I'll tell you the *real* story about Bonn Creek, but you won't find it in any history book—yet."

She wiggled deeper under her covers, pulling them up all the way to her nose. "Okay," she said timidly, as though she wasn't sure if she did, in fact, want to hear it.

"Bonn Creek was named after Charles Bonn, who discovered this land and brought his family and friends from London to live here," I explained. "But then most of the settlers...um, left town and went to a better place." I chose my words carefully, not wanting to share the grim truth that only one settler survived while the rest drowned in Bonn Creek. The last thing I wanted was for her to have nightmares for months on end.

"Only one person stayed in Bonnville, as it was once called, and then people from nearby towns eventually moved here and changed the name to Darlington Hills." I leaned in, lowering my voice to a whisper. "And here's a little secret, which you can't tell Bobby Watson or anyone else at camp: the woman who used to live in this house, Irma Murdoch, was related to the man who discovered this town. How cool is that?"

It was so cool, in fact, that a cable TV channel was planning to film the Ladyvale Manor next month for a series about the nation's iconic historic homes.

Kinsley smiled, and I saw the lingering fear fade from her eyes. "Is Irma famous?"

"No, not yet."

"Why not? Did she leave town too?"

"Yes, sweetie. Irma also went to live in a better place. But before she left, she wrote a book about her family's history. I'm sure a lot of people would like to read it, but no one can find it."

"That's a problem," Kinsley said, and for a moment it was as though I were looking at a tiny version of Dennis, with her furrowed brows and pensive expression. It was a look that meant business, and even though she was only five, I knew better than to underestimate her intelligence. Dennis himself had been blown away by her precocious reading skills.

"Sure is," I agreed. "Irma hadn't even printed her book yet. She probably kept it in her computer, but then her computer flew out a window and went kablooey—so no more book."

The covers moved up and down as Kinsley shrugged her shoulders. "Maybe it isn't in her computer. My mommy and daddy keep computer things in the clouds. Don't ask me how it gets up there, or why it doesn't fall, but they say it's a better place to keep stuff."

Her words hit me like a bolt of lightning. "Of course!" I exclaimed. "The *cloud*!"

Dennis's footsteps sounded down the upstairs hallway at five minutes before one o'clock in the morning. Floorboards creaked and groaned as he walked towards his room, pausing briefly to peek into Kinsley's room.

I rolled over in bed and listened as he opened his own door and turned on the water for a shower.

After leaving Kinsley's room tonight, I had decided to finish my emails tomorrow when I wasn't nodding off every few seconds. But as soon as my head hit my pillow, my mind shifted into overdrive, thinking about everything from what I still needed to get done before the Christmas Eve brunch, to how I would explain to Dennis why I hadn't told him about my slashed ankle. Then I mused over the possibility that Irma had kept her book file in a cloud storage site. And even if she had, how would I know which site she used and what her username and password were?

Rosie van Pelt, the President of the Darlington Hills Historical Society and overseer of tours at the Ladyvale Manor, had been good friends with Irma. Rosie wanted more than anything to find the book because she knew how much effort Irma had put into it. She wanted the world to see it.

Not only that, but the book likely contained never-before-seen information about the town's past, since her ancestors had deep roots in its history.

I must have drifted off to sleep while Dennis showered, because I jolted awake at the sound of a creaking floorboard in his bedroom. Propping myself up on an elbow, I turned to look at the clock on my nightstand.

Two o'clock! How was he still awake?

Maybe, like me, he had trouble shutting off his mind before bedtime. Or maybe he was an insufferable night owl, always busy at work on a case. It would explain why I'd caught him yawning so often recently.

And I thought I had a bad habit of staying up too late!

I sat up, abandoning the glorious warmth of my thick down comforter, and turned to face the wall behind my headboard—the wall dividing his room and mine. Turning an ear towards it, I strained to listen for any other sounds.

Because if he was still awake, maybe a cup of chamomile tea might help him unwind. A cup of tea, a quiet conversation in the family room—just Dennis and me, with only the light from the floor lamp near the leather loveseat.

I wouldn't tell him about my ankle over tea. Even though *I* would sleep better after fessing up, I didn't want him to stay up worrying about it.

Footsteps sounded once again in his room, softer and slower this time—like he was pacing around the room, walking the perimeter as if he were on a patrol of his own quarters. I swung my feet over the side of my bed, deciding that tea and a bit of company were exactly what we both needed.

Shivering slightly, I slipped into a robe and pair of slippers, then checked my hair in the bathroom mirror and brushed my teeth for the second time since midnight.

The hallway felt longer in the dark, and the distance between my room and his seemed to grow with each step. His door was slightly ajar, revealing a dark room inside. I tapped gently on the wood before turning to peek into Kinsley's room, hoping I wouldn't wake her up. She was sound asleep, and Razzy was nowhere in sight.

I waited several moments for Dennis to respond, unsure whether I should knock again. Either he'd already fallen asleep, he hadn't heard my tapping, or he was ignoring it, though I doubted that was the case.

Just as soon as my feet turned back toward my room, a single creak sounded from within his room.

"Dennis?" I whispered, "are you still awake?"

Nothing. No answer, no sign that he had heard me.

If he was asleep, then what was making the wood floor groan inside his room? The house settling? Or—

"Razzy!" I whispered. "Here, kitty kitty. Let Dennis get some sleep. This is not social hour."

After waiting several more moments, I let out an exasperated sigh and peeked inside his room, searching for my mischievous cat. My eyes froze on Dennis's bed—on his still-made, not-yet-rumpled, *empty* bed.

Where *was* he?

I walked to the end of the hallway, peering down at the dark house below, then went back to my room and climbed into bed again, wondering where Dennis had run off to at two o'clock in the morning.

CHAPTER EIGHTEEN

I felt like a kid on a school field trip, eager to leave the classroom and venture to somewhere more exciting.

Grand-mère led all seven of us down the pathway from the cooking school to the back of the restaurant, lecturing us as we walked. "Don't touch anything, don't distract anyone, and whatever you do, don't remove your apron or hat."

A heavenly, intoxicating wave of garlicky goodness greeted me the moment Grand-mère opened the door and led us into the employee break room. We walked past a wall of lockers to our left, and tables holding empty coffee cups to our right, before stepping into the kitchen. *This* was what heaven must smell like.

"Wonderful, wonderful, right on time," Madame Balleroy sang when she saw us at the door. "Welcome to my kitchen, the center of my world, and the beating heart of my beloved restaurant. As you can see, it's another busy night and my staff is hard at work preparing dinner for our guests."

It was noisier and more chaotic than when I'd seen it before on the tour with Chloe, but it still had the same energy, the same orchestrated frenzy. Chefs removed steaming dishes from ovens while servers pivoted through the kitchen's tight corners carrying trays, amid the clanging of plates and the rapid staccato of chopping knives.

Madame Balleroy ushered us through the kitchen towards an empty prep table near the back wall. Cooks nodded in greeting as we passed, some offering smiles amid their focused preparations. "This kitchen boasts top-of-the-line equipment and cookware, unlike many restaurants nowadays," she said. "I've hired only the best chefs in the industry to work here with me. If you look around, you'll notice that it's almost identical to the one in my cooking school."

Hal chuckled next to me. "I'd say you have a mighty loose definition of 'identical.' Everything's bigger in here, and there's more of it—prep tables, stoves, refrigerators. And don't get me started on the stacks of dishes over there. I've never seen so many. I'll consider myself lucky I never have dish duty in this joint."

Madame Balleroy blushed and pressed her thin lips together, clearly flustered. "If you ever refer to my restaurant as a 'joint' again," she scolded, "you'll be scrubbing dishes for the rest of your life."

"Madame, you're needed at Table Five," interrupted a woman dressed in a black suit dress. "Our guests would like a photo with you before they leave."

"Another one?" she asked, looking equally pleased and bewildered. "I'll be right there." Madame Balleroy signaled to Natasha, who stopped talking with another chef and came over. "Natasha, please chat with my students while I visit with some guests. I'll only be a minute."

Natasha's bright, expressive eyes turned toward us, and her amiable smile told me she didn't mind stepping away from the chaos of the kitchen to entertain us while Madame Balleroy posed for photos. "What recipe are you cooking tonight? Is it the roasted pork shoulder?"

As Natasha spoke, I noticed something odd—only one chunky

gold hoop hung from her right ear, its mate conspicuously absent. I almost pointed it out, but didn't want to embarrass her in front of my classmates.

"No, the pork shoulder is tomorrow," Mitzy said. "Tonight, we're making golden mashed potatoes with fresh thyme and lemon butter."

Delight danced in Natasha's eyes. "Ooh, that's a good one! It's perfect for holiday meals. Your future Christmas dinners will never be the same, and your family will be thankful you learned this recipe. They won't be able to get enough of it. Even children like it—I promise."

She went on to describe which meats, sauces, and wines paired nicely with the potatoes, but I couldn't focus on her words. My mind was stuck replaying her earlier comment: "your future Christmas dinners."

Who would sit at my table for Christmases yet to come? I used to think it would be Ricky, and then I'd hoped it would be Reid, and now...well, now I couldn't picture who would sit by me at holiday meals. Would there be children to gobble up these mashed potatoes, as Natasha had promised?

Would I regain Aunt Deb's trust enough to host Christmas at my house, or would she insist on cooking holiday meals forevermore? If a certificate of completion from Madame Balleroy's cooking school didn't vindicate me, I didn't know what would.

"I'll give you a few pointers before you get started tonight," Natasha whispered conspiratorially. "Then you can impress Madame Balleroy with your knowledge."

She hustled over to the enormous walk-in refrigerator in the back corner of the kitchen, then returned with two Yukon gold potatoes and some thyme sprigs.

"Let's start with the herbs," she said, placing everything on the prep table in front of her. "Can anyone tell me the best way to chop the teeny leaves off the stem?"

"With a teeny knife," Hal joked.

"It's a trick question," I said. "You don't need a knife at all. You just pinch the end of the sprig and run your fingers down it." Of course, it was also helpful to have a gorgeous house guest standing behind you, guiding your hands as you worked.

"That's right!" Natasha said, her eyes full of surprised delight. With a skilled hand, she showed us how to pull off the leaves in the opposite direction of their natural growth. "Awesome job, Hadley. You win the award for top student of the night. Perhaps there's a future for you in the culinary arts."

Grand-mère frowned at Natasha's over-the-top praise. "This isn't rocket science. Everyone knows how to remove thyme leaves." With a loud sigh, she walked off into the sea of culinary chaos. Despite Grand-mère's dismissive comments, I felt proud. Thanks to Dennis, I'd impressed a culinary superstar.

While watching the pile of thyme leaves grow on the cutting board, I could almost feel Dennis's arms around me, his breath soft against my ear. The memory of my thyme-cutting lesson brought a pang of regret for choosing to attend the cooking class instead of staying home with Dennis and Kinsley. Each passing day brought him closer to solving the money laundering case, which also meant I would have to return to cooking alone in my quiet kitchen.

Today was my first day of vacation, and I'd woken up early to get a head start on my errands. Dennis had beat me to the kitchen and was making scrambled eggs with tortillas. He was more alert and energetic than he'd been since they came to stay with me, and although I was thrilled he seemed so well rested, I also found it strange, considering his habit of pacing around his room late at night.

After Dennis had left to drop off Kinsley at camp, I ran around Darlington Hills, ticking off my long list of errands. I finished almost all my Christmas shopping, bought a new dress for the Christmas Eve brunch, and even treated myself to a pedicure.

At three-thirty, I texted Dennis and offered to pick up Kinsley early from camp since he was still working at the station. I took her to Whisks and Whiskers, where we visited with Erin and indulged in a slice of Paw-some Raspberry Brownie Cheesecake. She was thrilled to eat the dessert that had inspired Razzy's name.

We had returned home just as tours ended for the day, and then Dennis joined us soon after. Unfortunately, I had to leave for cooking school, putting a bit of a damper on an otherwise amazing day.

Kinsley had then begged Dennis to take her through the labyrinth again. With a groan, I admitted I was tempted to skip class for the night and join them instead.

"Why don't you and I take a walk through there later tonight?" Dennis had suggested as he peered out the kitchen window at the massive hedges beyond, illuminated by the low-level landscape lighting. "After you-know-who goes to bed."

That thought alone had been enough to motivate me to go. The labyrinth was a magical place at night, and the idea of walking through it with Dennis made me want to leave Madame Balleroy's as soon as possible. Tonight, I'd be mashing those potatoes on turbo mode.

A loud clatter of pots and a subsequent chorus of swearing made all of us jump. Natasha laughed, then hollered at the crew on the other side of the kitchen to get their act together.

"Is the kitchen always so...busy?" Eileen asked. She was being polite. It wasn't just busy, it was frantic. Like a circus, or perhaps an anthill that someone had stepped on, causing outright mayhem.

"Busy—yes. Chaotic—no," Natasha explained. "The restaurant has been booked for almost a week now. Considering the recent homicide, we couldn't explain why it was so packed. Until yesterday, when a group of dinner guests told me the reason: last week, a man spotted—well, claimed to have seen—Seth's ghost inside the restaurant, peering over the shoulder of Madame Balleroy as she greeted guests at tables. The news spread like wildfire on social media, and we've been slammed every night since."

Ah. So that must have been the customer "sighting" Jared referred to when he spoke with Seth's fiancée last week. It was better than another beetle, I supposed.

Hal let out a low, amused chuckle. "So that's why guests want photos with Madame Balleroy tonight?"

Natasha checked the double doors. "Yes, but I don't think she knows this yet. Let's keep it between us, okay?" Once we nodded in agreement, she plucked one of the gold potatoes from the table and tossed it playfully into the air. "All of this ghost business is nonsense, of course, but it's been beneficial for business during what we expected to be a slow period. Not only has the restaurant been packed, but we've also sold out of tickets for our Christmas Eve brunch."

After giving the potato another couple of tosses, Natasha returned it to the prep table and removed a knife from the shelf below. A KnuckleKnight tool was affixed to the blade, shielding Natasha's fingers as she cut the potato.

With each swift slice, a sharp twinge shot up my ankle, reminding me of my run-in with the sharp *thing* under the hedges Saturday night. What, exactly, that *thing* was had nagged at me ever since. Every time I flirted with the idea of returning to the playground to investigate, the lingering pain in my leg held me back.

"Here are some tips for slicing potatoes," she said, demonstrating as she spoke. "Always start by cutting a small slice off one side. This creates a flat, stable base so it won't roll around when you're cutting it. And be sure to use a sharp knife, since it's safer and requires less force—"

"*Seriously*, Natasha?" Jared, who had just pushed through the kitchen doors, stopped next to us and gestured to the Knuckle-Knight. "That useless piece of junk was never intended for professionals like you. You should know how to use a knife without cutting yourself."

I winced at his words, wondering if he'd seen Eileen before making his harsh comment. It was likely Cindy had told her about the falling out between Seth and Jared, and although Eileen might have understood what prompted the insult, her narrowed eyes told me she didn't at all appreciate it.

Lifting her chin, Eileen pulled herself up to her full height and looked Jared in the eye. "I'd hardly call the KnuckleKnight junk. I'm sure Seth would be thrilled to see it's being used, even by esteemed chefs like Natasha."

"Thanks, Eileen," Natasha said, giving Jared a pointed glance that signaled him to leave. "I couldn't agree with you more. Cooks of all skill levels can benefit from this tool. Even Seth nicked his fingers from time to time."

Madame Balleroy swept into the kitchen, a proud grin peeking through her stern demeanor. "I adore my guests. Nothing pleases me more than seeing their smiling faces." Instead of stopping next to us, she continued strolling towards the back door, motioning us to follow. "Many thanks, Natasha; you are a dear. Class, follow me, please. It's time to return to the classroom."

We thanked Natasha and turned to follow Madame Balleroy. Slipping a hand into my apron's pocket, I retrieved my phone and discreetly placed it on the corner of the prep table before leaving.

Once outside with the others, I gasped. "Oh, no! I left my phone inside. I'll catch up with you after I grab it." Without waiting for permission, I slipped back through the door.

I jogged over to Natasha, who was cleaning the prep table where she'd given us the demonstration. "One more question about the KnuckleKnight," I said hastily. "Do you know if anyone else at the restaurant invested in Seth and Jared's invention?"

Natasha kept her eyes on the prep table, her voice little more than a whisper when she answered, "Both Madame Balleroy and Grand-mère."

My eyes widened. "Do you know how much?"

She looked up from the table, opening her mouth to reply, but her gaze darted to something over my shoulder.

"Hadley!" called Grand-mère's shrill voice. She had seemed to materialize directly behind me, her approaching footsteps undetected in the noisy kitchen. "We don't have all night to wait on you. I told you not to touch anything, much less leave a dirty phone on our prep tables! Come on, let's go."

"Coming." Returning my phone to my pocket, I walked toward Grand-mère, then cast a quick glance over my shoulder at Natasha, who mouthed to me, "A lot."

CHAPTER NINETEEN

"I hope you know your way around this thing." Dennis stopped walking and eyed the tall, dense hedges surrounding us, illuminated only by tendrils of light from small lamps scattered throughout. It was a cold, moonless night, making it even more difficult to navigate through the maze.

"Um..." I started. Twirling around to get my bearings, I saw nothing but the endless corridors of greenery. "Yeah, I've got this. Sort of. No, not really," I laughed. "I think we're close to the middle of it, but I don't come out here a lot—and never at night by myself."

Dennis shivered, despite his black leather coat and matching winter hat. "It *is* a little spooky," he admitted. "Kinsley and I didn't walk more than twenty steps into the labyrinth before we decided it was best to head back inside. Have any tourists ever... not returned from this thing?"

I gave his arm a playful nudge. "What a terrible thought! I think you're joking, but I'm not sure. Besides, *you* would be the first to know, Detective Appley, if people were disappearing from my backyard."

"If we ever get a report of a missing person, I'll know where to look first." Dennis wrapped a hand around the back of his neck and rubbed it. "I believe your house is in that direction," he gestured with his thumb behind him, "so if we continue in this direction," he pointed confidently ahead of us, "we should reach the exit on the opposite side. Right?"

"Yes, in theory. Unless you're wrong about where the house is. Sorry, but I lost track of our turns." I'd been too distracted by the feel of his arm brushing against mine and indulgent thoughts about another tickle session inside the labyrinth. "We'll find the exit eventually," I promised. "If not, tourists will find us tomorrow."

"I hope you're right, because I have some bad guys to catch."

"Bad *guys,*" I mused. "So, you're thinking Seth's killer is a male?"

His sea-blue eyes twinkled with barely suppressed laughter. "'Bad guys' is an imprecise, ambiguous term we use when we don't want to reveal details of our investigations to nosy onlookers."

Matching his look of wry amusement, I dropped my voice to a silky whisper. "I'm not nosy, I'm *friendly.* I talk to people, and they talk to me. I'm like a gossip magnet. People just tell me things."

Fighting a smile, he crossed his arms in mock defiance. "Okay, 'gossip magnet,' what's the scoop today?"

I narrowed my eyes, tapping a finger to my chin in mock contemplation. "Well, Detective, you might find this tidbit particularly interesting. Tonight, Natasha told me Madame Balleroy and Grand-mère helped fund Seth and Jared's KnuckleKnight invention when they were developing it. She said they invested 'a lot' of money."

His smile vanished. "Natasha Antonov told you this?" He couldn't have looked more surprised.

"Yes, during cooking class tonight. She didn't have time to

give me details before Grand-mère dragged me away from the conversation."

"Okay, I'll follow up on it," he said, then rubbed the back of his neck again.

"The KnuckleKnight gadget keeps coming up in conversations about the homicide. Seth's fiancée told me Jared 'went nuclear' when he found out Winterbridge Supply Company stole their invention without compensation. But maybe Jared was mad because he found out Winterbridge actually did compensate Seth. And what about Madame Balleroy and Grand-mère? They must have been expecting a return on the money they invested. And come to think of it, Seth's fiancée told me she had also invested in it. What if any of them found out Seth had lied and didn't share his profit?"

Dennis nodded as he listened to me, wincing as he dug his fingertips into his neck and shoulders. When he didn't respond to my musings, I stepped behind him and cupped my hands around his shoulders, then worked my thumbs into his tight muscles.

He let out a low moan, which told me I'd found the right spot. Closing my eyes, I breathed in his intoxicating scent as my hands moved along his neck and broad shoulders. I was sure I'd crossed the line between friendship and something more, and although I might regret it later, I couldn't resist the under-the-moon massage session.

"That feels amazing," he murmured, leaning back into my touch as though silently pleading for more. I traced the contours of his spine, massaging my way down to his lower back before refocusing my efforts on his neck. Being this close to him, hearing his soft groans and sighs, made my heart thunder against my ribcage. My poor, damaged, confused heart that didn't know what it wanted—or rather, knew all too well, but was scared to admit it.

When Dennis spoke again, his voice was low and rough. "Yes,

it is possible the KnuckleKnight is tied to the motive for the homicide."

I froze. Had he really just talked to me about the case? "Oh? What makes you think so?" I didn't expect him to answer, but it was worth a shot. I pressed my thumbs deeper into his tense shoulders.

"It was a shady business deal. I did some digging after you told me about the conflicting reports of *how* the culinary supplier acquired Seth and Jared's KnuckleKnight invention. I questioned the CEO of Winterbridge Supply Company, who then conducted his own internal investigation into his company's acquisition of the product."

"The CEO wasn't involved in the process initially?" I asked.

"Only at a high level, since it was a relatively insignificant business transaction—at least compared to their other products. This deal was handled solely by their acquisitions team, which was headed up by a man named Arnold. When I talked to Arnold, he owned up to circumventing the company's vetting process with the KnuckleKnight deal. He cut some corners and agreed to some questionable terms."

"Like leaving Jared out of the transaction?" I pressed my thumbs into a tight knot in his neck.

Giving a soft, appreciative moan, Dennis rolled his head forward until his chin touched his chest. "Arnold claimed he didn't know Seth had a partner, which I'm inclined to believe since he expedited the deal and was so sloppy about everything. He felt rushed because Seth had told him two other companies were interested in buying it. So, he agreed to Seth's request to keep the details of the transaction private."

"Because Seth didn't want Jared to know the company paid him."

Dennis nodded. "That's my guess."

"So much for Arnold keeping the details of the transaction confidential," I laughed. "Clearly, he blabbed about it to people within the company because one of their sales reps told Erin about Seth's hefty payout. And if Erin knows…"

"Then it's possible Jared found out too," Dennis said, completing my thought.

"Exactly. It just goes to show that secrets don't stay secret for long. People like to talk too much."

Dennis's back went rigid—even more so than before. "Speaking of which, I need *you* to keep quiet about everything I just told you."

I gave his shoulders a reassuring squeeze. "Don't worry, I will."

"I trust you."

I winced at that statement. My still-sore ankle was proof of just how trustworthy I was. For the past three days, I'd struggled with whether to tell him about it. I went back and forth between deciding I would, then chickening out, then convincing myself it was merely a sharp branch that had cut me.

Deep down, I knew I should tell him. He *trusted* me to not withhold such information, but I wasn't ready to admit I'd lied about it because I didn't want to ruin North Pole Night.

And the more days that elapsed, the more rotten I felt about not telling him.

"It's interesting that Madame Balleroy and her grandmother invested in their employees' side business," Dennis said. "Seems like a conflict of interest."

"I don't understand why Seth and Jared needed their funding." As I spoke, my fingers found another cluster of knots under his right shoulder. I worked at it with a gentle but firm motion, and his body relaxed under my touch. "They hadn't started producing the KnuckleKnight yet, and they hadn't spent money on a patent attorney. What other expenses did they have?"

"Prototypes," he said simply. "Not just one, or two, or three, but *four*. According to Arnold, prototype development is very expensive. Seth invested a considerable amount of his personal money in the invention, as did his fiancée."

"What about Jared?" I asked.

"No money; he only invested his time."

"Maybe that's why Seth felt entitled to the entire payout from Winterbridge," I offered.

Dennis's shoulders rose and fell as he let out a deep sigh. "It's possible. I need to find out how much Madame Balleroy and her grandmother invested."

"To gauge their potential motive?"

"Something like that."

I rubbed harder and deeper, sensing that his willingness to share information was dwindling. "What about Seth's fiancée, Cindy? Is she a suspect? Because if she found out Seth was involved with Chloe, then that could be a motive right there."

He shook his head. "We've confirmed her alibi."

"Well then, what about Chloe's husband? If he knew his wife was cheating on him with Seth—"

"Nope. He was on a flight to London the night of the homicide—not home cooking salmon, as Chloe claimed."

"Then who's your primary suspect?" I said. "Does anyone *not* have an alibi?"

Dennis turned to face me. He placed a finger over my lips and smiled, but remained silent. My pulse quickened as I looked into his eyes, feeling my insides flutter with excitement. Was he about to kiss me?

The labyrinth seemed to fall away, its twists and turns no match for the complexity of my conflicting feelings about him. I wouldn't kiss him first—that was a risk my heart wasn't ready to take. But if *he* kissed *me*...

"It's best if you don't know," he said. "For your safety, Hadley. Please understand how important it is to me that you don't get hurt." He gave me a heart-stopping wink, then turned around and walked toward an opening in the hedges that led to another long corridor.

I took a deep breath, then caught up with him. "I've been meaning to tell you, when your family returns from Africa, they're welcome to stay here if you think your home is unsafe."

Dennis's cheek dimpled. "I appreciate it, but I'm finalizing my evidence against the suspects in the money laundering case. I should have warrants by the end of the week. Once that happens, Kinsley and I can go home."

The end of the week. Only several more days with them. My stomach dropped with disappointment, but I forced a wide grin on my face. "Well, congrats on wrapping up your case. I can imagine it isn't easy juggling two big cases at once. And I'm excited to meet your family at the Christmas Eve brunch—or maybe even sooner, if you don't get those warrants."

"My family can't wait to meet you. I may or may not have told them everything there is to know about the wonderful and stunning Hadley Sutton. So don't be surprised if they treat you like family right off the bat."

My heart did a funny flip-flop. Wonderful and *stunning*? And he'd talked about me to his family? What had he told them? "I hope you didn't hype me up too much."

"Trust me, any embellishments were unnecessary. You're amazing, through and through."

"Thank you." It was all I could manage, my voice nothing more than a shy whisper.

He grinned at my response. "As for the brunch, I wouldn't be surprised if people are hesitant to come. Our group might be one of the only ones to show."

"Oh! You haven't heard? Madame Balleroy's restaurant has been booked since last week, and she sold out of tables for brunch. It'll be a packed house—or barn, technically. Everyone wants to see Seth."

Dennis blinked. "What do you mean?"

"Someone claimed to see his ghost while eating dinner at Balleroy's. They posted it on social media, and suddenly we've got a town full of ghost hunters wanting to catch a glimpse of him."

I laughed, but Dennis didn't. His expression turned serious as he asked, "Who told you that story?"

"Natasha. She said a customer saw Seth's ghost peering over Madame Balleroy's shoulder in the restaurant."

He shuddered. "Well, if you run into Seth—or through him— you might as well ask who killed him," he joked. His expression, however, didn't carry even a flicker of humor. His eyes were fixed on the dark, tunnel-like path of the labyrinth ahead of us. "We'd better hurry. I don't want to be gone too long while Kinsley's inside by herself."

"If you want to cheat, we can look at the labyrinth map on my website for tourists," I admitted sheepishly. I hadn't brought it up before, since I had selfishly wanted to prolong our time inside the labyrinth. "After a few tourists complained about the complexity of this maze, I paid a guy with a drone to map it out."

His eyes locked with mine as a smile crept along his lips. "You *wanted* us to get lost, didn't you?" he said, his voice rumbling with amusement. "You...sneaky, cunning thing." Dennis closed the distance between us. "What did you have in mind for when we got lost?"

There was a two-chimed beep, and Dennis broke eye contact with me before grabbing his phone from his pocket and raising it to his ear. The conversation lasted less than thirty seconds, during which Dennis swore, cringed, then nodded curtly as he listened to the deep voice on the other end. Finally, he ended the call with a simple, "Be there in ten minutes."

"Something wrong?" I asked.

"Let's see that map of yours. I need to grab my keys and go. Jared Bernardi was found dead outside his apartment."

CHAPTER TWENTY

Vincent stood by the barn entrance, frantically waving his hands to direct the moving crew. "Be careful with the blue crates," he warned them. "No, no! Don't stack them on top of the yellow ones. See where it says 'fragile' on them? There's glass inside!"

He turned to me, shaking his head. "Is it too early in the morning for common sense?"

"No, but apparently it's too early for patience," I teased.

Nine months ago, when I started working for Vincent, I wouldn't have dared to say such a thing to him, but our relationship had evolved into a more friendly and upfront one. On days like this, when he was the grump of all grumps, he needed someone to keep him in check.

Vincent sighed. "I overslept and only got one cup of coffee."

This was his way of apologizing, I guessed. "You slept in because you're already in vacation mode. If I hadn't sprung this opportunity on you at the last minute, you'd still be in bed dreaming."

His expression softened. "It's a great marketing opportunity for Walnut Ridge. I'm glad you told me about it."

"Of course," I chirped, motioning him further into the barn, where it was warmer. "I'm always looking out for you." I stopped next to the yellow crate that now sat next to the blue one, removed the lid, and retrieved a bubble-wrapped glass lantern. Its minimalistic frame was made of brushed brass that carried a touch of rustic charm. The sides were glass, allowing a clear view of the chunky red candle I would place inside.

Madame Balleroy's staff had already set up the tables, chairs, and bone-colored, raw-edge linen tablecloths. Now came the fun part—decorating.

Vincent followed me as I strolled over to the closest round table, placed a candle inside the lantern, and then set it down in the center of the table. I draped a lush garland made of pine branches, holly, and mistletoe around its base, then scattered small pinecones, cherry-red ornaments, and matte-gold baubles around the garland before tying a wide, festive tartan-patterned ribbon around the small handle at the top of the lantern.

I had to move quickly. The Christmas Eve brunch was in three days, and there was a long, long list of things to do before then. I didn't need Vincent here for all of it, but I wanted to get his thumbs-up on any decorations that included Walnut Ridge items.

"What do you think?" I asked, tilting my head towards the table. "Everything looks good?"

"Do you want to add a candelabra next to the lantern?" he asked.

I pretended to consider his suggestion for a few moments, instead of immediately shooting down his idea. I'd learned this was the best way to handle any of his less-than-stellar design ideas. "I love your new line of brass candelabras, but I'd prefer for the centerpiece to focus on just the one candle inside the lantern. We also have the globe lights"—I pointed to the crisscrossing strands above us that crews had hung two days ago—"so I don't want too many competing light sources."

He gave a curt nod. "Makes sense."

"Okay, then let's talk about the place settings. Once the guys bring in the wood-slab chargers, I'll place them around the tables and see how they look with the flatware and linen napkins." I'd included the chargers in the place settings since they were a recent edition to the Walnut Ridge catalog. "I'm planning to tie a sprig of holly to each napkin to give it a rustic touch. Thoughts?"

Vincent scrutinized the table for a moment, his gaze taking in every detail. "There sure are a lot of chairs," he said, not answering my question whatsoever. "Most events like this have tables of eight or ten. But *twelve*? Don't you think the table will look crowded?"

I shrugged. "I can't do anything about the table size. They're Madame Balleroy's. She uses them for all her events, probably because they're nice for large families. My aunt has filled all but one seat at our table for the brunch—speaking of which, we'd love for you to join us." Ever since Vincent told me he planned to spend the holiday with Lexi and Lexi alone, I'd felt like I should extend the invitation. The thought of him being alone with a dog all Christmas didn't sit right with me.

Vincent looked surprised, maybe even a little flustered. "I appreciate that, but I wouldn't want to impose on your family meal. And with the two homicides and no one in custody, are you certain the brunch will still happen?"

"The brunch is completely booked. Someone claimed they spotted the ghost of the sous chef in the restaurant recently, and now everyone wants to dine at Madame Balleroy's. There are a lot of superstitious people around here."

Vincent snorted. "Oh, I'm fully aware I'm living in a town full of lunatics."

I laughed. "Come on, join us. It won't be an imposition. It'll be my aunt, her fiancé, and some other friends who have nothing better to do." When he still didn't look convinced, I pressed, "It's Christmas, Vincent. Please join us. If for no other reason, you can take pictures of all the amazing Walnut Ridge decorations and send them to your social media manager."

He smiled. "You had me at please. Thanks for the invitation."

I clasped my hands together. "Great! I'll add your name to Madame Balleroy's guest list." I glanced toward the open barn doors, wondering if she would stop by the barn to meet Vincent, since he was sponsoring her brunch.

But there was no sign of her or anyone else from the restaurant. Although the scattering of cars in the restaurant's parking lot told me the kitchen crew had arrived, the property was uncharacteristically quiet this morning, void of the typical hum of preparations that came before the restaurant opened for lunch.

Most likely, everyone was still in shock from Jared's brutal death just four days ago. A resident of his apartment complex had found his body on the sidewalk leading to the parking lot, a short distance from his own unit. The cause of death was a severe blow to the head.

I'd cried when Dennis told me about the news in the labyrinth on Tuesday night, and when he asked for my statement the following day, my tears continued to flow. I had seen Jared in Madame Balleroy's kitchen hours before his death, and despite his mocking remarks about Natasha's use of the KnuckleKnight, I was devastated to learn of his murder.

Since Dennis was now working on two homicide investigations, he hadn't wrapped up the money laundering case like he'd planned. He'd mentioned several times this week that he hoped he wasn't wearing out his welcome. I sensed he was eager to go home.

Even so, we enjoyed being around each other. We fell into a routine where he brought Kinsley to her camp before work, I ran errands and relaxed in the morning and then I picked her up shortly after lunch and took her to whatever kid-oriented activity I'd found through Google searches that morning.

Then, Dennis would come home and I'd leave for cooking

class, during which I watched the clock more than the stove—much to the chagrin of Madame Balleroy. After class, Dennis and I worked alongside each other in the kitchen to get dinner on the table. I didn't know why he waited so late to eat, but it sure was nice to not have to eat alone.

After our bellies were full and dishes were in the sink, we hung out in the family room for another hour or so. Dennis and I talked while Kinsley watched a TV show. Eventually, she would doze off and Dennis would tuck her into bed. I usually went to my room at the same time as Kinsley and skimmed through the food safety book Madame Balleroy gave me, but Dennis stayed downstairs working on his laptop for Lord knows how long.

Last night, as I lay in bed struggling to fall asleep, I heard Dennis's deep voice floating up from the kitchen. And this morning, when I emerged from my room at six-thirty, he was having another animated phone conversation from behind his closed bedroom door. Despite his late hours and early mornings, he didn't seem as tired as he had during his first week of staying with me.

"Why don't we move on to the buffet table?" I suggested to Vincent before he could think of more suggestions for the centerpieces. "I'd like to show you how I plan to arrange the collection of our new hammered metal flower boxes."

"But don't you need to do the rest of the table centerpieces?"

"I'll take care of them later, after you go home and get another cup of coffee." I gave him a quick smile, then took off toward the left side of the barn, where long rectangular tables were placed end to end, each of them draped with the same raw-edge linen tablecloths.

Vincent plucked a small ornament from a box, turning it over in his slender fingers. His black and gray eyebrows furrowed. "When did you start decorating for parties? Surely you've got bigger client projects than this?"

Heat crept up my cheeks. "Yes, I recently wrapped up several large-scale residential redesign gigs. This job"—I gestured around the barn—"is more of a punishment than a client project."

Vincent's eyebrows shot upwards. "A what?"

I told him about the salmonella-laced Thanksgiving dinner I made, the resulting cooking school punishment, and the deal that Aunt Deb had worked out with Madame Balleroy to cover the cost of my tuition. Vincent's lips were pressed together so tightly they trembled, his eyes raging with hilarity, cheeks red as red could be. He was on the verge of losing control.

I thrust a hand to my hip. "It's not funny, but whatever. I'm sure Reid told you about my cooking skills...or lack thereof."

Vincent's eyebrows arched in feigned innocence. "He said nothing of the sort. Reid thought you were a great cook. He especially enjoyed the peanut butter and jelly sandwich and can of baked beans you cooked up that one time."

It was then that Vincent erupted into uncontrollable laughter, hunching over and holding onto his thighs as if trying to catch his breath in between deep, rolling guffaws.

I stood there with my arms folded across my chest. "That was *one* meal, and it was right before Hurricane Heath. I had stocked up on canned goods and non-perishable foods as any reasonable person would do before such a storm. Reid and I had just finished nailing plywood to the windows, and I didn't have time to prepare a grandiose meal. Your brother was hard to please."

Vincent looked up from his doubled-over position. "It's one of his many shortcomings." He straightened his back, shaking his head. "If anyone tried to enroll me in cooking school, I would have said no." His words were interrupted by short bursts of laughter as he struggled to compose himself.

"Even if it meant losing the privilege of cooking holiday meals forevermore?"

"Uh, *yeah*. Especially if it meant never cooking again." Vincent cleared his throat, as though forcing himself to stop laughing. "You know, it would be unrealistic to expect to be good at everything, Hadley. You're the most talented designer I've ever worked with. Don't beat yourself up for not being just as skilled in the kitchen. I usually just make myself a sandwich for dinner...only without the can of baked beans."

I groaned. "You'll never let me live that one down, will you?"

"Never."

Laughing, I headed for the collection of miniature planter boxes in the center of the buffet table. They were of various sizes, each made of hammered steel with a shiny copper finish. "The florist will transfer the arrangements I selected to these planters early Tuesday morning—"

My words hitched in my throat as swirls of blue and red lights bathed the bone-colored tablecloth in front of me. I whipped my head around towards the barn door, through which I saw a line of police vehicles charging down the narrow road toward the restaurant's parking lot.

Vincent swore. "Not another one," he whispered in disbelief.

I stuffed my hand in my coat pocket, removed my phone, and called Dennis. No way had there been another homicide. *No way.*

"What's going on?" I demanded when he answered. "I'm in the barn and I'm seeing a lot of police cars."

"Stay in the barn, Hadley," came his clipped reply. "Don't leave until I say you can. We're here to make an arrest for the murders of Seth O'Boyle and Jared Bernardi. We've nailed our woman."

CHAPTER TWENTY-ONE

After I hung up with Dennis, Vincent and I abandoned our decorations discussion and hurried towards the open barn door. Vincent told his crew to stop working and wait inside, but didn't explain why. They rested at a table while Vincent and I stood near the barn's entrance, peering around the right side of the gaping door at the police activity near the restaurant.

Trees and shrubs obscured part of the walkway leading to the restaurant, but we counted seven police officers who stormed through the front doors of Madame Balleroy's restaurant. Dennis followed behind them, phone pressed to his ear, his movements quick and deliberate.

Nailed our woman. His words played over and over again in my mind. Which woman? Madame Balleroy, who had disappeared for five minutes that night while Chloe and I waited in the barn? Or, perhaps, was it Grand-mère, who fired Seth moments before his murder and gave him the dreaded Roma tomato? Surely it wasn't Seth's fiancée, Cindy, unless her alibi wasn't as solid as Dennis initially thought.

As for motives, either Madame Balleroy or Grand-mère could have been bitter if they found out Seth lied about the large sum of money he received for the invention in which they invested. And, according to Natasha, Madame Balleroy was likely jealous of Seth's fame.

"Any idea who they're arresting?" Vincent whispered, his voice close to my ear. His cologne, so similar to that of his brother's, hung between us. I'd never noticed it before, but then again, I'd never stood so close to him. And while Reid's musky scent filled a room, Vincent's was more subtle—perhaps only one spray instead of three.

I stepped out from behind the side of the door. Though it was colder where I stood now, I no longer had to inhale the scent that threatened to crumple my heart once again.

"Most likely, they're here for Madame Balleroy or her grandmother," I said, glancing back at the workers sitting near the wall of hay bales, each staring at their phone, clueless about the arrest in progress.

Vincent craned his neck a little further around the side of the open door, but didn't move closer to me. "They've been in the restaurant for a while. How long does it take to arrest someone?"

"Hard to say. It's been a while since I've been arrested," I joked.

His face lit up with a smirk. "You've got a history with handcuffs, then? You failed to mention that during your job interview."

I side-eyed him. "Because I was too busy solving your ridiculously hard math problem."

Vincent gave a simple shrug. "It was something I found on Google that morning. Seemed like a good challenge for a candidate."

I rolled my eyes as I laughed, then returned my focus to the front of the restaurant. It had been about fifteen minutes since Dennis called, and my face now felt numb from the icy wind blowing in through the open door.

"Less than ten minutes," I blurted out, "for the cops to arrest someone—at least from what I've seen."

"You do have a way of getting into the middle of these things," he muttered.

"Unfortunately, yes. But you were there when they arrested Willy's murderer. The cops had him in handcuffs in five minutes. Not sure what's taking them so long today."

"We might have to load everything back onto the truck if one of the Balleroy women goes to jail. They can't host a brunch from behind bars."

I huffed out a laugh. "Oh, I'm sure they'd find a way to do it. Nothing seems to come between them and their—"

Vincent and I saw him at the same time. Officer Stevens exited the restaurant, running, *sprinting* down the sidewalk and around the other side of the restaurant. Seconds later, two more officers shot out of the restaurant and followed Officer Stevens.

I whispered, "What's happening?"

Anxiety gnawed at my stomach. I had to use all my willpower to resist calling Dennis to make sure he was okay. The pink, swollen scar from the bullet was still fresh on his forearm, and even fresher in my mind. I wrapped my arms around my chest, hugging my now-shaking body. If only I could see what was going on, see that he was safe, I wouldn't feel so panicky.

I took a cautious step outside the barn, my eyes scanning the surrounding area for signs of danger. If I hid in the herb forest, concealed by its thick foliage, I might have a better view of the restaurant. With a deep breath, I took another step away from the barn.

Vincent's hand wrapped around my arm, gently tugging me back inside. "Whoa there. The cop you talked to told us to stay in here. Probably for our safety."

"He's a detective," I said, but my whispered words were likely lost in the wind. I stopped in the middle of the open door, not once removing my eyes from the restaurant. Vincent stood next to me, remaining silent as we waited.

And waited. And waited.

Just when I thought my wobbly legs would give out, the restaurant's front door swung open and Dennis emerged, his expression cool and smug, as though he'd just achieved some great victory. The sound of heated voices drifted from the restaurant just before a throng of officers spilled out the door, clustered around a pinch-faced Natasha.

I jolted upright, my eyes widening as she struggled against the officers holding onto her arms. "*Natasha?*" I stammered in disbelief. "She couldn't have."

Vincent gaped at me. "You know her?"

"Enough to know she wouldn't kill anyone."

Dennis said a few words to the officers, then turned and started towards the barn. Vincent told his crew that their break was over, then led them to their truck while recounting the excitement they had missed.

I stayed put and waited for Dennis.

"Enjoy the show?" he asked as he neared, a faint smile resting on his face.

"It wasn't Natasha. There's *no way* she could have committed murder."

He stopped in front of me. "My evidence suggests otherwise."

"But she has *children*! And a husband. What motive could she possibly have?" My loud voice caught Vincent's attention as he stood near the truck in the parking lot, causing him to turn and head back to the barn.

Dennis didn't flinch or look insulted that I'd questioned him. He glanced at his watch. "That arrest took longer than it should have. She bolted right before Officer Stevens cuffed her." He smiled to himself, shaking his head. "None of us expected to play a game of chase this morning. She's a speedy one; good at hiding, too. But cops always win in the end."

"Except for when they're wrong about a suspect." I kept my voice steady this time, trying not to imagine the horrified faces of Natasha's children when they learned their mom was in jail and would spend Christmas without them.

"I understand why you're so surprised, but there have been plenty of convicted felons who have children." His voice was low and matter-of-fact, as though he were an expert at detaching himself from the emotions of a case.

"Okay, but how many of those killers wear silly holiday sweaters with pink snowmen on roller-skates while taking their kids to North Pole night?"

"What?" He cocked his head. "Snowmen on roller—"

"Never mind. I'm just saying I can't believe—I *don't* believe Natasha killed two of her co-workers. What evidence do you have against her?"

Dennis sighed heavily, looking away for a moment before meeting my gaze again. "I can't share those details. You know that. Sometimes I think you forget you're an interior designer."

Vincent stopped several feet behind Dennis, looking a little surprised by Dennis's somewhat prickly tone.

I clenched my jaw, attempting to contain my frustration. Now wasn't the time to push him to talk, especially with Vincent nearby, but I needed to know what evidence they had against Natasha. I needed to help her.

Sure, she had been next in line for the sous-chef position, and she seemed like a motivated, ambitious woman—but a killer? It didn't add up. One way or another, I'd convince Dennis to tell me about his evidence. Even if I had to massage his back all day.

Dennis's expression softened, the lines of authority on his face giving way to the beginnings of a smile. "When I left Kinsley with your aunt, I promised I'd take her to the town square after dinner and treat her to a hot cocoa sundae. I hope you'll join us?"

"Sure. Let's celebrate your almost-successful arrest. Because even a step in the wrong direction brings you closer to the right one." I flashed him a grin, and he let out a small laugh.

"I'm heading to the station now," he said. "I'll pick up Kinsley when I'm done. We should be home well before five. I'll cook tonight because you've done enough of that lately."

Now Vincent looked *really* surprised, his eyes skewed with confusion as he processed Dennis's words, likely assuming I'd not only started a new relationship so soon after splitting up with Reid, but also that Dennis was now living with me. Oh, how embarrassing!

Fiery heat crawled up my neck, searing my cheeks. I kept my eyes on Dennis as I replied, "That sounds great, and I'll pick up Kinsley if I finish before you do."

In less than a heartbeat, Dennis stepped closer to me and gave me a swift kiss on the cheek. "Thanks, Hadley. I know she'd appreciate it. Let's try to get Kinsley to bed earlier tonight. Then you and I can—"

Vincent cleared his throat, making Dennis and me jump. We pivoted towards him in unison.

"The guys have six more crates to unload before returning the truck to Richmond. I'll head out when they do, so Hadley, if you need me for anything else, now's the time." Vincent seemed to fight a smile as he spoke, his gaze flickering from Dennis to me.

Dennis stepped towards Vincent and gave him a strong-armed handshake. "Good seeing you again; it's been a while. You might want to reconsider giving Hadley so much time off over Christmas. We need to keep her busy decorating, so she doesn't have time to play detective." Dennis threw me a wink, then started back down the path back towards the parking lot.

"New boyfriend?" Vincent asked.

I turned to him, smiling sheepishly. "Let me explain."

CHAPTER TWENTY-TWO

"Why did Santa start eating ice cream instead of cookies?" Kinsley asked with a sneaky grin, bouncing on her toes as the three of us waited in line at the Frosty's Sundae Stop, which was currently parked just a short skip away from the fountain in the town square.

"I dunno," Dennis drawled. "Because he got tired of cookies?"

"No!" Kinsley squealed. "Because he wanted a *cool* change!"

Dennis and I laughed. "That's very clever, Kins," he said. "Did you just now come up with that?"

"I just now read that sign over there." She pointed to a rustic A-frame chalkboard easel to the right of the food cart.

"Creative," I said. "If their sundaes are half as good as their riddles, then we are in for a treat!" Judging from the length of the line winding through the cobblestone street, I guessed their desserts would indeed be delicious. "I don't remember seeing this cart at North Pole Night. They would have made a *killing*. And speaking of killing, I am one-hundred percent sure that Natasha did not—"

"Hadley," Dennis warned, raising his brows in feigned reproach. "I'm not going to discuss the case with you. And as for

Frosty's Sundae Shop, they didn't come to North Pole Night because they were at a much bigger festival in Richmond that day. I follow them on Instagram."

"Ah, so you're a fanatic?"

"A shameless one. I tried to recreate it at home, but it didn't quite compare to Frosty's."

"Then you should keep trying," I urged, my words saccharine sweet. "Because even if you don't get things right the *first time*, you should always give it another shot. Be receptive to others' ideas and feedback, Dennis, and have open conversations about your process so others can assist you in perfecting it."

He closed his eyes as understanding dawned on him. "We're not talking about sundaes, are we?"

"You tell me," I cooed. "You're the detective."

Laughing quietly, Dennis stepped up to the festive food stall and whipped out his wallet. "Three hot cocoa sundaes, please." He slid a credit card across the smooth, weathered wood of the countertop towards the middle-aged man wearing a sweatshirt featuring the food stall's snowman logo.

"Sorry, sir, but our credit card machine is down tonight. Cash only, I'm afraid." He pointed to a small, handwritten note taped to the front of the counter saying just that.

Dennis peered inside his wallet, thumbing through a slim stack of bills. "Looks like I only have enough cash for two sundaes. Hadley, do you have any cash on you?"

I shook my head. "Only a card. But it's okay, I'll skip the sundae tonight."

"I didn't drag you out here just so you could watch us enjoy a sundae. Let's share one."

When the cashier handed Dennis the sundaes, he grabbed two plastic spoons from the utensil caddy and stuffed one into each beautiful swirl of peppermint candy-sprinkled ice cream.

One spoon in our sundae.

I felt a rush of flutters in my stomach, then did an immediate mental head-slap. *Why* was I excited about sharing a spoon with Dennis? This was far from the first time I'd shared a utensil—or, let's be honest, a little more—with a guy.

But swapping a little spit with *Dennis*? That was new territory.

We found a place to sit on the wide ledge of the fountain, not too far from where Chloe and her unpleasant husband, Kraig, had sat exactly a week ago. Dennis gave one bowl to Kinsley, then dug his spoon into our bowl.

"You'll love it," was all he said as he held it up to my mouth.

I leaned in, allowing the frozen sweetness to hit my taste buds, and there it was—pure bliss. It was as if Frosty's Sundae Stop had extracted the very essence of winter cheer and infused it into cream and sugar. I closed my eyes for a moment, savoring the flavor.

"Best ever?" he asked, talking through his own bite of hot cocoa-flavored ice cream. He dipped our spoon into the bowl once again and lifted it to my lips.

A rush of anticipation—over a *spoon,* of all things—zipped through my veins as if I were sixteen again and about to kiss a boy for the very first time.

Only tonight, I wasn't so lucky. I had to settle for a plastic utensil that touched his lips.

"Absolutely the best," I agreed, shivering as the treat sent chills through my body. I pulled down my knitted hat further over my ears for extra warmth. My coat was thicker than Dennis's leather one, but he seemed completely unaffected by the cold.

"Hey there, little nugget," came a deep male voice nearby. Dennis, Kinsley, and I looked up, searching for whoever had spoken.

My gaze landed on Hal, sporting a tailored wool overcoat and blue jeans. He chuckled and waved at us as he strolled by, hand in hand with Sheila Moody, whom I recognized from Aunt Deb's hiking group.

Dennis sat up straight, his eyes narrowing at Hal. "'Little nugget?' Is he talking to you or Kinsley?"

"Unfortunately, me," I laughed. "He thinks it's funny that the chicken nugget is my signature ingredient."

A fully loaded spoon paused halfway to Dennis's mouth. "Really? Chicken nuggets? Your signature ingredient?"

"According to Madame Balleroy, it is. Do you have a signature ingredient?"

He slid the spoon into his mouth, considering my question. "Who says you can only have one? I have lots of them—essentially anything from my garden. It's my schtick in my cooking videos."

"I haven't told you the worst part. I have to—"

Dennis spooned another scoop of ice cream into my mouth, laughing as bits of crushed peppermint fell onto my coat. I picked them off one by one and tossed them into my mouth. "I have to make a dish for the Christmas Eve brunch and somehow incorporate nuggets. It's the final assignment for her cooking classes."

Kinsley squealed. "I want to try some! I usually have to eat boring stuff on holidays."

"It won't be the dinosaur nuggets you're used to," I confessed. "Madame Balleroy would never allow that. I need to bread the nuggets myself."

"Okay," she said cautiously. "Just don't ruin it with green things."

I looked at Dennis, raising a brow.

"Vegetables," he explained.

Laughing, I held out a gloved hand to Kinsley. "I pinky promise, no veggies."

"Have you planned your chicken nugget dish yet?" Dennis asked.

"Ugh, no. I've been so caught up with…well, everything. But I still have two days to come up with something."

"Two days is plenty of time for a miracle," he quipped as he scooped more ice cream from the bowl. "There's no need to panic."

"I'm not panicking, Dennis. I'm *apprehensive*. Speaking of which, the suspect you *apprehended* today—"

Without warning, he thrust a gigantic spoonful of sundae into my mouth, causing it to overflow from the corners and trickle down my chin.

The taste of hot cocoa and peppermint lingered on my lips as we headed back to the Ladyvale Manor, when Dennis carried a sleepy Kinsley to bed, when he then asked if I wanted to watch a movie, when the walls of caution shot up around my heart, and when I finally stepped into the shower, wishing I wasn't so scared of getting hurt again.

Now, as I hid under a mound of soft, downy blankets and watched the shadows of bare branches sway on my bedroom wall, doubt inched its way into my thoughts.

I had panicked when he asked me. Between one heartbeat and the next, a flood of questions raced through my mind as I imagined sitting on the downstairs sofa with Dennis. How close would we sit to each other? Would his fingers trace along my arm, my cheek, my lips? Would he kiss me...would we even watch the movie at all? As exhilarating as that scenario was, the thought of what might come after was equally frightening. Could I trust him with my fragile heart?

Tonight, I had chosen caution over opportunity; I had hidden behind that invisible but deeply felt wall I'd built from past heartbreaks.

And the look on his face when I turned him down! His smile hadn't dipped, but for a fleeting moment, I saw something crumble beneath the warmth of his eyes. Maybe it was disappointment, maybe even a little pain...as if my rejection had reached deeper than intended. He'd covered it quickly with a half-hearted joke about being an early bird kind of guy anyway, but I knew that wasn't true. For the past week, I'd heard him walking around his room late at night, floorboards grunting under his quiet footsteps.

Just as he was doing tonight. It was a little past midnight, and he'd been pacing ever since I got out of the shower. It was one reason I couldn't fall asleep. I couldn't stop wondering if I had something to do with his sleepless nights.

I rolled onto my stomach and gazed at the wall behind me. Dennis was so close, with only thin layers of sheetrock separating my bed from his.

And yet, he felt so far away—more so tonight, after I turned away from him. Turned my back on a good man who was not only gorgeous but also caring and kind.

It was the first time I'd ever shied away from a relationship. I'd never been guarded, and I certainly never would have turned down a movie night with a man I had a huge crush on.

But this was more than a crush. It was me wanting to rush home from cooking class to spend as much time with him as possible; it was craving his body against mine while cutting herbs, and wanting to get lost with him in the labyrinth. It was admiring the adoring way he cared for Kinsley, and the way his laughing blue eyes made me hope he never solved his money laundering case.

That was why I was so terrified. And though I rarely flinched from a challenge, love was one feat that seemed impossible for me to conquer.

I propped myself up on my elbows, considering Carmella's advice last week. What if she was right? That I could miss an opportunity for love if I played it too safe? *All relationships are doomed to fail,* she'd said, *except for the one that isn't.*

Slowly, quietly, I pushed myself up to my knees and crawled closer to the headboard, placing my hand flat against the painted

194

sheetrock. What if the wall wasn't there? Not only the one separating our rooms, but the one shielding my heart?

What if I let my heart loose, allowed it to love Dennis with everything in me?

I could get hurt again. But *would* I?

The memory of Dennis's hands gripping my waist on the dance floor, as if he never wanted to let me go, encouraged me to toss the blanket off my body and leave the warmth of my bed. I shoved my feet into my furry slippers, thinking about how he asked about my day at work each afternoon, then truly seemed interested in my retelling of it. Then, thinking about his sweet words the night of the dance, how I brightened the darkest month of the year, I mindlessly slipped on my robe and tied it around the middle.

Dennis cares about you, Carmella had said.

Something inside me shifted, like a key unlocking a forgotten door. It was too late to watch the movie with Dennis, but I still had time to tell him I regretted my decision.

I stepped out of my room and tapped quietly on his cracked door. "Dennis?" I whispered. Hearing nothing, I knocked a little louder.

So strange. Only minutes ago, I'd heard him pacing inside his room, but now he was asleep or gone. Just like last Saturday night when I knocked on his door.

I peeked through the crack into his room, but didn't see him in bed. I pushed the door open a little more, calling out his name.

Hearing nothing, I stepped into his room and looked around: rumpled bed spread, black boots just outside the closet, wallet on the nightstand—

I laughed out loud, then clamped a hand around my mouth so I wouldn't wake up Kinsley. Judging by the haphazard way Irma's porcelain dolls were on the shelf, with all of them facing the wall, I guessed she had snuck in here to play with them at some point, despite Dennis's initial warning that they were only meant to be looked at.

Shaking my head, I scolded myself for putting Dennis in this room instead of Kinsley. *Duh*. I removed a doll with blue eyes and brown hair—remarkably similar to sweet Kinsley—from the shelf, then walked into her room, placing it on the dresser for her to find in the morning.

Out in the hallway again, I peeked inside the other upstairs rooms for Dennis, and finding them empty, canvassed every room downstairs—the formal parlor, dining room, kitchen, drawing room, family room, and even the historical society's office, though I didn't at all expect to find him there.

I returned to the entry hall, slowly turning a full circle, wondering if I'd missed a room.

He must be at the station, I told myself as I unlocked the front door. Maybe, after all my pestering, he was reconsidering whatever evidence he had against Natasha. I stepped out onto the front porch and looked toward the small gravel parking lot.

His unmarked police car was parked next to mine, exactly where he'd left it when we returned from our sundae outing. Scrunching my forehead in confusion, I retreated inside and locked the door behind me.

Perhaps an officer had picked him up on their way to a crime scene? It was possible, but not at all likely.

Or, and this thought made my stomach drop like a rock, maybe it was a woman who had picked him up. Maybe he and Akari had rekindled their relationship—or any other woman in town who wasn't stupid enough to turn down a movie night with the sea-blue eyed heartthrob.

CHAPTER TWENTY-THREE

Where had Dennis gone off to last night?

It was the question playing on my mind the minute my alarm woke me up, as I got dressed for church, and as I glanced inside his room before heading downstairs.

Nearing the staircase, the divine smell of bacon told me precisely where he was now. I followed my nose to the kitchen but paused at the doorway. In slim-fitting blue jeans and a navy-blue crewneck sweater, Dennis stood with his back to me in front of the stove, busily turning bacon with a pair of tongs.

My heart melted a little. Dennis was nodding his head to an upbeat Christmas song, playing from his phone on the kitchen island. I joined in by bopping my head in rhythm and crept closer, eager to give him a surprise hug from behind. The walls around my heart were lowered, and I was ready to embrace the joy bubbling up inside me.

But then I stopped as my eyes fell on his laptop screen, which displayed a close-up photo of a chunky gold hoop earring.

Natasha's earring.

I abandoned my plans for the surprise hug and scurried over

to the island for a closer look. What was so important about her earring?

With a quick glance at Dennis, I pressed the right arrow on his keyboard to advance to the next photo in his file folder. Another photo of her earring popped up, this one even closer. It lay on what looked like grass—brown, dead grass that hadn't survived the last cold snap.

I pressed the keyboard once more, bringing up a photo taken from above. My breath caught in my throat. It was a crime scene photo, displaying a section of sidewalk cordoned off by police tape and a patch of withered grass where Natasha's earring rested.

Impossible.

I backed away from his computer, my hands now shaking. How had her earring ended up near the crime scene?

Dennis turned, then jumped when he saw me. "Hey! I didn't hear you come in. How'd you sleep?" His bright eyes bounced over to his open laptop, and in two casual steps, he made it to the island and flipped down the screen. He pointed to his laptop. "Did you—"

"I slept okay. How about you?"

"Great. Never better."

"Really? Interesting. By the way, why is Natasha's earring in your crime scene photos?"

Dennis's jaw tightened. "You looked at my computer?"

"Well, I couldn't *not* see it. It's sitting right there on the island."

"Everything on this computer is confidential," he said calmly. His eyes met mine, and I saw a hint of frustration in them.

I dipped my chin. "Sorry, I should have looked away, but curiosity got the best of me."

Dennis wrapped a hand around the back of his neck and pressed his fingers deep into his muscles. Maybe *I* was the source of his recent neck tension.

I gave him another apologetic look. "Listen, I'm not trying to be annoying; I'm being persistent because I really, *truly* believe Natasha is innocent."

"I understand it's upsetting to think a woman with small children could commit such brutal crimes, but I wouldn't have been able to get an arrest warrant without enough evidence. I'm not making educated guesses here."

"I'm not either."

Dennis leaned a hip against the kitchen island, pointing the pair of greasy bacon tongs at me. "Then what's your evidence?"

"Well, at first it was a just a gut feeling—call it intuition if you'd like—because I simply couldn't think of a logical motive. Sure, Natasha is driven and ambitious, but with young children at home, I can't imagine she would jeopardize everything by committing a crime just to become the next sous chef."

"Intuition doesn't get us very far in the police world—"

"But," I continued, "after seeing the photo of Natasha's earring in the middle of the crime scene, it seems even more likely she was framed."

He shook his head. "It's not very often that someone is framed. It happens a lot in movies, but in reality, it's difficult for someone to pull it off."

"Who says they were successful?" I arched an eyebrow, emphasizing my point. "Natasha was missing an earring *before* Jared's death. Several hours before, my cooking class toured the restaurant's kitchen, and Natasha gave us tips on making mashed potatoes. That's when I noticed her missing earring."

"Are you sure?"

"I almost pointed it out to her because, honestly, she sort of looked like a pirate with only one gold hoop, but I didn't want to embarrass her."

Dennis remained silent, not even acknowledging my comments with a nod. He turned and flipped each strip of bacon in the pan. Finally, after setting the tongs on the spoon rest, he faced me again. "That is interesting, and I will follow up on it.

But it proves nothing. It's possible Natasha found her earring after she talked to your class, put it back in, and then lost it again outside Jared's apartment."

"But is it likely?" I mused.

"My sister used to lose earrings all the time. She looked like a pirate too." His expression softened, and I even detected the beginnings of a smile. "She'd complain that once the back part got loose, it would continue to fall out until she found another back. Sometimes she'd use a pencil eraser."

"I'm impressed you know her beauty hacks. Sounds like you were just as observant back then as you are now."

"You're pretty observant yourself." His voice was low and even, and it no longer held traces of frustration.

I let out a slow breath, grateful he wasn't irritated that I questioned his investigation. Because ticking off Dennis wasn't what I had in mind when I woke up this morning. I'd hoped to find out where he went last night, and if it wasn't with another woman, then I wanted to suggest watching a movie tonight to make up for the one I'd missed.

But now wasn't the right time to talk about any of that, not with this tension now hanging between us, thanks to my sneak-peak of his evidence.

Easing onto the stool in front of the island, I kept my gaze locked with his. "If you have other evidence against her, can...can you tell me about it? I might be able to help, since I've interacted several times now with Natasha."

"Nope, the earring is all we got on her," he said, giving me a playful wink as he ambled towards me.

"Come on, seriously. You said it yourself—I'm 'pretty observant.'"

"I never said that."

"You said it ten seconds ago."

"You misheard me. I said you're pretty and I like to observe you."

I groaned, fighting the smile threatening to break across my face. "Flattery will not get you anywhere, detective. I'm serious about helping Natasha. I believe she's innocent."

Dennis studied me, his brows furrowed in thought. "There are a couple more pieces of information I can share," he said at last, "but only because you might have insight into them that I don't. Besides, you've already undermined our most compelling evidence; why not try to dismantle our entire argument against her while you're at it?"

"I wasn't trying to—"

"I'm kidding. It was an impressive observation."

Dennis took a seat on a stool next to me, his face turning serious once again. "I need you to promise me you won't tell anyone about this. Ever." I nodded in agreement before he continued. "When officers searched the restaurant after Jared's death, they found a printout of Seth's work schedule among Natasha's belongings. The schedule from the week he was killed. And next to it was a sheet of paper with Jared's address written in Natasha's handwriting."

"Where did they find it?"

"Inside Natasha's locker in the staff break room."

I leaned forward, placing my elbows onto the countertop and resting my chin on one hand as I thought back to the restaurant's break room. We had walked by the lockers on our way into the kitchen. There were at least twenty of them, all a dark gray that blended into the walls. Each one had a label with an employee's name printed with what appeared to be a label maker, and silver pull handles, which gleamed dully under the fluorescent lights, were...empty.

"The lockers didn't have locks," I said.

He nodded. "Which is probably why Madame Balleroy referred to them as 'cubbies' when I questioned her."

"Anyone could have put the address and schedule in there. Whoever slipped the note into my container of dessert loaves was really sneaky—not one person noticed them do it. It's possible the same person planted the so-called evidence in Natasha's locker."

"Our handwriting analysis software confirmed the handwriting matches the samples we collected from the suspect's home," he said.

I pointed to his laptop, smiling coyly. "Do you have a photo of the address you found?"

Dennis studied me, his mind likely churning through all the reasons he should *not* show me, but he reopened his laptop with an exaggerated sigh of defeat. He moved a finger against his laptop's trackpad, clicked to close the image of the earring, then opened a closeup photo of a sheet of notebook paper with the handwritten address.

"Purple ink," I said, my breath catching in my throat. "Natasha wrote a note on my recipe card when we made lobster bisque, and she used a purple pen." I slid off my stool and retrieved my recipe binder from the cabinet next to the sink, removing the card from the binder's clear front pocket.

I held it up next to the screen, shifting my gaze between the handwritten address on the screen and Natasha's helpful note on my recipe card.

"The handwriting looks the same," I agreed after a while.

"Yes, and several members of the kitchen crew, including Madame Balleroy, told me that Natasha and Seth had a contentious relationship. They said Natasha thought his ego interfered with his cooking."

I grimaced. "Natasha and Jared didn't seem to get along well either. The night Jared was killed, he gave her a hard time for using the KnuckleKnight attachment, and then she gave him a dirty look—one that made it clear she wanted him to leave. I'm pretty sure I mentioned this when I gave you my statement."

"You did, as did several others from your class."

"But I'm still not convinced Natasha really wrote down the

address. I mean, who puts addresses on paper these days? Do you? I always enter them into my phone's map app, which then takes me wherever I want to go. So why would she have written the address and then left it in her locker where someone could find it? She's not an idiot."

"It was cleverly hidden, along with Seth's work schedule." He closed the photo of Jared's address and opened another one, which showed the inside of Natasha's locker. She had stuffed more than just a few personal items in there. "It's a mess, right? Well, at the bottom of this mess, officers found this—" Dennis tapped the right arrow key, bringing up a photo of a bright red oven mitt. "Seth's schedule and the address to the apartment complex were at the bottom of the thumb section of the mitt, crumpled up into tiny balls."

Chill bumps pricked my neck and arms. Slowly, I tore my eyes away from the red oven mitt until they met Dennis's. "Someone planted that evidence." Dennis stayed silent, waiting for me to explain. "Do you use oven mitts?"

"Of course," he said. "These hands aren't made of steel."

I nodded. "I use them too. Want to know who doesn't? Natasha. Or any of the other chefs in the kitchen."

He pulled back his chin. "Why not?"

"I don't know; I didn't ask. But I didn't see a single mitt in the restaurant's kitchen. They all use dish towels—the same ones used to wipe the counters and clean up messes. We use mitts in the cooking school, but two weeks ago, when Natasha removed someone's burnt lobster from the oven, she pulled a dish towel from the pocket of her chef coat. Not an oven mitt."

Dennis still looked skeptical, so I grabbed my phone from the side pocket of my dress and searched: 'Do professional chefs use oven mitts?'

He moved closer to me, resting his hand on the smooth granite countertop of the kitchen island. The faint scent of his shower-fresh scent filled my nose, making it tempting to put down my phone and talk about last night instead—about the movie I should have watched with him.

But I was a woman on a mission: help Natasha get out of jail before Christmas.

I thumbed through the search engine results that popped up, clicking on several legitimate-looking pages. We huddled over my phone for the next five minutes, absorbing all the information we could find on how professionals handle hot cookware.

Website after website said the same thing: many professional chefs prefer to use a folded kitchen towel rather than an oven mitt when handling hot pans. They argued it's more convenient to keep a towel in their apron pocket and more hygienic since towels can easily be replaced and washed in hot water at the end of each day.

Dennis drummed his fingers against the countertop. "Interesting," he said, looking up from my phone, his face still close to mine. "None of Balleroy's chefs wore oven mitts?"

"None that I saw."

"Okay, I'll follow up on it." He rubbed his jaw, feeling the scruff that had grown over the past few days. "I won't lie, I'll be ticked off if I made a mistake, but I appreciate you pressing this. You have a knack for piecing things together, Hadley."

He stepped away from the island and returned to the bacon, carefully placing each greasy strip onto a plate covered with paper towels. I watched the way his muscles flexed and rippled underneath the smooth fabric of his navy-blue sweater. Would I have leaned against those arms last night if we'd watched a movie? Would they have wrapped around me, pulled me in closer?

"Thank you," I said, studying the mysterious man before me. If only I could piece together why he disappeared after midnight.

CHAPTER TWENTY-FOUR

Throughout the day, I'd tried half a dozen ways of asking Dennis about his mysterious midnight vanishings, but all my attempts were too subtle and he revealed absolutely zero information on his late-night whereabouts. I couldn't directly ask him without admitting I had peeked into his room.

Over breakfast, I brought up the chilly nights and asked him and Kinsley if they needed additional blankets. That attempt failed, since both assured me they were fine.

I'd lost track of time during breakfast and didn't make it to church with Aunt Deb, so I joined Dennis and Kinsley instead. I wanted to spend the day with them anyway since he'd booked rooms for his family once they arrived tomorrow afternoon so he wouldn't further impose on me.

On our way to church, I'd brought up the popping noise the heater makes when it kicks on, and I asked if it ever bothered him.

"Not at all," he'd replied, which was likely the truth if he had gone elsewhere to sleep.

Then, when a young couple holding hands strolled by us during our picnic lunch at the park, I casually asked if he'd started dating anyone new since Akari. He'd seemed puzzled by my question and chuckled as he shook his head no.

It went like this the rest of the afternoon and into the evening, when he told Kinsley she had to go to bed early. Not only did he want to get her back on a decent bedtime schedule before his family arrived, but he said he also needed to work on his investigation.

It was the first time he'd mentioned his case since I challenged his evidence this morning, though his mind seemed to be elsewhere for most of the day, likely buried in the morbid trenches of the homicides.

After he tucked in Kinsley and retreated to his room with his laptop tonight, I felt even more regret than I had this morning. Had I blown my chances with him when I turned down movie night? Had I irritated him by second-guessing his evidence? Given how strongly I felt about Natasha's innocence, I couldn't help but share my opinion with him.

Now, while sitting on the edge of my bed, I scrolled through my friends' social media updates on my phone while listening to the sound of the shower running in Dennis's bathroom. Since my attempts at asking him where he disappeared to had failed, I would find out for myself.

My plan was simple: once he finished showering and pacing around his room, I'd keep an eye on the small crack in my door, hidden in the darkness of my room, waiting for him to pass by.

Then, I'd slip out of my room and follow him, acting slightly surprised to see him out of his room at the same time. I'd use the lame excuse of needing a late-night cup of tea and would oh-so-casually ask what he was up to. My plan was a little short on specifics, but I would figure out the details later when he inevitably started pacing.

The sound of water stopped, and there was a soft thud as his shower door swung shut, followed by the sound of drawers opening and closing.

I slipped my phone into the pocket of my robe and stretched my legs in front of me. It was too dark to see my toenail polish, but I would need to repaint them before the brunch.

I'll paint them red tomorrow, I decided. *Red for Christmas—*

The sound of Dennis's footsteps suddenly echoed in the hallway, each step landing softly on the long, narrow rug. They came to a halt just before my door as though—why had they stopped? So he could see if I was still awake?

His footsteps resumed and, for a fleeting moment, I saw Dennis's shadowy frame through the crack in my door. It was too dark to make out what he was wearing—if he was dressed to go to the station…or somewhere else.

I gave him a fifteen-second lead so he wouldn't think I'd been sitting in the dark waiting for him—how humiliating would that be!—and then I stepped out into the hallway.

Something jingled in a distant room down below, telling me he had a sufficient lead. I descended the stairs slowly, straining to hear any other sounds that might give away his location.

My bare feet hit the cold marble tile just as Dennis strolled into the entry hall. He was wrapped in a blanket and had a pillow tucked under his arm.

"*Dennis?*" I exclaimed, just a little too loudly.

Shrieking, he leapt a foot in the air at the sound of my voice, dropping the pillow and blanket in the process. His eyes were enormous as he spun around towards me, now wearing nothing but sneakers and boxer shorts covered in little reindeer. Hanging from his pinky finger was a set of car keys—my car keys.

"Where are you going?" I demanded.

"Outside." He leaned over and snatched the blanket off the floor, clumsily wrapping it around his body again.

"Wearing only that?" I asked, making no effort to look away from his abs, which even in the dim light of the entry hall, were undeniably well-defined.

"Yes…I…um—could you *not* stand right there?" His tone was

adamant, if not a little harsh, but his eyes flickered with something more raw. Perhaps...fear?

"Why not?" I folded my arms.

"Because that's where Irma..." His voice trailed off as he leaned against the front door. His eyes were fixed on the marble tile just behind me, where the previous owner of Ladyvale Manor had met her murderous death.

"Oh!" I cried, taking a giant step forward. "I didn't know that spot...bothered you." I couldn't think of a better word. Disturbed? Scared?

"How does it *not* bother you? I can't get it out of my head, seeing her twisted body on the marble. Right there, two feet from where you're standing." His face, already white as bone, paled even more. "How can you sleep at all in this place?"

My eyes drifted to the pillow still on the tile and then to the keys in his hand.

Oh.

"So you've been sleeping outside? In my car?"

Despite the cold air surrounding us and his wet hair that probably made him even colder, droplets of sweat dotted his forehead. "My car smells like—well, like a police vehicle. Yours smells like vanilla. So, I slept in yours. It's the only place around here I could get away from the noises. I didn't sleep at all my first week here. I tried going downstairs in the family room, and then on the fancy couch in there"—he gestured to the formal parlor— "but I still heard them."

I scanned the dark, still house around us, suddenly wishing I had a blanket of my own to wrap around me. Stepping closer to him, I whispered, "What noises?"

"The ones upstairs at night. Sometimes they're downstairs."

"The popping sounds coming from the heater? I thought you said they didn't bother you."

"Not the heater. The...other noises. You don't hear them?"

When I shook my head, he looked baffled.

"Maybe you're used to them," he said. "I told myself all old homes make noises, and that it wasn't dangerous for us to stay here. I mean, you sleep here every night—although not in the bedroom of a recently murdered woman."

Oh. Good. God.

I had put a man *who was scared of ghosts* in Irma's old bedroom. Sleeping *in her bed*.

I could have slapped myself. "I am so, *so* sorry, Dennis. I had no idea you were afraid of ghosts."

"Neither did I," he said ruefully. "And it sounds so emasculating, by the way, when you put it that way. But those dolls of Irma's—it's like they're watching me...watching with their freakish beady eyes." He gestured wildly, causing the blanket to slide further down his chest. "I turned them the other way, but even that didn't help me sleep."

No wonder he'd been so tired initially! At least he was able to get some sleep in my car, even though he'd paid for it with stiff muscles. "I wish you would have told me, Dennis. I would have given you a different room." Kinsley probably would have been fine in there, but I kept that thought to myself for the sake of his ego. "Well, this explains why all the dolls were facing the wall."

"Yes, and last night, one of those creepy little things *moved*. Into Kinsley's room. And it even *looked* like her. Light brown hair, blue eyes. She swears she didn't do it; she said they're too dusty to play with—" Dennis closed his mouth, straightening his back while giving me a strange look. "Hang on. How did you know the dolls were facing the walls?"

"I saw them last night when I went looking for you. I figured Kinsley had been playing with them, so I moved one into her room."

Dennis's eyebrows inched higher, and suddenly he didn't look panicky at all. "You were in my room...looking for me?" He sounded rather intrigued by the idea.

I blushed. "I wanted to tell you how much I regret—"

An ear-splitting, chandelier-rattling scream shot through the house, loud enough to split it into two—Kinsley's scream.

Dennis and I shot up the stairs, taking them two at a time. Kinsley stood in the middle of the hallway, her face red and slick with tears.

"What happened?" Dennis demanded, scooping her into his arms.

"I couldn't find you! Or Hadley. I had a bad dream and when I went into your room, you weren't there. Hadley was gone too." Her cries became muffled as she buried her face into the blanket wrapped around his shoulders.

"It's okay, Kins. It was only a dream and you'll be okay. We didn't go far—just to the bottom of the stairs—but we're here now."

She lifted her face, frowning at him. "Why were you downstairs? It's the middle of the night."

Dennis wasn't ready with a quick reply, so I said simply, "We were talking."

"In the dark?" she asked.

"Yep," I squeaked.

She frowned. "About what?"

"Things," Dennis said.

"What *things*?"

I tensed every muscle in my face to keep from laughing at her rapid-fire questions, which reminded me so much of her uncle it was almost unbearable. Like Dennis, she expected the truth, and she expected it *now*.

Neither of us would give it to her, of course. I couldn't imagine the fallout that would ensue if we told her we'd been talking about ghosts and possessed dolls and all the late-night noises within my house of horrors.

Dennis started back towards Kinsley's room, patting her back reassuringly. "Uncle Dennis also had a bad dream, and Hadley was making me feel better," he said.

Kinsley peeked up over his shoulder and grinned at me, as though she were genuinely impressed. "Then maybe Hadley should put me back to sleep."

It took Dennis and me thirty minutes of whispered reassurances that there was not, in fact, a headless horseman galloping through the streets of Darlington Hills at night, as her fearmongering little camp friend had claimed. Perhaps there was the ghost of a homicide victim in the room across the hall, but neither of us mentioned that.

When her eyes finally fluttered shut, Dennis gave her a gentle kiss on the top of her head and signaled for me to follow him out of the room. Out in the hallway, he let out a long exhale. "Thanks for your help in there," he whispered. "She adores you, Hadley."

My heart swelled with warmth. "You have an incredible niece. I feel so blessed to have had the opportunity to get to know her."

Dennis's eyes shifted to his feet, and I sensed he wanted to say something more. Instead, he turned towards his bedroom with a simple, "Good night."

In one step, I was by his side. "You don't have to sleep in Irma's room. I can throw some sheets on the sofa in the upstairs TV room for you."

"It's okay, I'll be fine. It sounded pretty absurd when I heard myself talk about it."

"Okay, but there's one thing I *will* do first—" Before he could object, I strode in front of him, slipped inside his room, passing Razzy on her way out, and headed for the shelves. In two giant swoops, I gathered the dolls into my arms. "I can't believe you've been sleeping in my car." I shook my head, imagining him curled up on the stiff leather seats, his long legs twisted like a pretzel.

"I only did it for the massages," he said with a wry smile. "You're quite good at those, you know."

"But an entire week of cramming yourself into my tiny car?"

"It was better than no sleep at all. And I don't give up easily."

"Clearly." I bent over to retrieve a doll that had slipped from my grasp, then headed toward his door.

Dennis stopped me in the middle of his dimly lit room, the only light filtering in from the moon through the blinds, casting faint, silvery stripes across the floor. His hand lightly rested on my forearm, holding me back for just a second longer. "And," he continued, "I couldn't pass up this chance to spend time with you."

Carmella's words rolled through my wary mind once again. *He cares about you, Hadley.*

Dennis took a doll from my hands, grabbing it by the hair. "You can leave them in here; I'll be okay."

"It's no trouble at all. I'll just put them—" I whipped my head to the right and sneezed half a second later. "Whew! Kinsley's right. These dolls *are* dusty. Anyway, I'll shove them into my—"

I sneezed again, my eyes watering from the cloud of dust swirling around us. "—I'll shove them into the hallway closet," I finished saying with a laugh.

Dennis removed another doll from my arms, then set the pair on the rug next to his bed. "Downstairs, right before Kinsley blew out our eardrums, you were getting ready to tell me why you came in here last night." He raised an eyebrow, prompting me.

I let out a shaky sigh, suddenly feeling nervous about admitting why I'd searched for him. But if I didn't tell him now, when would I?

"I wanted to say I should have watched the movie with you. I was kicking myself for turning down the offer."

His smile was warm, his eyes shining with affection. He took the remaining dolls from my arms, set them down by the other two, then stood in front of me again. "I'd be lying if I said I wasn't disappointed."

I swallowed hard, fighting the lump swelling in my throat. I would not let myself get emotional. "It's been hard, so soon after Reid. And even though I've gotten over *him*, I haven't gotten over the fear of getting hurt again. But"—I held up a finger—"I decided last night, I refuse to let those worries control me. That's why I came to talk to you."

Dennis took my outstretched hand and held it against the soft blanket covering his chest. "I understand you feel that way, but I'm not here to hurt you. In fact, quite the opposite."

His tone, softer and more sincere than ever, made my breath hitch. This wasn't just Dennis flirting with me; this was real and heartfelt. He had slept in my tiny car all week and before that, endured sleepless nights in Irma's bed just so he could spend time with me until his house was deemed safe.

My heart instantly calmed down. I inhaled his scent, lingering from the shower, and felt his warmth spread through my cold hands.

Removing one of his hands from mine, he touched the bottom of my chin, guiding it upwards. "I don't want this to end when I go back home. I want more dinners together, more walks through the labyrinth...more of *you*—"

I pulled away from him. His eyes widened. He had heard it too. Slowly, we both turned our heads towards his bed, toward the wood floor that had just creaked.

The noise had been soft—not nearly as loud as when Dennis traipsed around his room—but it was distinct.

"See?" he whispered, his voice so quiet it was barely audible. "Noises." His gaze slid from the wall down to the pile of dolls next to the bed.

I nudged his arm playfully. "It wasn't the *dolls*. It's only the house settling. Probably." I glanced again toward the bed. "That's what you've been hearing?"

"Yes, among other noises. Sometimes they're in this room, sometimes in the hallway or downstairs late at night. The first time I heard them, I peeked into Kinsley's room and yours, thinking it was one of you. But both of you were asleep."

I shuddered at the thought of the old house alive with noises while I slept. "I must be a really heavy sleeper."

His eyes remained on the dolls. "You've seriously never heard them?"

I giggled. "They only thing I hear is you pacing around your room every night."

Dennis said nothing. He didn't need to. The fear on his face, the way he flinched at my words, said everything I didn't want to hear.

Dennis was not a pacer.

Something moved under his bed, making the wood groan again.

Dennis and I leapt back simultaneously, an electric thread of fear ripping through us. We stared at the gap under the bed, neither of us breathing.

"What the—" he started.

"Maybe it's Razzy?" I whispered, though I knew it couldn't be. The cat had run past me on my way into his room. Had we missed seeing her come back inside and run under the bed?

Unable to think of any other logical explanation, I got down on my hands and knees and called out, "Razzy? Here, kitty kitty."

"You see her?" Dennis was at my side, one hand on my back protectively.

I peered into the dark space beneath his bed. "I see...something. It's moving, I think. Razzy?"

The thing under the bed sneezed.

"*Not* a cat!" I hissed, scrambling backward as Dennis seized me under the arms, yanking me away from the bed. The sneeze had been too loud, too human, to belong to Razzy.

Dennis must have thought so too, because he ran towards the nightstand, yanked open the top drawer and snatched his pistol, then aimed for the gap under the bed.

"You have three seconds to come out or I'll start shooting," he hollered. Then, glancing at me, "Turn on the light, and don't let Kinsley come in if she wakes up."

There was a whimper under the bed, followed by more scuffling sounds. I flipped on the light and stood by the door, ready to intercept his niece if needed.

"Show me your hands first," he demanded. "Both hands. If I see anything else come out first, I'll put a bullet hole in it."

Two hands slid out from under the bed. Long, slender ones with bubblegum pink polish.

Not Irma's hands, praise be.

"Now, the rest of you," he ordered. Keeping one hand on the gun, he fished through the nightstand and yanked a pair of handcuffs from it. In one graceful swoop, he snapped them shut around the slender wrists.

"What are you *doing?*" came a woman's panicked voice.

Dennis grasped her arm and pulled until a wiry figure with disheveled blonde hair and wide, beautiful eyes emerged. She was perhaps in her late twenties, wearing a grubby oversized sweater and jeans that had seen better days. Her feet were bare and filthy, as if she'd been running outside without shoes.

Dennis dropped her arm and stepped back. "Who are you?" he demanded, keeping the gun steadily trained on her.

The woman looked up at him, her eyes widening in amazement as they roamed over his bare chest, exposed by the fallen blanket. "I'm Carrie," she said breathlessly. "I'm your biggest fan."

Dennis swore.

I stepped forward. "How long have you been here?"

The woman's eyes narrowed when she turned them on me. "Who are *you?*"

"I own this house, and you are trespassing."

She ignored me, swinging her pretty face back to Dennis. "I've watched your videos hundreds of times, and I've made all your recipes. I'm totally obsessed with your pineapple jalapeño salsa—"

"I don't care what you've cooked," Dennis snapped. "You broke into this house—"

"I didn't break in; I came in with a tour group. I have a ticket to prove it."

"*When* did you arrive?" His voice was loud but even, and if he was flustered, I couldn't tell.

"The same day you and the little girl did," she said sweetly.

Dennis clamped a hand over his mouth, stifling a sound that was somewhere between a moan and a growl.

I gawked at the woman. "You've been here for *two weeks?*"

"Yes, but not under the bed the whole time." She said it as though I'd asked the dumbest question ever. "And I'm not a criminal; I didn't steal anything, so don't accuse me of it."

"Except for bread," I pointed out. "We've been flying through loaves—milk, too. And toilet paper, I assume."

"Yes, but those things aren't expensive."

My eyes grew as I thought about everything of mine this woman might have used in the past two weeks. "Did you use my shower? My towels? My toiletries?" I thought I might lose my dinner, then and there.

She scrunched up her nose. "Ew, no way. I used his."

Dennis paled. "You're going to jail." He turned to me. "Do you have your phone? Mine's downstairs."

I removed my phone from my robe's pocket, entered the passcode, and tossed it to him. Carrie gawked as it flew across the room.

"You're calling the cops on me?" she shrieked.

"I am a cop."

"He's a detective," I clarified.

"But, but...you're really with the *police?*" She was utterly dumbfounded.

He smirked. "That's what I said. And you are a lousy stalker if you don't know that by now."

"I'm not a stalker; I'm in love with you! Don't you want to get to know each other before you make that call?"

"No," he grunted.

"Well, if you really are with the police, why aren't *you* taking me to jail?" she challenged.

Dennis was busy talking to whomever he'd called, so I stepped towards her. "He drives an unmarked car without a cage, so you won't get to ride with him to jail. Too bad for you," I taunted.

"They're on their way," he announced, crossing the room and handing me my phone. "Could you stay here with Kins while I follow them to the station?" he whispered. "I want to question this lunatic."

"Of course," I said, as he pulled Carrie to her feet and escorted her down the stairs.

I stayed on the top step, not wanting to stray too far from Kinsley. Within minutes, the familiar swirl of red and blue police lights streamed through the front windows, and a thunderous knock sounded at the door.

Before Dennis opened it, I called out to Carrie, "Just so you know, you're not his number one fan. *I* am."

CHAPTER TWENTY-FIVE

"So…" Dennis greeted me the moment I walked into the kitchen Monday morning. "I might not tell my sister about you-know-what." Holding a finger to his lips, he glanced at Kinsley, who was busy stirring a bowl of batter at the kitchen island.

"Tell her about what?" I asked with mock ignorance, joining him next to the stove, where he was drizzling oil on my griddle pan. "About Kinsley's two-week streak of late bedtimes? Or her new chicken nugget-only diet?"

His eyebrows hung low over his eyes in mock anger. "Very funny."

"Or perhaps you're talking about the crazy stalker woman who hung out under your bed for two weeks," I whispered.

Dennis grunted. "She was literally right under my nose." He took a sip of coffee, shaking his head.

"Don't feel bad; she was an expert in her field. A stalking guru, of sorts."

"Chief Mansfield doesn't see it like that. He could not comprehend how it took me two weeks to notice a woman sleeping two feet below me. You wouldn't imagine the jokes going around the station."

It had been bad enough when Officer Stevens and Akari responded to Dennis's call last night, both doubling over at the sight of his sneakers and reindeer boxer shorts ensemble.

"Did you tell Chief Mansfield you thought the noises were from…a ghost?" I whispered.

Dennis gave me a look. "No way. I would never, *ever* hear the end of it." He then chuckled, his eyes crinkly with amusement.

At least he could laugh about it. His sense of humor was one of the many things I loved about him.

Loved?

The word slipped into my mind as easily as a breeze through an open window, and with it came a shiver of terrifying, exhilarating realization. My feelings for him extended beyond the typical bounds of friendship. And though Dennis's stalker had claimed she hadn't taken anything of value, she had robbed me of something far more important than milk or slices of bread. She'd stolen my opportunity for a kiss with Dennis. He would leave for the hotel today, and I might not get another opportunity like the one I'd had last night.

"I'm ready for the chocolate chips," Kinsley announced.

"Okay, kiddo, coming right up." Dennis tore the corner off a bag of chocolate morsels, then poured a heap into her bowl. "These will be the best pancakes ever."

"I'll be sure to give you a five-star rating," I promised Kinsley, which made her erupt into a fit of giggles.

Of the three of us, she was the only one who looked more than half-awake. I'd only gotten four hours of sleep, and I guessed Dennis got about half as much, since his bedroom door didn't open until sometime after five o'clock.

But we were all up before seven, since we both had a hectic day in front of us. He had to get himself and Kinsley packed and ready so they could pick up their family from the airport at noon. I needed to finish setting up for the brunch today, and then tonight, I had my tenth and final cooking class.

219

Dennis lifted the bowl from the kitchen island and carried it over to the stove, where he poured several large dollops of batter onto the skillet.

I leaned my elbows against the counter, looking up at him. "How'd it go when you questioned Carrie last night?"

"She confessed to stalking me—and even admitted to breaking into my house."

My heart sank a little. This really was his last day here. Some small part of me had hoped it would still be too dangerous for him to return home after his family returned to Texas.

"That's great news!" I said, as enthusiastically as possible. "I guess this means your family won't have to stay at a hotel for Christmas."

Dennis was silent for a moment, mindlessly poking the corner of a spatula through the tiny bubbles that appeared at the top of the batter. "I'm not convinced it's safe to go home yet. It's strange—Carrie confessed to breaking into my bathroom window and looking through all the drawers in my house, but she swears she didn't mail the threatening letter."

I pressed my lips together, considering. "Either she's lying, or someone else mailed the letter."

"Right. And I didn't get the sense she's lying."

"Are you still thinking it could be the suspects involved in your money laundering case?"

He slid the spatula under the pancakes and flipped them over, revealing perfect golden edges. "Considering the way the letter was worded, yes I do. It sounded personal, like the sender had every intent on carrying through with their threat."

My stomach twisted at the idea of someone hurting him. "What did the note say?"

With swift, practiced motions, Dennis gathered the pancakes from the skillet and slid them onto a waiting plate, then added more batter to the skillet. He set down his coffee mug and spatula, and removed his phone from his pocket, sighing heavily as he tapped the screen.

With a hushed voice, he turned the screen towards me and said, "This is the work of a true madman. Most criminals wouldn't even think about threatening someone in law enforcement."

I let out a shaky breath as I examined his photo of the threat. The sender had used a bold, black font and typed everything in capital letters.

"To Detective Dennis Appley," I read with a shaky voice. "I have not been pleased with your actions of late. Your blindness to the truth will cost you dearly if you continue your path forward. Until you remedy your actions, you will not be safe. I know where you live, and I've been watching you through your windows. Consider yourself warned. P.S.: You need to fix your wooden horse."

I narrowed my eyes, focusing intently on that last sentence. "What is that supposed to mean? 'Fix your wooden horse'? Is that a metaphor?"

"No, it's proof that whoever wrote this really had been looking through my windows. I have a horse figurine—a wooden one—on an end table in my family room, and it's missing a leg. I accidentally broke it a couple of months ago and haven't had time to fix it."

I read the note again and again, my eyes hitching on the first sentence. "'—your actions *of late.*' It sounds so...so..." I snatched the phone from Dennis and moved my fingers against the screen to zoom in on the photo, scrolling all the way to the bottom of the note.

My blood turned to fire as my heart exploded with fury.

"I know who sent the threat."

I switched off the stove with a swift flick of my wrist. "Grab a pancake for the road, if you'd like. There's somewhere we need to go."

It wasn't until after we dropped off Kinsley at camp—only for a few hours, Dennis had promised her—that Dennis asked, "You really think you know who threatened me?"

"Yes." I turned into a parking spot next to Detective Sanders's unmarked vehicle.

Dennis eyed his partner's car, drawing his brows together. "I don't understand—you want to share your theory with Sanders and me at the same time? Why not tell me first, and then I'll brief him on it?"

"Let's go." I threw open the door of my car, tossing the keys into my bag as I marched towards Aunt Deb's leasing office.

Dennis jogged after me. Aunt Deb was seated behind her desk while Detective Sanders perched on its edge. They stopped talking the moment we entered.

Before I could open my mouth, Aunt Deb shot to her feet and cried out, "Oh Hadley, I can't believe what happened last night! That crazy, crazy woman."

"I'm not here to talk about the stalker," I huffed. "I want to know—"

"Would you like a cup of coffee, hon? Dennis, how about you? What a week you two have had! And how's your foot, Hadley? Michael said you might have injured it?"

I froze. How did Michael know? Carmella was the only one I'd told, and I was positive she hadn't blabbed to him about it. Dennis looked at me, his eyebrows raised in silent question.

"It's fine," I said.

Aunt Deb laughed. "Michael will be home soon; you'll have to ask him where he got that story from. Apparently a friend of his —well, you know Zach from the Tea Bone Café he used to work at—he saw you limping down Orchard Road—

"My foot is fine," I snapped. "What I want to know is why you threatened Dennis."

Dennis let out a strange laugh. "You think your *aunt—*"

"I don't think it; I *know* it. She's been up to no good *'as of late'*," I said.

He frowned. "As of late?"

"Those are her words, not mine. They're from the letter she mailed you. I knew it as soon as I read it because she's the only person I know who talks like that. And the only person who would threaten a police officer."

Aunt Deb stool tall. "I would never!" she declared, a twitch of a smile playing on the side of her mouth.

I snatched a stack of papers from her desk and held up the top sheet. "See the funny-looking smudge in the lower right corner?" I slammed it onto the table and grabbed the next one in the pile. "Another funny-looking smudge in the lower right corner." I held up another one and then another, finally tossing the rest of the pile onto the desk. "Your printer is ancient. It has printed that tiny smudge for as long as I can remember. Little things like that drive me insane, though not as much as an aunt who finds amusement in torturing my friends. Do you have any idea how much money Dennis would have wasted on a hotel room if I hadn't invited him to stay?"

"Oh, but I knew you would," she replied, her sly smile widening.

Roy looked incredulous. "Why would you threaten him?"

She shrugged. "I thought Hadley and Dennis would enjoy getting to know each other better."

Roy smiled, then laughed, then gripped the edge of the desk as he howled. "Woman, you sure do stir up a lot of trouble, don't you?"

Aunt Deb giggled. "You should have seen me in high school!"

Dennis just stared at them, probably wondering who was

crazier—my aunt, or his partner, who had asked for her hand in marriage.

Aunt Deb turned to Dennis. "I would have fessed up sooner, but then Roy told me someone broke into your home. So, then I figured it wasn't safe for you and sweet Kinsley to stay there anyway."

"How did you know Dennis's horse was broken? Did you look through his windows?"

Dennis whipped his head toward my aunt, his entire body stiffening.

Aunt Deb shrugged. "I brought some homemade cookies to his house after you food poisoned him. He was nice enough to offer me a cup of coffee, and we chatted for at least an hour on his sofa. I had to gather intel about his house to make this work; to make it look like the threat was genuine."

Dennis flinched. "Wait. This note was pre-meditated?"

"I don't really care for that word," she said. "Pre-meditated sounds too criminal. I'd say it was pre-*designed*, and all for a very good reason."

"You know what this is? It's—" Dennis pressed his lips together and worked his jaw furiously. "Never mind. I'm leaving before I say something that isn't very nice."

I piped up, "*I'll* tell you what this is, if he won't. It's too much. *Too much*, Aunt Deb. You went too far this time. Dennis was not comfortable at my house, not for a single minute. But he stayed there anyway because it was his best option." I bent over and snatched my Prince Charming nutcracker from where he stood and tucked him under my arm. "Let's go, Dennis."

As I turned toward the door, Michael came through it, followed by Akari. Dennis grunted, then exchanged awkward nods with them.

Michael's eyes dropped to my feet, and he frowned. "How's your foot? I ran into Zach yesterday and he said you were hobbling down Orchard Road last week before North Pole Night. Was everything okay?"

"It-it was fine," I stammered.

Dennis looked at me. "Before North Pole Night? I thought I noticed you limping."

"Zach said you were screaming," Michael said, grinning like it was the craziest thing he'd ever heard. "But I told him I saw you two days ago when you picked up Kinsley and you were just fine."

I kept my eyes on Michael, but I felt the weight of Dennis's gaze on me, his mind likely racing with questions.

"Running down the street? Screaming?" Something in Dennis's voice told me he was piecing together the fragments of the story I wasn't ready for him to see.

I cleared my throat, searching for an explanation. None came.

"I need to go." I strode past Michael and Akari. I couldn't have this conversation with Dennis in front of everyone, especially Aunt Deb, who I couldn't even look at. "I need to go to the barn. Need to finish decorating—"

Dennis was right behind me as I pushed through the door into the crisp morning air. "What was that about? Was it true?"

I remained silent.

"Tell me what happened, Hadley," he insisted. "I don't like being kept in the dark, especially when it concerns you."

I stopped then, the cold bite of the winter air sharp in my lungs. Dennis wouldn't let this go—not now, not after what he'd heard.

"I just..." My voice trailed off as I swallowed back the fear that had gripped me that night. "I...got cut. On my ankle," I said, motioning to it. "Right after I texted you about the playground and slides, something cut me. But it's not a big deal; it was probably nothing more than a cat scratch or branch."

"People don't run screaming from branches." Dennis knelt and lifted the frayed hem of my jeans, but I moved my leg away.

"Let me see," he insisted, reaching out with a careful hand to pull it closer. He peeled back the corner of my bandage and flinched at what he saw. He looked up at me. "This isn't a cat scratch."

"A branch, then."

He stood, shaking his head. "If you really thought that, you would've told me Saturday night."

I shifted my weight, avoiding his gaze. If only I'd told him on our way home from North Pole Night, or the next day or the next. "Something...or maybe someone, came out from under the hedges by the park on Orchard Road and cut me. I ran back to my car and drove to Carmella's to patch it up."

Dennis's face was red, his jaw tight as he ran his fingers through his hair. "You thought someone *slashed your ankle*, and you didn't think it was worth mentioning? What if it was the same person who slipped the note into your container?"

"I reassured myself it was just a cat or sharp branch, and... well, I figured you'd assume the worst and ditch our plans to go investigate."

"Yeah, well, I probably would have, because that's my *job*. Just like it's your job to tell me if someone slices your leg!"

I stepped back, bristling at the harshness of his tone. "As I said, it could have been a branch—"

"Did you see anyone? Hear anything?"

I turned away from him, my eyes stinging. "Something ran off in the opposite direction, towards the playground. I didn't see what it was."

Dennis huffed out a laugh. "I really can't believe you didn't tell me about this—and all because you didn't want to miss out on some corn dogs at North Pole Night. Wow."

Corn dogs! I wanted to shout. *It wasn't corn dogs I wanted that night; it was* you.

"You may have hindered my investigation, Hadley. How could you be so reckless? And selfish—just like..." His gaze jerked over towards the leasing office. *Just like your aunt*, is what he was thinking.

Through my tear-blurred vision, I saw a red SUV pull into the parking spot next to mine. *Gayle.*

I turned away from the car, wishing I had a pair of sunglasses to hide my wet eyes. "Less than an hour ago, you said you don't want to tell your sister about the stalker who camped out under your bed, right across the hall from Kinsley. How is what I did any worse?"

Gayle's car door closed, followed by the dainty clipping sound of her heels. I held up a hand to Dennis, signaling him to pause our conversation. Gayle was the last person I wanted to overhear us.

"Good morning, Hadley. Officer Appley," she said, as she strolled by us, her enormous sunglasses hiding whatever sneer lay behind them.

"*Detective* Appley," I corrected.

Gayle turned slowly, then sauntered toward us. She peered at me over the top of her sunglasses, smirking when her gaze landed on the Prince Charming Nutcracker tucked under my arm. "I understand you've been busy lately," she said to me. "I had a lovely chat with Madame Balleroy yesterday evening when I dined at her restaurant. She explained why she hired you to decorate for this year's event." Gayle laughed quietly through her nose. "Though I suppose 'hired' isn't the right word, is it?"

I closed my eyes with a grunt. Every interaction with Gayle felt like a battle, her words sharp and hostile. Her words were like punches, my ego her punching bag.

But I gave an equally haughty laugh, deciding to pretend her insult hadn't stung. I wouldn't give her the satisfaction of it. "I've certainly never bartered my design services for cooking classes before. But there's a first time for everything." If Gayle hadn't been a customer of Aunt Deb's, my response wouldn't have been so diplomatic.

"Though technically, it was your aunt who bartered on your behalf."

I smiled sweetly. "Technically."

"And your boyfriend, of course."

"Boyfriend?" I shook my head. "Reid and I broke up last—"

"Come on, Hadley," Dennis urged. He placed a hand on my back and guided me towards the car. "We need to go. Busy day ahead."

I took a few more steps before stopping abruptly and turning to face Gayle. "What makes you think Reid was involved in negotiating with Madame Balleroy?" I asked.

A small smile formed on one side of her mouth. "I wasn't talking about Reid. Everyone knows how *that* turned out. I'm referring to Detective Appley, of course."

I blinked. "Dennis? He didn't have anything to do with it."

"Oh, yes he did," she chirped. "Your decorating services were an added throw-in to the deal, although she was far more interested in the partnership videos with him." She gestured gracefully towards Dennis, who stood there motionless. "And speaking of that, Detective, congratulations on the partnership. I'm sure it's a fantastic opportunity for both you and Madame Balleroy. To have such a renowned chef working alongside you! Your subscribers will skyrocket, I'm sure."

"It's not a partnership," he said cooly. "It's only three videos, which I agreed—"

"You *what*?" I gaped at him.

"Ooh, look at the time, my dears," Gayle cooed as she backed away from us. "I'd stay and chat, but I need to speak with Deb about renting a third storage unit. Merry Christmas and—"

I spun around before she finished talking and marched toward my car. Dennis caught my hand, but I snatched it away. "You conspired with my aunt to send me to cooking school? Because I'm that horrible of a cook? Or because you'll get more subscribers out of the deal?"

"That's not why I did it. It was your aunt who came up with the idea. She'd already worked out a deal with Madame Balleroy, and she just needed my approval. Your aunt said it was the only way she could cover the cost of your tuition."

His words gutted me. "Am I not allowed to make a mistake? Yes, I messed up and didn't cook the stuffing long enough. Yes, we were all miserable the next day. But do you have *any idea* how much thought I put into that dinner? How excited I was to host my first big holiday meal? How much time and money I spent preparing for it, or how many times I went to the store because I'd forgotten this or that ingredient?"

"Hadley, please. Please just listen—"

"The only reason I went to those classes was because I felt terrible for what I'd done. I thought I would somehow redeem myself." Laughing at my stupidity, I opened my bag and looked for my keys, but it was hard to see through the tears clouding my vision.

"We haven't filmed the videos yet; I'm holding off until I wrap up the homicide investigations. Would you want to join us?"

"You know, I'm not shocked my aunt approached you with the behind-my-back negotiation, but I'm torn up that you went along with it and didn't tell me."

Dennis winced. "We didn't want you to feel bad about what I was contributing. Your aunt said you'd refuse to take the classes if you knew I was pitching in. I thought I was doing something nice for you, that you would *want* to take the classes."

"Is that why Aunt Deb went to your house with cookies—so the two of you could talk about the deal?"

He hesitated for a moment before nodding. "Yes. She came over to ask for my help."

I narrowed my eyes at him. "How can I trust anything you say? For all I know, you helped plan the threatening letter scheme so you could stay with me and monitor my progress in the kitchen, giving me your pro tips and cute little herb-cutting lessons."

"That's ridiculous. We wouldn't have stayed there if we didn't have to."

A sob finally escaped, and a slew of tears along with it. "Of course you wouldn't have. No one ever does." I thrust my hand deep into my bag, fishing desperately for my keys.

Dennis took a step closer, his hand outstretched as though he wanted me to take it. "I didn't mean it like that."

My fingers closed around my keys, and I pushed the button to unlock my car, then ran to the driver's side. "To think I almost kissed you last night! I'll have to thank your stalker for saving me from that mistake."

CHAPTER TWENTY-SIX

I dawdled as much as a dawdler can dawdle—and then some.

An enormous chafing dish lay before me on the prep table in the cooking school's kitchen, filled with my fresh-from-the-oven dish for Christmas Eve brunch guests, who were already sitting at their tables, talking with friends and family while waiting for the buffet to open.

Among those seated inside the barn were Aunt Deb and Dennis, both of whom had called and texted me repeatedly yesterday. Aunt Deb had texted me a heartfelt apology of epic length, admitting her inappropriate interference and begging me to come to today's brunch and Christmas dinner at her house tomorrow.

Dennis's texts hadn't been so wordy, with his shortest one only two words—"I'm sorry"—and his longest one topping out at a whopping five words: "I think we're even now."

I'd ignored them all—every text, call, and voicemail. The only reason I'd decided to attend the brunch was to say goodbye to Kinsley before she flew back to Texas tomorrow, and because I'd invited Carmella and Vincent and would feel horribly rude if I didn't show up.

I wasn't looking forward to seeing Dennis or my aunt. I intended to arrange the breadcrumbs on top of my dish, crumb by tiny crumb, for as long as I could get away with it.

The moment Madame Balleroy breezed into the kitchen and scowled when she saw me still fiddling with my dish, I knew I'd have to go out there and face them.

"Why haven't you finished?" she demanded. "You've had plenty of time." She wasn't wrong. I'd arrived at seven o'clock and had been working on my dish for the past four hours. Making her way towards me, her eyes grew larger when they landed on my culinary masterpiece. "I specifically told you not to use frozen chicken nuggets. I said *hand-breaded*, Hadley. Did you really think you could fool me? They're shaped like dinosaurs!"

"I've never made nuggets from scratch, and I've been too busy lately to learn how." I leveled my eyes at her dark brown ones. "Look around inside your barn. At the lights, the centerpieces, the enchanted forest photo backdrop. *That* is my passion. Not cooking."

Madame Balleroy's expression softened a little. "Well, you did an amazing job with the decorations. My barn has never looked this charming. I've received countless compliments on it already today. I'd like to hire you for next year's brunch, if you're available."

I smiled as I imagined Gayle's face when she heard the news. "I'd be happy to help. As long as it's not in exchange for more cooking classes."

"Heaven's no. I believe I've done all that I can for you." She kept her eyes on the golden-brown dinosaurs topping my dish, and I could have sworn I heard her growl. "Please tell me you didn't heat those things in the microwave."

"I used the oven."

She didn't look at all relieved, but she nodded anyway. "Please head to the barn now. My kitchen crew will transport your casserole to the buffet table. Did you write the name of your dish on the placard I gave you?"

I fished it out from under the chafing dish and held it up. With the help of Google Translate, I'd written it in French and then provided the English translation below.

Madame Balleroy read the card, then closed her eyes. Taking that as my cue to leave, I slipped out of the kitchen before she could say anything.

Sounds of lively chatter grew as I neared the cabernet-colored barn. I stepped inside and grinned at what I saw. The place had looked stunning last night when I'd finished decorating it, but this morning, with all the beautiful smiling faces and jubilant Christmas music filling the area, it was nothing short of magical.

I headed for my table on the far right side of the barn, waving to familiar faces as I passed by. My empty chair came into view, and my smile vanished. It was between Dennis and Carmella, and directly across the large round table from Aunt Deb.

A middle-aged woman with shoulder-length, sandy-blonde hair rose from her seat on the other side of Dennis and approached me with outstretched arms. "You must be Hadley! We've heard so much about you, and I'm thrilled to finally meet you. I'm Dennis's mom, Mindy, and that's my husband, Dale."

I would have guessed Mindy and Dale were Dennis's parents, even if she hadn't introduced them as such. Mindy shared Dennis's large, expressive blue eyes, and his dad was clearly the one responsible for Dennis's dimpled smile.

Dennis stood to greet me, giving me a quick kiss on the cheek before enthusiastically introducing me to his sister, Kate, and brother-in-law, Nicholas, while pretending like nothing was wrong—like he hadn't gone behind my back and betrayed me for his own selfish motives...like he wasn't angry with me for not telling him about my ankle.

"I'm sorry I'm late," I told the group. "I was finishing my dish for the cooking competition. It's for students of Madame

Balleroy's cooking school, and if I had to guess, I'd say it's intended to drum up more interest in her classes." I gestured toward the small table on the other side of the barn, completely separated from the main buffet table that held Madame Balleroy's exquisite French dishes. An aproned waiter was placing my chafing dish next to those of my classmates.

"Which one's yours?" asked Dennis's dad. "I'll be sure to vote for it."

"Thanks! It's the one on the very end. My dish is called 'Je ne mange que des nuggets de poulet.'"

"Ooh, it sounds fancy," Kate said.

Vincent snorted, coughing on the iced tea he'd just sipped.

I laughed with him. "Ah, so you speak French."

"And clearly, you don't," he sputtered. "Your accent is terrible."

"Google translated it for me," I explained, then turned to the others. "It's French for, 'I only eat chicken nuggets.'"

"What's in it?" Vincent asked.

"It's a layered casserole with a base of crispy tater tots, a layer of macaroni and cheese, all crowned with chicken nuggets and melted cheese." I slid my eyes over to Kinsley and grinned. "There are no green things in my dish, as promised."

"Green things?" Carmella asked.

"Vegetables," Kinsley's parents replied in unison.

The Christmas music stopped. Madame Balleroy's sophisticated voice flowed through the speakers. "Good morning!" she sang, pausing for the chatter to die down. She stood on the small stage at the front of the barn next to Grand-mère, both wearing their standard white chef coat attire, their hair pulled back into tidy chignons.

Madame Balleroy continued, "My grandmother, Zelia Balleroy, known to many of us as Grand-mère, joins me this morning to thank all of you for attending this year's Christmas Eve brunch. We're delighted to see so many returning guests, as well as some new faces in the crowd. As I'm sure you've heard, this has been a difficult month for my team, and I'd like to dedicate today's brunch to the memory of Seth O'Boyle and Jared Bernardi—two of my esteemed colleagues who were like family to me and everyone else at the restaurant."

As she spoke, I glanced at Dennis. He was tracking Madame Balleroy as she walked from one side of the stage to the other, his eyes narrowing at her poignant remarks about Seth and Jared.

Madame Balleroy returned to the center of the stage. "Before we open the buffet, I'd like to direct your attention to the table in the back, where you'll find dishes prepared exclusively by students enrolled in my December cooking classes. Please sample their creations, then vote for your favorite dish using the slips of paper on your table. When you're done, place it in the cherry-wood box next to my students' dishes. We will announce our winner at noon." Madame Balleroy invited all those eager to enhance their cooking skills to sign up for her January session, then announced that the buffet tables were open.

What I'd thought would be a painfully awkward meal turned out to be unexpectedly enjoyable. I talked with Carmella and Vincent most of the time, successfully avoiding any conversation with Aunt Deb or Dennis. The only time I looked in his general direction was when his mom asked about the labyrinth in my backyard, or when Kinsley told me to watch her dinosaur nuggets climb the mountain of fruit piled on her plate.

The food from Madame Balleroy's kitchen was exquisite—eggs Benedict, cheese soufflé, coq au vin, chocolate crepes—and I almost moaned while trying the quiche au fromage. My classmates' dishes were also amazing, especially Mitzy's baklava cheesecake, with its layers of flaky phyllo dough crust and creamy filling.

Everyone at the table sampled my chicken nugget dish, politely oohing and ahhing over it, but Kinsley's reaction was the only one I suspected to be completely genuine. Michael's too, since he'd gone back for seconds.

At twelve-thirty, Madame Balleroy's voice boomed through the speakers once again, when she announced that voting would close in five minutes.

Kate picked up the pile of red slips from the center of the table, took one, then instructed everyone to write my name on it. Like Dennis, she had a big personality and an even louder voice— one she no doubt used to boss around her little brother while growing up.

We passed a pair of pencils around the table, and just as Detective Sanders was getting ready to write down his vote, he stopped and glanced down at his phone, reading something that had just popped up on the screen. Dennis did the same, then exchanged poker-faced glances with Sanders, who then resumed writing on the piece of paper.

"Can I talk to you for a minute?" Dennis's whispered words were warm against my face. He gestured to a vacant spot near the haystacks. "Privately." When I didn't agree immediately, he added, "It's about Natasha."

I stood and headed for the hay without waiting for him.

He joined me a moment later, glancing around as though looking for any eavesdroppers. "After you cast doubt on the evidence we had against Natasha, I called Sanders—" he paused long enough for his eyes to travel down and then back up my body. "You look amazing today, by the way. Stunning, actually, in that red dress—"

I flipped up a hand. "You don't need to flatter me. You were saying?"

"Oh, right. I told Sanders everything you observed, so he contacted a forensic document examiner and asked her to analyze the handwritten address found in Natasha's oven mitt along with confirmed samples of her writing—even though our analysis software had confirmed a match. Well, our expert just texted; she does not believe Natasha wrote the address."

I gasped. "Natasha's off the hook?"

"Not entirely," he said, lowering his voice even more. "But we no longer have sufficient evidence to keep her detained."

"She's going home for Christmas!" I squealed loud enough to turn a few nearby heads. "This Christmas just got a whole lot merrier." The thought of Natasha spending the holiday with her family made my face split into a smile. "But how was someone able to mimic Natasha's handwriting enough to trick your software?"

"Our expert suspects someone used an app to scan and digitize Natasha's handwriting, then printed out the address, put a sheet of paper over it, and traced it. Notebook paper is thin, so it wouldn't have been too hard to see through it if the lighting was right."

I considered this. "Then it must have been someone with access to something Natasha wrote."

"Which could be just about anyone."

"Does this mean you're back to square one?"

"Close to it, if you ask me."

"That's because you're a pessimist—" I stopped as my eyes fell on Vincent, whose face was lit up like a kid at Christmas as he talked to Carmella. She appeared every bit as engaged in the conversation, nodding and laughing as he spoke. The two of them seemed to inhabit a world of their own, and I was suddenly hesitant to return to the table and distract them from each other. I needed to talk to Dennis a little longer.

"There's something else I need to tell you." With a heavy sigh, he leaned a shoulder against the haystack.

"I don't want to talk about it. You teamed up with my aunt and plotted against me, all for your own personal gain."

Dennis rubbed the back of his neck, frowning. "Wow, it sounds terrible when you put it that way. But that's not why I went along with it. I wanted—"

"I said I don't want to talk about it."

He titled his head as he studied my face. "You're one of the kindest people I know, Hadley. I would've thought you'd be slightly more forgiving."

I blinked. What could I possibly say to *that*?

"Anyway," he went on, "that's not what I wanted to talk about...not here, at least. Yesterday, after you drove off and left me at your aunt's house, Sanders and I went to the playground on Orchard Road and looked around. I stood on the sidewalk near the hedges you described. Want to know what I found?"

"A cat, I hope? An angry, feral one that swats at innocent people passing by?"

He folded his arms. "Not a cat. But there was a broken branch jutting out from the bush's undergrowth. It was about ankle-high, sharp enough to slice through skin, and it was stained with what appeared to be dried blood."

"No way. Seriously?" I narrowed my eyes at him, unsure if he was just teasing me.

"It appears as though you were assaulted by a vicious, blood-thirsty branch. We arrested it immediately, and I will personally ensure it is punished to the fullest extent of the law."

"But what about the glint of light I saw? And the thing that ran off when I yelped?"

He shrugged. "It had rained a lot that day, so it could have just been the streetlights reflecting off the wet leaves. And there were signs of raccoons in the area, so you likely spooked one of them."

I slumped back against the haystack, feeling an instant, over-whelming sense of relief. "The streets will be safer now that the branch is behind bars," I said, playing along with his charade. Turning to face him, I looked into his steady gaze as the playful-ness faded from his features.

"I know you don't want to talk about my video deal with Madame Balleroy, but let me just say that I should have told you. She is desperate for fame, and I—"

The Christmas music cut out, replaced once again by Madame Balleroy's voice.

"I'd like all students in my December cooking class to come to the stage, please," she said. "It is time to announce the winner of our favorite dish competition."

"You'd better get going," Dennis said with a smile. "Good luck."

I turned, and his hand brushed against my arm. But I strolled towards the stage, leaving too many words left unsaid. Guilt was already nipping at me—for not being more forgiving and for not apologizing to him for withholding information about my ankle.

There were so many thoughts and feelings tangled up inside me, but now wasn't the time to sort through them. I'd have plenty of time this afternoon, tonight…tomorrow on Christmas, when I was alone in my quiet house.

I stood between Hal and Eileen, listening as Madame Balleroy raved about her 'remarkably talented' students, and how our once-clumsy hands, so unsure and tentative, now moved with newfound grace, as though guided by an unseen spirit of culinary wisdom.

Looking into the crowd, I wondered if anyone who had eaten my chicken nugget dish was calling bluff on Madame Balleroy's exaggerated praise.

But she seemed to have no qualms about overstating our cooking abilities. Like Dennis had said, she was desperate for fame.

Desperate. It was a good word to describe Madame Balleroy the day she yelled at Jared in the barn after Chloe postponed the news article about the restaurant and cooking school. Not only that, but Natasha had hinted at Madame Balleroy's envy towards Seth's success, revealing that she felt overshadowed by his rising fame.

Just *how* desperate for fame was Madame Balleroy?

Enough to kill Seth?

Enough to murder Jared for failing to secure enough media attention?

With swan-like grace, Madame Balleroy held up a folded, white chef coat wrapped in a wispy tulle bow. "I am honored to present this year's Junior Chef Award to a student who created a dish that not only defied convention but also left everyone with a taste of something truly extraordinary. This dish is a symphony of ingredients and a celebration of flavor."

I glanced over at Mitzy, whose lips were already trembling with a smile. She knew her dish was the best. Even I would have voted for her if Kinsley hadn't been standing over my shoulder when I filled in my ballot.

"Please join me in congratulating Hadley Sutton for her creative, if not unconventional, chicken nugget dish, 'Je ne mange que des nuggets de poulet.'"

Instantly, the barn filled with high-pitched screaming as the entire under-twelve crowd celebrated. Kinsley stood on top of her chair, jumping up and down as the adults at our table tried to usher her down.

"Are you sure?" I heard myself saying as I walked towards Madame Balleroy at the front of the stage. She untied the bow and held out the chef coat.

"Put it on," she whispered.

I did just that and smiled broadly at the sea of people applauding me.

Maybe I'd won because every child in attendance voted for my dish while the adults' votes were split between the other dishes. Or maybe Aunt Deb had found a way to rig the voting. I wouldn't put it past her.

Either way, a win was a win, and I hadn't had a lot of those lately—especially in the kitchen.

I'd take it.

CHAPTER TWENTY-SEVEN

My classmates and I stood on the stage, surrounded by a dazzling display of camera flashes. My cheeks were sore from smiling so much, but my smile never wavered. Achy cheeks were totally worth this moment of culinary glory.

Madame Balleroy spoke into the microphone again, announcing that coffee service would continue for another hour. "Please feel free to stay and visit with family; there's no need to rush home. And if you haven't already, be sure to snap some photos in front of our enchanted forest photo backdrop. It's a keepsake worth waiting in line for."

Stepping down from the stage, I headed for my table, only to be intercepted by three women in their mid-to-late thirties who said they were curious about the cooking classes. I shared the high points of my experience before realizing they were more interested in the gossip surrounding the two homicides than the culinary skills I had honed.

For the next twenty minutes, I visited with Dennis's family about everything from the wildebeest migration they'd witnessed in Africa, to a story about the time Dennis snuck out his window on Christmas Eve and climbed on their roof so he could watch

Santa land on the roof, to my retelling of how I reacted when Dennis informed me I'd inherited an enormous estate earlier this year.

I told them the fairytale version of the story, omitting the fact that Dennis had been dangling his handcuffs in front of me, ready to use them if I said anything to incriminate myself.

Now, as Dennis's family rose to leave, the tiniest of lumps swelled within my throat. It would be a long time before I saw sweet little Kinsley—*if* I ever did. And amid my wild dash to leave my house early this morning, I'd forgotten to bring her Christmas gift. It was something I'd found last week that I knew would make her smile.

Kinsley bounded from one chair to the next until she reached me, tossing her arms around my neck and squeezing. "I get to feed Sadie when we get back to Uncle Dennis's!" she said by way of farewell.

"Sadie is one lucky goat!" I replied with a laugh as I mussed her disheveled tangle of curls. "Thanks for inspiring my award-winning dish. I wouldn't have won without you."

She leapt from the chair, weaving in and out of the adults at our table who were busy exchanging farewell hugs. Except for Carmella and Vincent, who still sat at the table, lost in their own little world.

I followed Dennis and his family out of the barn, ready to gather my things from the cooking school and go home. When they turned left down the path toward the parking lot, I waved again before heading in the opposite direction, toward the kitchen's back door.

Peals of high-pitched laughter drifted on the breeze, growing louder with each step towards the herb forest. The giggles were accompanied by a man's deep, whisper-smooth voice, and though I couldn't make out what he was saying, I had a pretty good guess at what they were doing.

Several steps later, I caught glimpses of the couple through small openings in the foliage, confirming my suspicions. They were locked in a passionate embrace, with their arms wrapped around each other tightly as they kissed.

It wasn't until they came up for air that I spotted Hal's lipstick-streaked face gazing broadly at the woman standing across from him. It took three more steps before the woman came into full view.

I nearly stumbled over my own two feet. It was Madame Balleroy, her once impeccably tidy chignon now a wild halo of black and silver curls around her flushed face.

I buried my face in the crook of my elbow to muffle the howling laughter flowing from my mouth. Hal and Madame Balleroy? *Seriously?* The two of them couldn't have been more different if they were from separate planets. Hal seemed like the kind of man who took everything as it came, with a shrug and a grin, and Madame Balleroy was precision and order personified.

Just last week, she had seemed flustered when she'd scolded him in the kitchen for calling her restaurant a joint. I'd assumed Hal had offended her, but now I realized it was simply his presence that made her blush. And the night Seth was murdered, when Madame Balleroy had returned to the barn after her five-minute herb-harvesting excursion, she was nearly out of breath, fanning herself despite the cold evening air. The bundle of dill she then gave Chloe—roots and all—had made me wonder if she could have been the one to murder Seth.

Considering what I'd just witnessed, I couldn't help but suspect that Madame Balleroy had abandoned Chloe and me for some alone time with Hal in the herb forest.

Which would mean she didn't kill Seth.

It made sense; if either Dennis or Detective Sanders had any inkling of her involvement, they surely wouldn't have allowed her to continue teaching classes.

I made it through the back door to the cooking school before letting my laughter loose. I dashed through the empty kitchen to my prep table and snatched my phone from my bag to text the surprising news to Aunt Deb.

But just as soon as I started tapping out my message, I hurled the phone back into my bag, suddenly remembering I wasn't talking to my aunt, much less sharing juicy tidbits of gossip with her.

I spooned what was left of my chicken nugget dish into the large plastic storage container I'd brought from home, smirking all the while. I'd hold the gossip hostage, I decided, until Aunt Deb convinced me she was truly sorry for both of her deceitful schemes.

The back door to the kitchen opened, and Eileen stepped inside, wearing a conservative green dress that fell beneath her knees. If she'd witnessed the same make-out session I did, her placid expression showed no sign of it.

"Nice coat, and congrats on your award." Eileen joined me at the prep table, removing her own plastic container from the shelf below.

I gazed down at my white button-up chef coat, which looked exactly like Madame Balleroy's kitchen crew. "I feel like an imposter in this thing. You won't see me wearing it around town."

Eileen walked over to the table where a server had gathered the remaining dishes from our meal, ready for us to take home and enjoy with our loved ones. Eileen's and Hal's were the last dishes remaining. I doubted Hal would come back to fetch his leftovers any time soon.

"It will be a nice souvenir—and a well-deserved one," she said, carrying her chafing dish back to our table. "If only I'd thought up a casserole like that when my daughter was little, she might have eaten more than hot dogs and peanut butter and jelly sandwiches."

I laughed softly, then turned a more thoughtful gaze towards her. "How's she doing today? I saw her at the brunch with you."

"These things take time. It was important to Cindy to attend today, and I can only hope it will help her heal." As she spoke, Eileen spooned leftover potatoes au gratin into her personal storage container. "She has always had an incredible spirit that refuses to be crushed, but Seth's passing hit her—hit us all—in unexpected ways. It'll be a long road ahead."

Eileen shook her head, as though trying to dispel a dark cloud of thought. "Anyway, thanks for asking." She set down the spoon and pressed on her container's lid. "Congrats again on your award. You'll forevermore be known as the town's top chicken nugget chef."

I stared at her lime-green container, my eyes widening. "You know what? I *do* make the best nuggets in town. They're always golden brown and perfectly crispy. It's all about paying attention to the details."

The details. Like, what excuse would I use for needing to leave the kitchen immediately? Would I turn right and head for the back door, or go left and aim for the exit through the classroom? Either way, Eileen stood between me and my way out. And once outside, where would I run to call the police?

Eileen looked at me, her eyes now sharp and alert. "What's wrong?"

"Nothing," I said innocently. "I just forgot that I need to get my..." I trailed off, unable to think of a single thing I would need to go fetch. But I set down my spoon anyway and turned to my right. The back door was closer. I could run to Madame Balleroy and Hal in the herb forest.

Stepping around the prep table, I ever-so-casually veered towards the door. The closer I got, the faster I walked. Eileen's footsteps were right behind me, her presence looming like a shadow.

"Are you sure everything is okay?" she asked, her voice rising with a mix of concern and suspicion.

"Actually, I need to get my...scarf. I must have left it at my table in the barn." What I really needed was my phone, but I wouldn't risk turning around to retrieve it from under the prep table. The kitchen held too many sharp objects, and I needed to get out of there.

"I don't remember seeing you in a scarf this morning." Eileen's voice grew so close that a sudden rush of adrenaline spurred me on, and I speed-walked the rest of the way to the door. With a quick pull, I swung it open and stepped outside, quickly turning right towards the herb forest.

"My family brought it for me in case, um, my neck got cold as it sometimes does. But I left it at the table and now my neck is cold." *What* was I saying? It was gibberish coming out of my mouth, and I highly doubted she believed me.

"Hal?" I called out as I approached the herb forest. "Madame Balleroy?"

No response. Were they hiding from me, too embarrassed to reply? With Eileen hot on my heels, I didn't want to go into the dense entanglement of herbs. People, and lots of them, were my best chance of survival.

I called out their names again, then peered into the rows of trellises as I passed by. They were nowhere in sight.

The red barn loomed in the distance. I followed the sidewalk towards it, now jogging as quickly as my heels would allow.

Eileen's shoes clattered against the sidewalk—frantic, *fast*.

Halfway to the barn, she caught up to me.

"Slow down," she demanded. "Your scarf isn't going anywhere."

It was then that I looked at her. Just one glance was enough to make my stomach drop. She'd brought her purse—a large double-zippered leather bag bulging with its contents.

What was in her bag, and more importantly, why had she brought it to run after me?

I followed the pathway to the left, where it sloped up toward the wide-open doors. A small group of older men stood just inside the barn, talking in a small circle.

I headed towards them.

But Eileen grabbed my arm, and I stumbled from the force of it. She pulled me close, her breath hot and ragged against my ear. "You and I need to talk."

My pulse thundered in my ears. "What's wrong? Are you jealous I won the competition? I'll give you my chef coat if it's that important." I tried to wrench my arm free, but Eileen's grip was iron.

"Don't play dumb. I see that look on your face." Eileen thrust her hand into her purse and kept it there. "It's the same look I saw on Seth's slimy roommate."

I lunged forward, breaking free from her grasp. In the span of several heartbeats, I considered my options: run back outside, where only a few people lingered in the distant parking lot; or stay in the barn, where several dozen people, including Carmella and Vincent, lounged at their tables while enjoying coffee and conversation. It was too risky to go near anyone inside; if Eileen had a weapon hidden in her purse, it could put them in the line of fire.

I darted to the right, aiming for the back of the barn.

Eileen hustled after me, hissing at me to slow down. I kept my eyes on Carmella, and when she finally met my gaze, I mouthed, *"Call the cops."* Even if she couldn't read my lips, I hoped my dire, panicked facial expression would relay the message.

No one seemed to notice my frenzied dash, or Eileen scurrying behind me through the center of the tables. People kept talking, laughing, sipping their coffee without pausing to give us a second thought.

Twenty feet from the stage, Eileen grasped my arm again. "Here's the funny thing: after you met my daughter, she told me what a sweetheart you were. A sweetheart! Those were her words. Cindy couldn't believe how many questions you asked about Seth and people he knew; she said it seemed like you wanted to solve the case yourself. She appreciated your concern. But I didn't," she snapped. "I didn't like you poking your nose around where it doesn't belong. This is *our* business." Suddenly, I heard the unmistakable clicking of the hammer on a revolver. "I already warned you with the note in your container. You should've listened." Eileen pressed her purse against my arm. "There's an exit in the back. Come with me, or—"

I broke away from her and ran for the stage. Madame Balleroy's microphone was where she'd left it, on top of the podium. I snatched it up, flicking the switch to 'on.' The barn was suddenly filled with the shrill feedback of the microphone that pierced the murmuring crowd.

"There is a killer among us!" I shouted.

That got everyone's attention. Some hid under their tables, some ran toward the exit screaming, and some, like Carmella and Vincent, stayed in their seats, with eyes wide and mouths agape. I threw my finger at Eileen. "Right there, in the green dress."

Eileen stood stock-still, her face ashen, her hand still buried inside her purse. From the stage, I saw the glint of a gun barrel. I didn't doubt she would use it.

But I pressed on, "Eileen Riggs murdered Seth O'Boyle and Jared Bernardi, both who were employees at Madame Balleroy's. Eileen was Seth's—"

"I didn't kill them!" she shrieked. "You have no right to accuse me of murder."

Carmella must not have understood what I'd tried to tell her moments before, but now she thrust her phone to her ear and cupped a hand around its mouthpiece. More people left their tables—some slowly backing away while others ran. The ones who stayed seated also had their phones to their ears, and I spotted a few people holding up their phone as though taking a video of me.

Eileen's eyes darted frantically from me to the crowd, likely calculating her chances of escape.

I kept the microphone close, my voice firm, even though my hands shook so fiercely I was certain I'd drop the mic. "Eileen's daughter was supposed to marry Seth this holiday season, but Eileen put an end to those plans when she stabbed him in the cooking school's kitchen."

"Don't you dare try to pin his death on me!" Eileen yelled. "I loved Seth like a son. I wouldn't take him away from my Cindy."

"You're lying!" I pointed the microphone toward her like an accusing finger. "Cindy invested her entire savings into Seth's KnuckleKnight invention, and when he claimed Winterbridge stole his idea without compensation, Cindy thought she'd lost all of it. She was so angry she broke off the engagement temporarily. You were furious at Seth for using, and then *losing*, your daughter's money."

"You can't prove that," she argued. "Young couples argue all the time. I was thrilled Seth would join my family."

"No, you weren't. Your daughter's florist said you weren't supportive of the wedding."

Eileen gaped at me. "That doesn't prove anything. This is insane. I'm not listening to you anymore." She turned and headed for the exit.

"If you leave, you'll look even more guilty. If I'm wrong, tell me why. Explain yourself to me and everyone else in this barn." I felt their eyes on us, felt the collective breath held in wait for what would happen next. "Oh, and while we're at it, let's talk about why you killed Seth's 'slimy' roommate, as you referred to him moments ago."

Eileen stopped and spun to face me, her eyes blazing with fury. "I did no such thing."

"You killed Jared because he, too, figured out you took Seth's life. On top of that, you framed Natasha. You found her earring in the restaurant's kitchen during our tour, then left it near Jared's body."

"*What?*" she shrieked. "I don't even know Natasha—"

"You knew she would make a logical suspect, since she got promoted to Seth's position. That's why you not only took Seth's work schedule from his apartment last week when you went to gather Cindy's belongings, but also forged Natasha's handwriting when you wrote down Jared's address. Then you stuffed the schedule and address into an oven mitt and slipped it into Natasha's locker."

Eileen's left hand clenched at her side. "That's not true. You have no evidence!"

"You wouldn't have chased me from the kitchen to this stage if that's what you really thought." I shifted my gaze beyond Eileen towards the barn's entrance, where Dennis rushed in with two officers by his side. As his eyes landed on me, he tilted his head in confusion, unsure of why I was on the stage.

I continued, "Not only were you angry at Seth for spending all your daughter's money, but then you found out he was cheating on Cindy with the reporter. The night of his murder, you stayed later than the rest of our classmates—one, because there are only two stoves at each prep table and you had to wait for the others in your group to finish baking theirs; and two, you're a slow cook. When you finally finished making your zucchini sticks, you went to the classroom to collect your coat and bag, and you overheard Seth talking on the phone with Chloe about their dinner plans for the evening. I know this because I was in the barn with Chloe when Seth called. I'm guessing you also saw the pomegranate seed necklace hanging from Chloe's purse—one that was just like your daughter's. Then, in an outrage, you went back into the kitchen, grabbed a knife, and stabbed Seth as he was leaving through the back door."

"That's not...no—you're mistaken," she said, stumbling over

her words. "As I told the police, I left the school with everyone else."

I shook my head. "No, you didn't. Our classmates went home shortly after I started the tour with Chloe and Madame Balleroy, which was approximately an hour before Seth was killed. You, however, stayed."

"*No, I didn't,*" she snarled.

Dennis and the two officers inched closer to Eileen, silently assessing our interaction. For a moment, I considered jumping off the stage and seeking safety behind them, but with the gun concealed in her purse pointed directly at me, I dared not make any sudden movements that might escalate the situation.

I gave a small laugh. "Deny it all you want, but the facts don't lie. Shortly after we found Seth's body in the kitchen, I talked with the police in Madame Balleroy's classroom. One officer was quite hungry and ate all my zucchini sticks, then moved on to another container sitting on the table and devoured those as well."

I snuck a quick look at Dennis, who looked puzzled and unsure of where I was going with this. I looked away and pinned my eyes on Eileen once again. "Officer Stevens sure enjoyed that second container full of zucchini sticks—crunching and crunching and crunching. And I didn't realize until tonight, when I saw you spooning potatoes into your lime-green container, that he was eating *your* zucchini sticks."

"So what?" she said sneered. "I accidentally left them behind that night."

Dennis and the two officers stepped closer to Eileen, their eyes fixated on the hand she held inside her purse. Carmella and Vincent had left the table, now standing at the back of the barn with their eyes on me.

I placed a hand on my hip. "You know, some people might have wondered how a lousy cook like me could have won today's cooking competition," I said. "Well, I'll tell you why my chicken nuggets are such a crowd pleaser. It's because they're perfectly crispy with just the right amount of crunch. I'm the master of crispy nuggets, and I learned the hard way eons ago that hot nuggets turn into soggy little meat sponges if they're not stored properly. I know you're lying because there is *no way* Officer Stevens would have been crunching so loudly on your zucchini sticks if you had left them for an hour in your container, which does not have a vented lid."

Dennis motioned to the officers at his side, and they pounced on Eileen. She yelled and flailed, dropping her purse to the floor. The contents scattered, revealing a host of items that clattered against the smooth concrete flooring—a phone, a lipstick, and a small revolver.

"Get her out of here," Dennis said. His voice was cool and collected, as though he was simply wrapping up another case on a typical Tuesday afternoon. "I'll meet you at the station in twenty minutes."

The officers handcuffed Eileen, who was still spewing denials and cursing under her breath. The barn had fallen into an uneasy quiet, with the remaining guests frozen by what they'd just witnessed.

Dennis strode to me, and I stepped off the stage and into his arms. He squeezed me tightly, holding me as he spoke. "She could have hurt you. Could have pulled her gun on you..." His words were clipped, his voice heavy with anger—though not directed at me.

I allowed myself to relax into his embrace. My knees trembled so much that I doubted I could stand on my own without his support. "I know," I said. "I got out of the kitchen as fast as I could. The barn seemed like the safest spot."

"You are amazing, Hadley." His voice was a deep rumble against my ear. "The crispy zucchini sticks? Officer Stevens's loud crunching? You don't miss a thing, do you?"

Madame Balleroy ran up to us, nearly out of breath. "What's

going on?" she demanded. Hal appeared a second later, standing next to her. "Someone told me Hadley accused Eileen of killing Seth and Jared."

Dennis turned to her but kept his arms around me. "Hadley didn't just accuse her of those crimes. She *proved* Eileen committed them."

"But, how—"

"Please wait over there," Dennis told her, motioning to a nearby table. "I'll explain everything in a minute. Right now, I need to talk to Hadley."

The two of them turned to walk off, but Dennis called out, "Hal—you've got a little..." Dennis swiped a finger against his own lips, smiling slightly as he did so.

Hal touched his mouth, looking perplexed for a moment before he understood. "Thanks, Detective." With a goofy grin, he turned to Madame Balleroy and whispered into her ear as they walked off.

"The night Seth was murdered, I'm pretty sure Madame Balleroy left Chloe and me in the barn so she could meet up with Hal in the herb forest," I told Dennis.

"That's exactly what she did. After you identified Hal's brake lights, I interrogated him again, and he owned up to his make-out session with Madame Balleroy, as you guessed. Neither of them admitted to it initially because Hal was also dating Madame Balleroy's best friend, Sheila Moody, and they didn't want to upset her." He gave a sharp laugh. "You'd think they were kids in high school."

I agreed with a nod. "This is why Hal the Heartbreaker is such a hot topic among the ladies in town."

Dennis took a step back, but kept his hand on my shoulder. "Are you okay? Do you need anything before I call Chief Mansfield and debrief Madame Balleroy?"

"I'll be fine," I reassured him with a shaky smile. "As soon as my legs stop shaking, I'm going home. Hopefully some snuggle time with Razzy will calm me down."

He tilted his head. "If you want me to come over later…" His voice was soft. Sincere.

"No, I'm fine. Really. Go deal with Eileen, then spend time with your family while they're in town."

"Actually, I wanted to ask if you would join us for Christmas at my house tomorrow. Are you free?"

My smile faltered as my mind dredged up the argument we had yesterday. The way he conspired with Aunt Deb. The secret deal he made with Madame Balleroy. "I…I'm having dinner at my aunt's."

"But I thought you were still mad at her. Or did I misinterpret the silent treatment you gave her during lunch?"

"Nope, you interpreted it correctly. I'm still upset with her. The only reason I'm going to her place tomorrow is because I don't want to be alone on Christmas."

Dennis pressed his lips together, thinking. "You're still angry at me, too." He wasn't asking; he knew it was true. When I didn't respond, he flashed me a crooked grin. "Since you're mad at both of us, why not spend Christmas with both of us?"

"I'm not following your logic."

"My family needs to leave for the airport by three in the afternoon, so we're having Christmas dinner at noon. Why don't you come over at ten and then head to your aunt's when they leave?" His eyes morphed into those of a puppy, and I could feel my resolve crumbling bit by bit under their pitiful gaze.

"Alright," I sighed. Despite my lingering anger, despite my narrow escape from death just now, I couldn't help but smile. Christmas with Dennis was too much to resist. "I'll bring a bottle of red wine, the gift I forgot to give Kinsley, and a steaming pot of stuffing."

CHAPTER TWENTY-EIGHT

I walked slowly up the steps to Dennis's door, my breath visible in the crisp, cold air of Christmas morning. It was scarf and hat weather. Gloves weather, too, but I'd forgotten those in my rush to make it to Dennis's house on time.

Beneath one of the front windows, the cushioned bench held a lanky elf figurine, dressed in glittery red and green fabric, its legs dangling off the edge as if ready to spring to life. As I pulled on the screen door handle, the scent of cinnamon and vanilla drifted past me, even before I knocked on the blue wooden door.

His house even *smelled* like Christmas morning.

I tapped on his door, then drew my coat closer around me. My cheeks felt flushed with both the cold and the excitement of seeing Dennis again.

Kinsley's loud squeal sounded inside, and a moment later, Dennis opened the door.

"Merry Christmas!" I exclaimed. My heart launched into a frenzied pace when I glimpsed his dazzling sea-blue eyes before pulling him into a warm hug. And that grin on his face! It was almost enough to make me forget why I'd ever gotten mad at him.

"Merry Christmas to you, Miss Hadley. You look amazing today."

My cheeks warmed even more as I stepped into his house. "Thank you! You said y'all keep Christmas casual, so jeans it is. And I love your T-shirt. It's so festive!" It was a souvenir, no doubt, from his family's recent safari. The vibrant red fabric featured a smiling zebra wearing a Santa hat with "Africa" written underneath in bold letters.

"Hadley, Hadley! Come see the toys Santa gave me!"

I turned towards Kinsley's excited voice, finding Dennis's entire family lounging in his family room, all of them wearing the same red T-shirt. Kinsley sat on the floor next to the Christmas tree while the adults occupied the chairs and sofa. I waved to them, wishing them a Merry Christmas, then slipped off my coat and hung it on a hook by Dennis's door. Turning to Dennis, I gave him a bottle of merlot and a box of assorted chocolates.

He thanked me, then stuck out his bottom lip as though disappointed. "No stuffing? I've told my family all about the last batch you made. They were hoping to sample some."

"Oh, Dennis! Behave!" his mom scolded, then turned to me, shaking her head wistfully. "Clearly, I have failed as a mother."

I laughed, nudging Dennis's arm playfully. "As an award-winning graduate of Madame Balleroy's School of Cooking, I didn't want my stuffing to overshadow whatever slop you threw together today."

Kate threw her brother an enthusiastic nod of approval. "I *like* her. You should invite her to more family gatherings." She winked at me while pushing herself off the sofa, then crossed the room and greeted me with a warm hug. "But here's a tip: next time, don't just nudge him when he teases you," she whispered. "Punch him, like this—" She balled up her fists and delivered several quick whacks to his upper arm. He stumbled back in mock pain, grinning all the while.

Kinsley pointed to the gift bag dangling from my finger. "Who are you giving that to?"

"Actually, it's a gift from Razzy, and since you're such an excellent reader, why don't you tell us who it's for?" I joined her on the floor by the tree, placed the bag in her lap, and gestured to the name on the tag.

"It's for me!" she declared. Not wasting any time, Kinsley thrust her hand into the bag, tossed out all the tissue paper, and peered inside. Her eyes grew wide. "It looks just like Razzy!" She removed the stuffed animal from the bag and held it up for everyone to see.

"If you push the button on its paw, it will purr," I explained.

Kinsley did just that, then wrapped her arms around it and squeezed. "Thank you, Hadley! Now I have a Razzy of my own."

Dennis sat next to me on the floor. "Okay, it's your turn." He dug through the gifts under the tree until he found a glittery red gift bag with green tissue paper. "This one's from my family."

Before he could hand it to me, Kinsley yanked out the tissue paper, which prompted Kate to remind her to use her manners. She smiled sweetly and promised she would, then stuck her hand in the bag and removed a folded red T-shirt. She jumped to her feet, holding it out for me to see. "It's just like mine!" she squealed. "We'll be twins."

I broke into a wide smile. "Oh, my goodness, I love it!"

Dennis gently pried the shirt from Kinsley's fingers and handed it to me. I slipped it on over my white sweater, then stood and modeled it for everyone. "Best zebra shirt ever!" I exclaimed. "Thank you."

Dennis's mom flashed me a smile. "Of course, dear. It's the least we could do. You were so kind to invite the two of them to stay at your house after he received that letter." If Dennis had told her about all of Aunt Deb's shenanigans, she didn't let on.

Kate cut her mom a sideways glance, her lips fighting a smile.

"Mom likes us all to match because she says it makes for better family photos."

His mom nodded. "Yes, and now Hadley won't look out of place in them."

Her words made me beam. Their gift wasn't just a T-shirt; it was an invitation into their circle—for today, at least. I had never felt so welcomed.

Dennis reached under the tree and fished around some more. I narrowed my eyes at the gray athletic long-sleeve shirt he wore underneath his zebra one, suddenly wondering if he'd worn it to hide his gunshot wound from his family—*oh, the irony*! But I decided not to mention it in case he hadn't told them himself.

His hands landed on a box wrapped in metallic red paper and adorned with a wide, silver bow. He held it out to me, a broad grin claiming his lips.

"Whoa," I said as I took the gift from him, feeling the weight of it in my hands. It was heavier than I expected, and for a moment I wondered if he'd packed it with bricks just to throw me off. I removed the tape slowly, being extra careful not to tear the pretty red paper. "A skillet!" I blurted out when I saw the box.

Not just any skillet, but a polished cast-iron one, just like those Madame Balleroy used in her commercial kitchen. With a squeal of excitement, I opened the box, pulled it out by the handle, and held it up for everyone to see. "Is this for cooking or self-defense?" I joked.

"Both, I suppose," he said with a laugh. "And this gift comes with an invitation: I will cook *for* you or *with* you any time you'd like. You are my favorite chef, and I really enjoyed cooking with you these past couple of weeks. I hope you'll take me up on my offer...just say the word."

Kinsley scrunched up her brows. "What word?"

"Any word," he replied.

So many emotions swelled within me. The skillet was such a generous gift, but it was his explanation, his invitation, that truly touched my heart. Without hesitation, I got up onto my knees and hugged him.

"Thank you, Dennis." I sat back down on my heels, giving him a sheepish look. "I wish I had brought your gift." I'd ordered him a bamboo cutting board, engraved with his last name, and although I was supposed to pick it up on Monday, I'd skipped that errand after our argument.

Kinsley poked her head between Dennis and me. "That's okay, Hadley. You can give him a kiss instead!"

My stomach lurched as my eyes flicked towards his, then just as quickly dropped to the ground. There was so much we still needed to talk about before I could even think about kissing him.

And in front of his family? If only life was as simple as it seemed through the eyes of a five-year-old!

I was certain he sensed my reluctance, but he played it off effortlessly. With a sudden burst of energy, he picked up Kinsley by her ankles and hoisted her onto his shoulders, then twirled her around before taking off on a sprint around his house.

There were no more make-out-with-Dennis propositions from Kinsley or anyone else as his family finished opening their gifts, when we posed for family photos—which everyone wanted me to be a part of—or when we enjoyed the meal Dennis had made, which was anything but slop. He served a beautiful dish of braised beef in wine sauce, three-cheese lasagna, turkey tetrazzini...and for Kinsley, a platter of chicken nuggets arranged in the shape of a Christmas tree.

After we finished the pecan pie Dennis's mom made, Kate's husband insisted on doing the dishes, so the rest of us grabbed our coats and went outside to feed Sadie. Kate and I waited along the perimeter of her pen, watching as the others took turns giving the goat pieces of leftover vegetables.

"Kins hasn't stopped talking about how much fun she had at your house," Kate said as she leaned a shoulder against a fencepost.

"I really enjoyed getting to know her. I'm sure she was disappointed about not staying at Dennis's house"—I motioned towards Sadie, who bleated happily as Kinsley fed her a carrot—"but at least Razzy helped to keep her entertained."

"Kins is crazy about your cat. You're lucky she didn't sneak her off to Dennis's house when they left. Oh, and this morning she announced that she's already started working on her Christmas list for next year. Right now, there are only two things on it, and one of them is a white cat with blue eyes, just like Razzy."

I chuckled. "Hopefully, the stuffed version will hold her over until next year."

"She'll have to wait a lot longer than that since her dad is severely allergic to cats."

"Bummer. Well, maybe Santa will bring the other thing on her list."

Kate smiled slyly, then hesitated. "Maybe."

"Oh no, is her dad allergic to this too?"

"No..." Kate glanced at the group inside the enclosure and lowered her voice. "She wants an aunt. One in particular...one whose name rhymes with gladly. And I won't tell you what's on her list for the Christmas after next." Kate let out a loud laugh, reminding me so much of Dennis's hearty chuckle. "I should probably start packing up Kinsley's stuff, since we need to leave for the airport soon."

Kate headed for the house, leaving me standing at the fence, reeling from what she'd just confessed. Why *had* she told me? Hadn't they all just laughed it off as the whimsical musings of an imaginative child?

I joined the others inside the pen for the next ten minutes, brushing Sadie as Kinsley fed her. When they started towards the house to get ready to leave, I hung back with Dennis, who was rinsing off Sadie's water trough.

"I'm going to head to my aunt's now," I told him. "I don't want to be in the way while everyone's saying their goodbyes."

Dennis snapped his head toward his house, where his family was climbing the steps to the front porch. "Hey guys, give me a few minutes," he called out to them. "I'll be in soon." His gaze fell on me. "Can we talk? There are some things I'd like to say."

My stomach swirled with nervous flutters. "Sure."

He set the water hose down into the trough to refill it, then wiped his hands on his jeans. "About the deal I made with Madame Balleroy...when your aunt approached me with the idea, I selfishly thought it would be in my best interest to go along with it. Sanders always talks about how Deb is a master matchmaker; how she's had a hand in so many relationships around town." He smiled guiltily, giving a small shrug. "I wanted to get on her good side. You know, in case she would try to set me up with you."

I groaned, but smiled nonetheless. "Just so you know, I hold the keys to my heart. Not Aunt Deb."

"Yes, but I'd already tried asking you to dinner several times this year, and since that didn't work, I thought it was time to try a different approach. Because the truth is, I fell for you a long time ago—as soon as you moved to Darlington Hills."

My mouth went dry, and a warmth spread across my cheeks. "You did?"

He nodded earnestly, his eyes locked on mine. "Yeah, I did. There's something about you that just...I don't know, it caught me." The steadiness of his voice faltered, now carrying a hint of nervous energy. "I'm sorry I didn't tell you about the deal with Madame Balleroy. I should have been honest about how I felt."

A sudden shyness overtook me, and I looked down, focusing instead on his dusty black boots. How had I been so oblivious? I'd always thought of Dennis as a good friend, and I assumed he flirted with me simply because he was a flirt. I never imagined he harbored deeper feelings.

I looked up at him, studying his earnest expression. "Dennis, I…" The words tangled in my throat. "I didn't know you felt like that. And I guess there's something sweet about the roundabout approach you took to win me over—conspiring with my aunt, asking me to be your fake girlfriend, pretending to think I was guilty of murder so you could keep me locked me up at your precinct—"

"Oh, I wasn't pretending with that one. I had evidence—"

"Anyway," I continued with a laugh, "our friendship…our *relationship* has been unconventional, to say the least. But somewhere between those handcuffs you threatened me with, the fake dates, and cooking alongside you every night, something changed for me too. These past two weeks were…I've never felt so…everything just felt *right*. That's why—"

My breath hitched as I tried to articulate my feelings. He reached for my hand and squeezed it, encouraging me to continue.

"That's why I didn't tell you about my slashed ankle. Yes, it was irresponsible and selfish, and for that I'm sorry. I knew you'd have to run off and investigate if I told you, and I'd been looking forward to North Pole Night all week. But it wasn't the corn dogs I cared about. I'd heard there would be a band and a dance floor, and I just wanted to dance with you again. Ever since the police banquet, I've wanted another dance."

"That makes two of us. It's why I invited you to North Pole Night. And if you had told me about your ankle, I would have gone to investigate. Not because I wouldn't want to dance with you, but because the thought of someone hurting you terrifies me." He paused as his eyes searched mine for a reaction. A smile tugged at the corner of my lips, softening the concern that had creased his forehead. "But, if I had missed North Pole Night, I would have made it up to you—a hundred times over. Hadley, I'll dance with you any time you'd like."

The trough overflowed, sending a small river cascading onto the dusty ground, but neither of us moved.

My smile grew. "I'm going to take you up on that offer."

"Any time, any place."

"You'll dance with me inside the labyrinth, when it's dark and we're lost?"

"*Especially* inside the labyrinth."

"In the middle of the town square?"

"In the fountain, if you'd like."

I laughed and took a step closer to him. "I promise I won't withhold important information like that again. Honesty from here on out. And I'll ask the same of you."

He blinked. I could have sworn a glint of surprise flickered across his expression before he regained his composure. "Yeah, I'll be honest too."

I tilted my head. "Is there anything else I should know?"

Dennis looked away, hesitating for a moment too long.

I took a step back and released his hand. "What is it?"

"Well, it's just that…there are things with my job…confidential things I can't share. For your safety and for the integrity of my cases. I need you to accept that—for now, at least."

"Are you referring to something specific, or is this a general statement? Does it involve me?"

Again, he hesitated.

"Dennis?"

"You're impossible," he said with a hint of flirtation in his voice. "Can't you just trust me?"

I took another step back, feeling those walls building around my heart again. Trust was something that had to be earned, and his words weren't doing much to help with that.

Dennis reached out for my hand. "Come on, Hadley. Please—"

I kept my hands by my side and dipped my head. "Thank you for inviting me over today. You have an incredible, amazing family. Merry Christmas, Dennis."

Before he could respond, I turned and headed for his house, where I said goodbye to his family, grabbed my skillet, removed my coat from the hook on his wall, and left. It wasn't until I was sitting in my car that I looked over at Sadie's pen. Dennis was spraying the outside walls of the water trough, his back to me.

I backed out of his dirt driveway, then turned onto the main road, swiping at tears threatening to turn my mascara to a soupy sludge. I'd come so close to forgiving Dennis…to trusting him; to letting down my guard yet again. But then he'd hesitated when I'd simply asked for his honesty and couldn't even give me a straight answer. In that moment, all my fears came flooding back, and I was terrified by the thought of jumping into another relationship built on secrets and half-truths.

Yet as the distance widened between Dennis and me, regret nibbled at the corners of my thoughts. Perhaps I'd been too quick to judge, too eager to re-erect the barrier around my heart. Though his words still haunted me—"confidential things that I can't share"—maybe I owed it to us both to allow some room for the unknown.

I took the long way to Aunt Deb's house, looping around the outskirts of Darlington Hills, before turning into a space in front of her leasing office. Turning off my car, I sat there and drummed my fingers against the steering wheel.

Dennis hadn't told me about the deal with Madame Balleroy —but I hadn't been upfront with him either. I understood why he hadn't told me, and I'd forgiven him. Just like he'd forgiven me. And the thought of him withholding secrets from me…it was an unsettling thought, but one I would have to get used to. The nature of his work was bound to come with complications. He was, after all, in the business of secrets.

I fished my phone from my coat pocket, dialed Aunt Deb's number, put it on speakerphone, then set it on the passenger seat.

It was Michael who answered. "Hey, Hadley! Merry Christmas."

I started my car and threw it into reverse. "Tell your mom she was right," I sobbed. "No wait—don't tell her that! It'll only encourage her. Tell her I…understand why she sent Dennis the letter; why she conspired with him."

"Hadley? Is everything okay?" Michael asked.

As I veered onto the empty street, my tears flowed freely, blurring the familiar landscape into a watercolor of greens and browns.

Trust must be earned, so said the old maxim. But what if, even though Dennis couldn't always tell me everything, I *chose* to trust him—offering it freely, without hesitation? Because he was a good man; relentlessly kind and generous…because he cared about me…and because I couldn't imagine even a day without seeing him.

"I'm more than okay," I promised. "Never been better, in fact."

"But you're crying," Michael argued.

I laughed. "Please tell your mom I love her, I forgive her, and I'm sorry to miss her dinner tonight. I'm spending Christmas with someone else this year."

"Okay, but you're sure you're alright? You sound like you're in a hurry."

"I am. I'm in a hurry to make things right."

After ending my call with Michael, I turned left onto Dennis's street and caught sight of the light blue minivan Dennis's family had rented. Kate was in the driver's seat, her mouth widening into a huge grin when she saw me. The entire family waved to me, clearly thrilled about where I was going.

I turned into his driveway, but didn't bother to turn off my engine before running to his porch and rapping my knuckles on the door.

Five seconds later, it started to open. "Did y'all forget something, or did you decide to stay another—Hadley! What are you—"

"Is now too soon for another dance?" I didn't wait for his

answer, but looped my arms around his neck and smashed my lips to his, pulling him into a kiss that seemed to stop time itself.

Dennis melted into the kiss, and his arms wrapped around me like a cozy blanket on a cold Christmas night.

Thanks so much for reading my book! I truly hope you enjoyed it. If so, can you please spend a couple of minutes leaving a review on Amazon? It would mean the world to me, and it helps other cozy mystery fans learn more about this book.

NEWSLETTER SIGNUP

Join my community of readers! You'll receive exclusive subscriber deals and giveaways, recipes and other fun printables, and news about upcoming releases. You can unsubscribe at any time.

Sign up for my newsletter at emilyoberton.com.

RECIPE

Hadley's Award-Winning
Chicken Nugget Casserole

This fun and hearty casserole is sure to be a crowd-pleaser—
especially for the littlest chicken nugget fans!

Ingredients:
- 1 (32 oz) bag frozen tater tots
- 2 cups prepared macaroni and cheese
- 1 (10.5 oz) can cream of mushroom soup
- 2 TBSP dry onion soup mix
- 1/3 cup milk
- 1 lb frozen chicken nuggets
- 1 cup shredded cheddar cheese (optional)
- Salt and pepper, to taste

Instructions:
1. Preheat oven to 350ºF (190 ºC). Lightly grease a 9x13-inch baking dish.

2. Spread the frozen tater tots evenly across the bottom of the baking dish.

3. In a small bowl, whisk together the cream of mushroom soup and milk. Season with a pinch of salt and pepper. Pour the mixture evenly over the tater tots.

4. Sprinkle the dry onion soup mix over the mushroom soup layer, then spoon the prepared mac and cheese on top. If you like it extra cheesy, sprinkle shredded cheddar cheese over the mac and cheese.

5. Arrange the frozen chicken nuggets on top of the macaroni and cheese layer, covering the entire surface.

6. Bake the casserole for 25-30 minutes, or until the chicken nuggets are golden and crispy and the casserole is bubbling around the edges. Let the casserole cool for a few minutes before serving.

ACKNOWLEDGMENTS

From the first word to the final sentence of this book, I've been surrounded by a village of supporters who inspired me, offered invaluable advice, and cheered me on. My heartfelt thanks goes to my mom, for her endless enthusiasm, and to my editor, Cindy Davis, for her insightful guidance and encouragement.

To my ARC team, thank you for being early readers and for sharing your honest feedback. I truly appreciate your candid opinion.

A special thank you to my amazing sisters-in-law—Vanessa, Sara, and Trish—who always listen patiently as I brainstorm ideas, whether we were fishing, hunting for arrowheads, sipping wine, or just visiting at a family get together.

And thank you so much—or shall I say, *merci beaucoup*—to my friend Audrey for assisting with the French translations in this story. Your reaction to the words I needed translated was priceless.

Noelle and Landon, I'm grateful that you continue to eat (almost) everything I whip up in the kitchen, even after I gave my characters food poisoning.

Thank you to my one and only, my happily ever after—Miles. You are the inspiration behind every thread of sweet romance woven into my stories.

Lastly, my deepest gratitude goes to the one who makes all things possible, Jesus.

BOOKS BY EMILY OBERTON

Hadley Home Design Mystery Series

Book 1 - *Lemon Yellow Lies*

Book 2 - *Pearl White Peril*

Book 3 - *Berry Purple Betrayal*

Book 4 - *Cider Orange Chaos*

Book 5 - *Wine Red Wrath*

Book 6 - *Misty Blue Malice* - Coming soon!

Sweet Romance (Written as Emily Bradford)

Holly Jolly Christmas Derailed

Want a **FREE** cozy mystery? Sign up for Emily's newsletter at emilyoberton.com

For the latest updates on new releases, follow Emily on Amazon and BookBub. Stay tuned for more twists, turns, and trouble!

ABOUT THE AUTHOR

Emily Oberton is the author of the fun and twisty Hadley Home Design Cozy Mystery series. She's also worked in news radio, corporate public relations, and as an independent PR consultant.

When she isn't concocting clever clues or crafting capers, you'll find Emily playing tennis, decorating her own home (not just fictitious ones in Darlington Hills!) and spending time with family and friends. She lives just outside of Houston, Texas, with her husband, two children, and orange tabby cat.

Want a **FREE** cozy mystery? Sign up for Emily's newsletter at
emilyoberton.com

Follow her latest book adventures here:
Facebook: facebook.com/obertonwrites
Instagram: instagram.com/emilyobertonbooks/
BookBub: bookbub.com/profile/emily-oberton
Website: emilyoberton.com

Made in the USA
Monee, IL
31 October 2024